Matters

TO ME

The Hart Series
book four

Cassie-
You matter!
XOXO
ME C...

M.E. CARTER

Copyright © 2020
By M.E. Carter

Editing: Erin Noelle
Cover Design: Murphy Rae
Formatting: Uplifting Author Services

ISBN: 978-1-948852-21-0

Matters
TO ME

The Hart Series
book four

To Janett, who absolutely would have adored this story and these characters. Here's to a life well-lived.

ONE

Lauren

"**P**ush hard, Lauren!"

Stepping back on my toes, I inhale deeply, slowing my breathing. I'll need all the oxygen here in three... two... one... LAUNCH...

"Go hard! Go hard!" My coach yells from the side of the mat, not that I'm paying close attention while performing. One of the first things you learn as a competitive gymnast is how to block out any distractions around you. Distractions mean mistakes, and mistakes can mean injuries. That doesn't mean Coach will stop yelling, though.

I run five steps...

Giant hurdle step...

Round off...

Back handspring, back handspring...

PUNCH my body in the air, pulling my arms in tight and twist...

Relaxing my arms before my feet touch the ground and...

"Dammit, Lauren!" His loud shout is unnecessary since I'm sitting on my butt instead of standing in a finish position.

I knew before my feet touched down I had underrotated. As soon as I landed, they slipped right out from underneath me, leaving me no way to stop my fall. It doesn't seem to matter how many times I throw it, no matter how many different arm placements I use, I can't seem to land that fucking double full with an extra half twist. The worst part is that no one in this gym seems to give a shit if I get it right or not. None of my so-called teammates are even pretending to watch. It kind of sucks.

All my life, I've lived and breathed gymnastics. My gym at home was a safe haven, the place I would go to for not just a workout, but also social interaction.

Until suddenly, my reputation was smashed to bits, and I discovered that one elite athlete who doesn't like you can pretty much ruin all your relationships in a matter of minutes. It was a hard lesson learned, but it also allowed me to change my dreams from being elite to joining a college team.

I had this fantasy that I'd get here, and we'd pull together as a team, our eyes on the common goal of kicking the ass of any other university that dared think they were more skilled than us.

Again... my dream was crushed. Turns out, a lot of college gymnasts are bitter and jaded. They put on a good show with their glittery makeup and cheerleader-esque bows. But really, they're Olympic rejects still grasping at one last chance of glory before the real world catches up with desk jobs and children. It makes it hard for anyone to feel like they fit in, especially if you're a walk-on like me.

In the beginning, I kept making sure that my deodorant was still working, and my smell wasn't why people stayed away. Then I figured it out... no scholarship means no respect. No respect means no value whatsoever. No value means no concern for your well-being.

It makes it extra hard to figure out how the hell I keep doing this skill wrong. Somehow, I keep underrotating. I wouldn't mind just adding another half to make a triple full, but I need the point value I'll get by putting two tumbling elements together. And I can't add another skill if I can't get the fucking rotation right.

2

Frustrated, I shake my head and trot off the mat to move out of the way for my teammate's tumbling pass. I try to shake off my lingering anxiety by remembering I still have a couple of months until this routine needs to be perfected. The season doesn't even start until after the New Year, so it'll be second nature by then, right?

Right. Keep telling yourself that, Lauren. Don't freak out. Don't get frustrated. Concentrate.

Using the techniques I learned in therapy to calm my anxiety, I take some deep breaths and remind myself that doing the skill wrong isn't a reflection of who I am as a person. This is just a small challenge to overcome. The best course of action is to figure out where the glitch is and fix it. Easier said than done.

"Lauren."

I look over at my coach, who is stalking toward me. He's not happy about my lack of progress with this skill. We've only been working on it for a couple of weeks, but we should have moved on to adding the connection by now. Putting my hands on my hips, I continue with my deep breaths, pretending it's from exertion and not nerves while he's talking to me. Or berating me. I briefly wonder which it will be.

"Lauren, we've talked about this." Berating it is. "You're underrotating because you're loosening up too quickly. You need to let your arms tighten up a bit longer. Do we need to do this on the trampoline again?"

I shake my head. "No, Coach. I'll get it. I can stay late and do it a few more times if I need to."

He shakes his head and I know what he's going to say before he does. "You know that's not an option. We're capped at twenty hours a week, and I'm not going to lose my accreditation because you can't land this skill."

I nod and look to the floor, biting back the sting of his words. He's right. The NCAA doesn't play, and if they say we can't practice more than twenty hours a week, including weights and endurance training, that's final. I can always try to sneak in some practice time at the local private gym, but if Coach caught me, I would be in serious trouble.

"Listen." His eyes soften a bit as he moves closer. For all his military-like instruction, Coach also knows how badly I want this. I'm the lone walk-on athlete. The only person on this twenty-four-member team who is here because I convinced him to give me a shot. I'm the only person who comes in every day because I want to be here, not because my scholarship dictates I have to. He knows I want to go beyond proving I can hang with the big dogs. "You have a little time before we have to change up the routine."

I wince. That's the last thing I want to do. I need the connection points or there is no chance he will even consider putting me in the line-up for the national championships. That's been my goal all along—to compete at nationals on the floor exercise. I haven't done it yet, and I only have two seasons left in my entire gymnastics career. To add even more stress to my life, since I'm not vying for an all-around spot, there're only two slots up for grabs.

I have to nail this skill. *Have* to. The intrasquad meet is coming up, and while we're only competing against each other, it's huge in determining who competes and who sits in the stands.

"That's our last resort, Lauren," Coach says gently, and I know he's picking up on my vibe of discouragement. "No getting ahead of ourselves yet. Now run the pass again."

Stepping up to the mat, I put myself in position again. Deep breath in three… two… one… LAUNCH!

Five running steps…

One giant hurdle…

Round off…

Back handspring, back handspring…

PUNCH…

I launch into the air, raising my arms overhead and immediately pulling them tight to my body, and twist once… twice… an extra half…

And land with two bouncing steps forward.

I step back and raise my hands to "finish" because even with it being a mistake, the skill has to be officially completed. One glance tells me Coach is still disappointed, but at least I'm upright this time.

Jogging off the floor, I hear, "You're overthinking it."

I blink a few times, trying to figure out if he actually spoke or if my schoolgirl crush has finally gotten the best of me and I'm hearing voices. "What?"

The cocky smile that has melted my panties since the day he walked into this gym is directed at me. Conrad Turner, the newest member of our team, has been impressing everyone since the day he graced our presence. Not just because he's more handsome than should be legal and prefers working out in just his gym shorts, which only serves to show off his impeccable abs, but because of his incredible skill level. His pommel horse routine is like nothing I've ever seen. The spins at the end of the horse are the stuff straight out of our guys' team's wet dreams. It's definitely caught the attention of our women as well. But how can it not? Those back and shoulder muscles are on display the whole time. That's the stuff our *women's* team's wet dreams are made of.

An elite gymnast for most of his teenage years, Con, as he prefers to be called, quit his Olympic bid when he decided he wanted the full college experience instead. Or so the story goes. That was two years ago. Since then, he attended Tennessee State, but for some reason, transferred here this summer. He's remained pretty tight-lipped as to why he left. The only thing he's said about transferring schools is we had a program he couldn't turn down.

My guess is we also had a scholarship he couldn't turn down, but hey, I'm not complaining. He brought the abs he's sporting with him, so I have no reason to be upset.

Strutting closer to me as he unwraps the tape from his hands, he says it again. "You're overthinking it."

I tighten my ponytail, which is just an excuse to arch my back a bit and push my breasts out. They're not big by any means, but they're there. His eyes flicker for just a moment. Con and I have been doing this flirtation dance for weeks now. He's easy to read.

"Funny. I don't usually overthink things."

Con flashes me a flirty grin, eyes completely trained on

me. I know how this goes. Flirting is like my second language, whether it goes anywhere or not. This time, though, feels different. We've had conversations before, but somehow the air feels more charged this time. Like things are shifting. I hope it finally goes somewhere.

"I bet that gets you in trouble sometimes, huh?" he asks, still inching closer until our bare feet are practically touching. "Just going with the flow."

I shrug nonchalantly. "Depends."

"Oh yeah? On what?"

"On if the trouble is worth the consequences."

He considers me for a moment, and I know he's trying to decide if I'm giving him permission to continue this sexually-charged conversation. At least it's sexually-charged on my end. And yes, I definitely give him permission. He's been on my radar since this summer. I've just been patiently waiting for him to look past the giant bows and glittery makeup to notice me. Flirting is easy for me. As I said, it's like my second language. It's seeing past the distractions of the other female options on the team that takes some time.

I wish I could say I love my teammates, because I'm sure some of them are great women. I just don't totally fit in with them, and no one seems to care that much. It's not just that I'm the only walk on. I'm also not into the cheerleader-esque routines. I'm more subdued in my performance wear. Sure, I wear the same competition uniform as everyone else. But the rest of the flash isn't my thing. I just want to tumble. That also means I don't stand out. But I'm not interested in first impressions. I'm interested in real ones.

Taking a small step back, Con refocuses the conversation back onto gymnastics.

One step at a time, Lauren. One step at a time.

"When you're in the air, I can practically see the gears in your brain spinning."

"You're probably right," I admit with a sigh. "But how do I fix it? If I don't pull hard, I won't get enough rotation and I'll land on my ass. I can't find the magic moment to let go of the motion."

"Maybe that's part of the problem."

"Meaning?"

"You're thinking so hard about when you should ease up, you aren't listening to your body. Or noticing where the floor is in relation to your rotation."

He's not wrong. I have a tendency to close my eyes on some of these tricks. But when you're spinning that fast, there's not much reason to look. You only need to feel where you are. He may have a point, though.

"I need to do the next pass with my eyes open, don't I?"

That megawatt smile is back. "And maybe loosen up a bit when you see the ceiling for the second time. That'll give you a full rotation to land. Because right now you're only giving yourself half the rotation."

Narrowing my eyes at him playfully, I put my hands on my hips. "How come you say the same things Coach does, but you say it in a way that suddenly makes sense to me?"

"Maybe Coach doesn't stare at you the way I do. Maybe he's not trying as hard as I am to figure you out."

Well doesn't that just make my lady bits shiver. I quirk an eyebrow at him. My reaction makes him laugh.

"Just try it," he encourages. "See how it feels."

"Alright," I say haughtily with a tilt of my head. "It's my last pass anyway."

Coach doesn't say anything as I step up on the floor, probably just waiting to see what this shit show is going to look like this time. I close my eyes and focus on what I'm trying to do—keep my eyes open and ease up when I see the ceiling.

Taking a deep breath, I launch myself forward.

Five running steps…

    Hurdle…

        Round off…

            Back handspring, back handspring…

            PUNCH…

I pull my arms tight to my body. But this time I concentrate, not on how straight my legs are or if they're together. This time I concentrate on the world around me, and the moment I see the ceiling for the second time, I loosen up ever so slightly.

And what do you know? I land on two feet with only a small hop.

Behind me, I hear my coach clap loudly and yell, "That's a way to do it, Lauren! Now get those legs straight!"

Turning to see Con's reaction, all he does is nod once, a smug look on his face. I shake my head at the cocky bastard. I'm not mad, though. I wish I could throw it one more time, just to make sure I've got it, but it's time to pack up and get out of here. Time limits are time limits, after all.

It's a nice end to practice, but after the day I've had, I need to let off some steam. What I wouldn't give for my best friend and roommate Annika to go out to a club with me so I can dance my worries away. I already know she'll decline my invitation, so I won't bother asking.

After being brutally raped behind a dumpster last year at our favorite club, she hasn't been able to pull together enough nerve to go out into that type of environment yet. We try helping her feel comfortable in public. Me, her new boyfriend Jaxon Hart, and his best friend Heath Germaine regularly go out together whenever they want to do dinner or the movies. We all want her to know we won't let anything happen to her again. It would be hard for anyone to get past those two college football players even if they wanted to. Although sometimes I think the bickering Heath and I do the whole time serves more as a sort of entertainment to Annika. He and I just can't seem to get along. But as long as our arguments keep her distracted, I suppose I don't mind hanging out with the guy.

Honestly, I don't blame Annika for her fear. The entire experience was awful for me, and I didn't even know about it until a few months later. I can't even pretend to know how she felt.

Fortunately, Annika is strong and bounced back to her new normal. There are some lingering emotional scars and overly crowded places still give her anxiety. It's not unusual for me to wake her up from a nightmare if her thoughts are accidentally triggered. But I credit Jaxon with helping her through most of the trauma. Not only did he stop the attack in progress, but he also stood with her during the aftermath. And then they fell in love.

Sweet, sickening, you know they're going to get married and have babies, kind of love.

It's actually the kind of love I'd like to find someday. That someday just hasn't happened yet, and I have a hard time believing it ever will. A girl can dream, though.

"Hey, Lauren." Con approaches me as I slip some Nikes on my feet for my trek across campus.

"Hey. Are you coming to gloat about your obvious superior coaching skills?"

"Nah. Although I'm glad you recognize them."

"Are you always this full of yourself?"

He stops, like he needs to think about his answer. "Uh… yeah. I guess so."

A laugh bursts out of me. I like Con. He's just arrogant enough to keep me entertained, but down to earth enough to help me out today. Not a bad combination if you ask me.

"I wanted to see if you'd like to go out tomorrow night."

That's not at all what I was expecting him to say. "Out? Like *out,* out? On a date out?"

Con shrugs and the movement draws attention to his traps. And they are very, very defined traps.

"Why not? You could introduce me to one of your favorite night spots. I'm still kind of new here. It could be fun."

I pause to consider his offer, although reality is, I'm not going to say no. I just want to see if I can make him sweat a little. When he holds my gaze for long enough that I feel satisfied he's serious, I make him an offer I hope he doesn't refuse.

"Do you like dancing?"

"What kind of dancing?"

I shrug nonchalantly. "Whatever the club is playing. Usually Top Forty, I guess. But they mix it up sometimes.

I haven't been in a while and my roommate won't go with me. And I have an itch to let loose. Interested?"

"Yeah," Con says slowly. "Yeah, I could go dancing."

"Great." I grab my gym bag off the floor and toss it over my back. "I'll meet you in the student union tomorrow at nine. Is that good for you?"

"See you then."

Without giving him a backward glance, I saunter away, swaying my hips just a bit more than normal for maximum flirt effect. I'm pretty pleased to have killed two birds with one stone—a date with my crush and a night at my favorite club. It doesn't get much better than that.

"Be careful with him," I hear from behind me as I stop to fill my water bottle. Ellery MacIlroy is standing behind me, the top off her bottle as well. I'm not sure if she's going for discreet or if she wants some water. Regardless, I don't like that she witnessed my whole exchange with Con or that she thinks it's okay to have an opinion on it.

Ellery is nice and all. We've roomed together at a couple of away meets. But we're still not close enough to consider ourselves friends.

"Why would you say that?"

She glances over her shoulder at Con who is hamming it up with the other guys like they do after almost every practice. While the women's team isn't necessarily close, the guys are clearly bonded.

"There are just rumors about him at his last school. And they aren't all good."

I keep from rolling my eyes because there's no reason to let her see how ridiculous I think she sounds. Rumors are everywhere. Hell, I was the subject of way too many of them in high school. What I learned is that rumors are just that—information people spread that has little to no truth to it. It's why I don't put much stock into them. Even coming from Ellery.

"Well, thank you. But I think I'll be fine." Popping the top back on my water bottle, I give her a quick wave and head toward the dorm. I've got some studying to do if I want to reward myself with this date.

TWO

Heath

Looking down the field, my eyes are trained on my target—Derrick Lucious. He's positioning himself to catch a pass, and my job is to stop him as quickly as possible.

As the starting cornerback for Southeast San Antonio State, this is what I live and breathe. Football is my life. My passion. And hopefully my ticket to financial freedom. Not that I've lived in poverty or anything. My parents have steady jobs that pay decent, but I've got three younger sisters who probably won't get a full ride to the university of their choice. They deserve to get a good education, whatever that looks like for them, and I know my parents won't be able to afford it.

In order to provide the basics for all of us kids, they needed two incomes. And my parents are nothing if not committed to the long-term future of their family. The evidence isn't just in how long they've worked in their respective industries, but in how long they've been together. Almost thirty years and they're still as in love as they've always been. It's nice to know that's what relationships can be like.

Not that I have time for a significant other right now.

I'm only twenty-two. It's not like I'm in a rush. Plus, the only love of my life is the game right now. I have goals to reach, and I'll be damned if I get sidetracked. Unfortunately for me, the stories about football groupies are true. It's not every woman, but there are enough who want to bag someone with talent on the field so they can bag that contract once the draft rolls around. An older player enlightened me when I was a freshman and I've never forgotten the warning.

For as long as I can remember, I've been playing defense. But what I lack in physical size, not that I'm small by any stretch, I make up for in speed. It's what makes me dangerous on the field and how I ended up as a starting cornerback. The other team can't score a touchdown if I knock their asses to the ground first.

I take off after Lucious but feel a tug at my shirt. It's a penalty for sure, but only if the ref sees it. Most times, he doesn't, so I have to rely on my footwork instead. Spinning to get away from whoever has ahold of me, I break free and keep trucking it as fast as I can. Lucious is reaching to snag the ball out of the air. If he gets it, the only thing holding him back from making it down the field and to the end zone will be tripping on his own two feet. And me, if I can get there quickly enough. But I'm too far back to catch up without him gaining some significant yardage first.

Damn my luck, the catch is clean, the carry is solid, and his feet do exactly what they're supposed to do, taking him step-by-step without so much as a wobble.

Fuck.

Pushing myself as hard as I can to catch him, I focus on making my legs go faster, my push off harder, my speed quicker. I thought I was giving one hundred percent before. If that was the case, I'm giving one hundred and twenty percent now because Lucious is headed toward the end zone and fast. I'm not the only one gunning for him, but I'll be damned if I don't get there first.

He's at the forty-yard line... the thirty-five... the thirty...

And I finally reach him, wishing I could just push him out of bounds but he's too far away from the line to risk it. Instead, I grab at his jersey with one hand while wrapping my other arm around his legs, bringing us both down on the field in a heap.

We both groan as we hit the ground and slide to a stop somewhere around the twenty-seven-yard line, whistles blowing on the sidelines.

Tossing the ball aside, Lucious flips over and looks at me. "What took you so long, man? I expected you at least ten yards ago. You stop for pizza or something? You're looking a little thick around the middle lately."

This is what we do at practice. We run plays. We encourage each other. And we talk a lot of shit. It's all in the name of pushing ourselves beyond our limits as we perfect our craft.

Standing up, I reach my hand down to help him up as well. "I got tangled up with your compadres over there. That was a nice catch, though. I'm impressed you didn't tackle yourself by tripping over your own feet."

He shoves me with a grin. "Shut up, man. That happened one time."

"One time is the difference between being drafted by the pros and being drafted by your local car dealership to sell automobiles with a smile."

Harsh words, but they're the truth for many of us. We all have dreams of playing in the NFL, but the reality is, not everyone makes it. Statistics don't lie and the success rate of playing professionally is close to zero. I remind myself of that daily. I work hard, practice hard, and am constantly trying to perfect my game, but I also know there is a chance it won't be enough.

But I'm solid at this point, so I haven't given up yet. I won't. Not until every last pro team I can find closes the door in my face. And even then, I may keep knocking until they give up and let me in.

Trotting downfield, I catch up to my roommate and best friend. "Fucking pissed, man."

"You saw his stats, didn't you?" Jaxon Hart and I have

been living together for more than three years now. He knows me better than anyone. I should have known he would figure out exactly what I'm talking about.

"Damn right, I did. How does this kid keep getting better and better?" For a year, Jaxon and I have been studying Abel Anders on the field. While he doesn't play on our team, he's still the biggest threat I have to my dreams. He came out of nowhere and suddenly was pushing ahead of everyone else on the draft board. Last year alone, he had close to a hundred tackles, a practically unheard of number. When it comes to players to watch, he's made a name for himself and fast.

"They grow 'em big in Minnesota," Jaxon responds, lacking enthusiasm with his words while pulling his helmet off and running his fingers through his sweaty hair. He looks off. His skin is weirdly pale, and his eyes are more sunken in than normal. Plus, he's been struggling through practice today. Jaxon is third string and content with that, as long as he's part of the team, but even with his lack of natural talent, he still can usually hang better than he is today.

Narrowing my eyes, I put my hand out to stop him. He looks back at me, confused.

"What?"

"Are you okay?"

He fiddles with the padding inside his helmet and pretends to ignore my concern. "I'm good."

Yeah. That's not convincing. "I don't believe you. What's going on?"

Cocking his head at me, I can already tell how this conversation is about to go. Denial, denial and more denial.

Jaxon survived cancer as a kid so those of us who know him best pay close attention when he gets sick. It's usually nothing—a pending cold, stress from finals, not enough sleep. But we can also peg when it's something more than that. And when that happens, it's best to remind him that he's not as hearty as someone who hasn't had toxic chemicals, also known as chemo, running through their veins. Add in the statistical data his father provided me of how many childhood cancer survivors end up battling the disease again in adulthood as well, and it's not something to be taken lightly.

I don't usually hound him. He's a grown-ass man and can take care of himself. But something about how he looks is triggering all kinds of alarms in my brain.

Running his fingers through his hair one last time, Jaxon positions his helmet on his head. "Nothing, Germaine. I'm good. I swear."

He tries to walk off, but I put out my hand again. I don't mind saying this guy is the greatest, but he's also stubborn as they come. And he becomes a whiny bitch when he's sick. The man-flu can be strong with this one.

Getting in his face, I make sure he understands I'm serious. "You know I leave you alone about your health because you get enough coddling from your parents."

He snorts a humorless laugh because that's the understatement of the year.

"But you don't look right. Your color is off. Your energy is low. And you look like you haven't slept in days."

"Maybe I haven't. I've been staying with my girlfriend for the past few nights, you know. There are benefits to having a solid relationship."

He's not wrong. After living together over the summer, I knew it would be hard for those two to stay out of each other's beds most nights. Thank god they mostly choose to stay at her place. Annika is great and all, but I draw a hard line at being in the room when they start getting all kissy face. I'm not sure how Jaxon can stand his girlfriend's roommate, Lauren. I have tried to get along with that girl, but she has way too much energy for me. It grates on my already frazzled nerves.

"Don't think I won't call Annika myself and tell her you're dragging from not getting enough sleep," I threaten.

He shoots me a glare and pushes away from me, heading back toward the line to set up for the next play. No idea who Coach is talking to or about, but so far, he isn't worried that we haven't joined the huddle yet.

"I'm serious, Hart," I call after him. "If this keeps up,

she's my next call, followed by your daddy."

His only response is a middle finger over his shoulder. He knows I'm not playing around. Their relationship has gotten so much better in the last year after they hashed out some miscommunications and the great Jason Hart finally eased up on his son. But they still butt heads about doctor visits. I stay out of it because Jaxon is my friend. I'm on his side, always. Unless something like this comes up. And one thing I have learned in my twenty-two years of life is that gut instinct is there for a reason. When I listen to it, life is a whole lot better for everyone.

Jogging up to the loosely-formed huddle, I catch the tail end of Coach's instructions.

"Let's run the play again with that one change. Line up."

As we head to our prospective spots, I ask Lucious, "What did I miss?"

He pats me on the back and replies with a cocky, "Don't worry about it, Germaine. Let's see if you can keep up with us this time."

I'm not happy to not know what play we're supposed to be running, and I'm a little miffed it's because I was trying to get Jaxon's head out of his own ass. But I remind myself I won't know what play is coming during an actual game so it's all about honing my skills. You can study game clips and a team as much as you want and inevitably, they're going to change things up on you. It's good to see if I can stay on my toes during the surprise plays.

Listening to the call, I know the ball is going to Lucious again. He's the one I've got my eye on. As soon as the QB yells his last, "Hut!" we're off.

Lucious is trucking it down the field, in position for a catch. But I'm having to keep my eye on Matt Denison when the ball is flipped to him first. I take my eye off Lucious for half a second. It's only that long at most, but it's long enough for him to cut toward the middle of the field, making my attempt to reach him that much harder.

I pump my legs faster than before and strain to get there in time. But it's no use.

Lucious is at the fifteen… the ten… the five… and in the end zone with me just a few feet behind.

"Fuck!" I yell and punch the air in my frustration.

Lucious flips the ball out of his hands and pats me on the back as he jogs by. "That was quick, man."

Not quick enough, though. If I'm getting an invitation to the combine this year, there isn't room to be a few feet behind.

I jog back to the line, determined to not be surprised again, and try to push that damn car dealership commercial out of my head.

THREE
Lauren

The bass pounds through my body as we sway to the music. It gives me the ability to let go of my thoughts and anxieties, and just feel.

It's why I like dancing so much. Annika thinks it's because I like to party, and I won't deny I enjoy that aspect as well. But to me, going to a club allows me to relax. To let go of stress. I don't know if the beat has some random neurological side effects to the type of anxiety I suffer from, or if I just enjoy it so much it has a calming effect.

I try not to think about it too much. I've been on an antidepressant to control my anxiety for so long now, I almost forget I'm the only person I know who takes them. Not that it's information I share with just anyone. There's no need. I perfected my ability to play off bad situations as insignificant to me, even if I feel like dying on the inside. It's why I have very few friends. It's hard not to look like a cold-hearted bitch when you can so easily pretend not to give a shit what other people think. Some call it a defense mechanism. I call it a superpower. I've learned people tend to talk less about you if their words don't throw you into a dramatic rage. The state of today's reality TV is proof enough of that.

Do people sit around watching *Desperate Housewives* for the tea and friendly conversation? No. Catfights and table flipping. That's what viewers want. And the reality is, the same viewers who love real-life gossip also have no interest in someone like me who doesn't succumb to the drama. Lesson learned the hard way.

None of that matters now, though. Right now, I have a beat running through my veins, and a warm body holding me close to him as we dance. My back is to his front as we sway to the rhythm, letting the music carry us away.

I feel his lips brush my shoulder, and I move my hair out of the way for him to get better access, raising my arm up to grab the back of his head and hold him closer. Generally speaking, this is not a dancing position I'm usually in. At just over five feet, most guys tower over me by well over half a foot minimum. But Con, being an elite gymnast is only a couple inches taller than me.

And yes, I know people like to make fun of male gymnasts because of their height, but their muscles and stamina are no joke. I don't know many guys who have the same kind of endurance a gymnast has. And that doesn't even include the flexibility. Cocky bastards know their strengths, too. Right now, Con's lips are definitely one of his strong points.

"There are too many people here," Con says in my ear. "What do you say we go somewhere to be alone?"

I nod because I really, really want to be alone with him. Thank goodness he's on the same page as me. Grabbing my hand, Con leads me off the dance floor and out of the club without looking back.

I assume we're on our way back to his dorm. It would make sense under the circumstances. While our flirting hasn't been intense, the attraction is definitely there. Small glances, cute comments, the whole shebang. Asking me out was obviously the next step, and we've had such a good time tonight.

It wasn't just the dancing, though. It was the conversation at dinner before. It was the similar interests, the coordinating class schedules, even when he asked questions about Annika having to speak at her rapist's trial and commenting on how much he admires her ability to do that. We just seem to connect. It's been amazing.

So, while going back to his place with him might seem like a big step to some, it seems completely natural to me. It's time to move this thing along, and I'm more than ready to see the muscles he's been keeping concealed under his workout shorts. I can already tell this is going to be the beginning of a beautiful thing.

It takes less time than I anticipate to get to his dorm where we can be alone. Con lucked out and got a single room. They're usually divvied out by first-come, first-served for upperclassmen, but when the original occupant backed out over the summer to move off-campus, Con had just secured his transfer and put in his application at the right time. Instead of messing with the waiting list, housing administration just gave it to him.

No hardship there. It just means we can be truly alone without worrying anyone will barge in on us. If this night goes the way I hope it does, I'd rather we not be interrupted.

The moment we step into the small room, Con immediately turns and pushes me up against the door, his lips crashing into mine. His intentions become crystal clear as his tongue delves into my mouth and his hands push my arms up over my head.

I like this position. Something about having my arms up gives me the feeling that I'm giving him complete control without losing any of mine. Maybe it's because my torso is more exposed now that my off the shoulder crop-top is hitched up more.

I gasp when his hands find the smooth skin on my stomach. The rough calluses slid up my sides as he lifts my shirt all the way up and over my head, dropping it to the floor as my hair cascades around us. The entire movement is sexy as hell and gives me a surge of hormones.

Cupping his cheek, I pull him back in for another kiss, my other hand grabbing at the hem of his shirt, my own intentions now very clear as well.

As soon as the offending article of clothing is gone, my hands have a chance to explore like they've been itching to do for months. Conrad Turner's body does not disappoint. Every muscle in his back, his obliques, his abs, his shoulders—oh wow, his shoulders are so fucking sexy. There is not one part of him that is not rock hard. And I do mean every. Single. Part.

Now that the frenzy has begun, there is no stopping it. I haven't had mind-blowing sex in—well, that's not relevant right now, and I am easily distracted from my thoughts when he picks me up under the knees, wraps my legs around his waist, and carries me to his bed. Slowly, using all that muscle strength he has, he lowers me onto the mattress. Holy shit that strength is sexy.

Our pace slows as we find our groove, hips beginning to grind as we seek friction. We kiss and suckle and nip, exploring each other's bodies, leaving nothing untouched. It's erotic and sensual and so fucking good. When the last of our clothes disappear from between us, my heart feels like it might burst from anticipation of the orgasm I'm hoping to have and the relationship that's just beginning.

"Condom," I whisper, because as much as I want him in this moment, I also know bad things can lay dormant in your bloodstream for years. I have Jaxon's new pre-med classes to thank for that piece of knowledge.

My demand doesn't bother Con, though, who reaches into the bedside table and pulls one out, sheathing himself quickly before stretching his body over top of mine.

He pushes inside and pumps fast and furious, his pace quicker than I anticipate and yet there is power behind his thrusts. So much power it drives me to seek my own pleasure as quickly as possible.

Reaching my hand between us, I find my clit and begin rubbing, trying to keep up with his pace. The look on his face tells me he won't last long, which is probably to be expected. With the intense sexual tension between us from the beginning, it's no surprise we've gotten this close this quickly.

Con lets out a groan of pleasure before I reach my

release and I begin rubbing even faster. "Don't stop yet, baby. I'm almost there."

But his movement becomes slower as his body comes down from the high. "I can't keep going, babe," he whispers. "So sorry, but I can't."

His body stills above mine as my orgasm fades away. I'm disappointed in this turn of events, but I'm not actually surprised. People like to pretend the first time with someone is this explosive moment where you feel like you float off in the sky as the orgasm rocks you to your core. But that is mostly fantasy. Good sex, *great* sex takes time. It takes practice. It takes getting to know your partner and what they like and don't like.

We have time to get it right, and personally, I'm looking forward to the practice.

Con gives me a quick kiss on the lips and wraps the now disheveled covers around us. "That was great babe, thanks."

I giggle and shake my head. He's got a few things to learn, *I think as I start to drift off.* But I'm more than happy to teach him.

• • •

The warmth of the sun on my face rouses me from my sleep. The warmth of the person behind me rouses my body as well.

I smile as the memories of last night infiltrate my mind. The dinner. The dancing. The sex.

It wasn't mind-blowing by any means, but it meant something to me. And there is nothing else in the world like the feeling of someone else with you in such an intimate position. His weight on top of you, his length inside you, his eyes staring into yours. Even bad sex is good when all those other factors are there.

Con begins to stir, his body lying face down and turned toward the wall. I run my foot down his leg, hoping to help wake him. "Good morning, Sleepyhead," I say quietly. "Did you sleep well?"

Before he can answer, the door flies open, at least six of our male teammates barreling in, laughing and shoving at each other.

"Hey!" I screech, pulling the blanket up over top of my very naked body. I know I wear skimpy workout clothes in front of these guys, but there are still parts of me I like to keep private.

Bryce Walker, partial scholarship recipient and complete douchebag, ignores me and jumps on the bed, slapping Con on the back to wake him up. "What are you doing in bed so late, man? We're supposed to drive into town today, remember? San Antonio Riverwalk for some guy time."

Holding one hand tight to the blanket, I use the other to push Bryce off the small bed. I catch him at the exact right angle as soon as he bounces and his feet leave the mattress, so he doesn't just stumble, he practically flies off to the floor, landing on his ass. The other guys burst out laughing at his less than perfect landing while he glares at me, venom in his eyes.

"What the fuck, Bagley? I could have been injured right before the season starts."

"You should have thought of that before you barged in here," I shoot right back at him. I've known Bryce since my freshman year and he's always been an entitled, elitist asshole. There's no love lost between us. Flicking my wrist at him, I add, "Can you guys leave so I can get dressed?"

"Please," he responds as he stands up and brushes off his rear end. "It's not like anyone cares to see those mosquito bites you call boobs."

I turn to Con who is propped up on his elbows, rubbing his hand down his face as he becomes coherent. I'm pissed now and hoping to get some back up from him because this isn't okay. But Con says nothing. He doesn't even look at me. Instead, he climbs out of bed, almost exposing my naked body to the room as he carelessly flings the covers aside. No one even takes a second glance at him despite his own nakedness.

"Seriously, Con? You're just going to let them hang out

in here?" I ask, getting angrier as Bryce grabs the remote and flips the television on.

Pulling his shorts over his hips, Con finally looks at me. "Um, yeah. They're my friends, and we have plans. But maybe it's time for you to go."

Several of the guys snicker at his dismissal and Ellery's warning comes back to haunt me. It finally hits me that all the weeks of flirting, leading up to last night, was just a game to him. It wasn't actual interest. It wasn't about dating and getting to know me. The goal was to get in my pants, and I fell for it.

Hurt and humiliation race through me, my anxieties skyrocketing. I'm so fucking stupid. I know better than to trust that any man has genuine intentions toward me. I'm not the girl you fall in love with. I'm the girl you bang until the one you want to be with comes along. Girls like me are a dime a dozen. I have never felt so strongly about that than I do in this moment.

I allow myself one deep breath. Only one to put my brave face on—to draw on my anger and my faux self-confidence so I can make it out of this room with the minimal amount of drama.

"I'd love to leave, asshole, but my clothes are over there."

The look he gives me chills me to my core. The shy glances and flirty winks are gone. No, this is complete indifference of me as a human being. As if being a decent person is wasted on someone like me.

"You put out on a first date," he says with a chuckle. "Since when do you care who sees you naked?"

The words hurt badly, especially after what transpired last night. But I refuse to lower my bravado. Instead, I mutter, "Big words coming from a five-pump chump," and I lean back against the wall, settling in. I would rather sit here in abject humiliation than get up and get my clothes. I don't trust any of these guys to not "accidentally" pull the sheet away from my body, and I certainly don't trust any of them not to record it while it happens. So here I sit, until they leave.

"Dude, hurry up and go shower the skank off of you," Bryce, the douche, remarks. "We need to hit the road in like ten minutes if we're going to get a good parking spot. I don't want to pay for parking."

"Yeah, yeah, give me a minute," he says, staring at his phone while he scrolls.

I shake my head and look away, trying to brush off the sting of Bryce's comment. I have known these guys for years. I have spent thousands of hours training with them. And yet, not one of them has been on my dating radar. Now, I know why. My gut may have failed me with Con, but it nailed it with everyone else.

I accidentally catch the eye of Kevin, the lone ginger on our team and probably the shiest of the bunch. He's standing with his back up against the door, like he might bolt at any minute. He gives me the tiniest of smiles before gathering my clothes and handing them to me, immediately returning to his preferred spot.

The gesture doesn't change the position I'm in or the anger I feel toward everyone in this room, but I feel a little less murderous toward Kevin. At least he has the decency to help me out. And he's staring at the floor now, too, ears bright red. I suspect if anyone understands how I must be feeling right now, it's him.

Doesn't change the fact that he's not standing up to his friends, but I'll at least give him credit for attempting to help me out. This time.

Getting dressed while staying covered under the blanket proves to be as difficult as one would imagine. My toes end up doing a lot of the work holding the cover in place when my hands are tugging fabric over my body. But I'm finally clothed and able to leave this nightmare behind.

The guys completely ignore me, too busy talking shop and about their plans for the day to give a shit that I've grabbed my shoes and clutch. Except for Kevin. He has the decency to move out of the way and give me a small smile before opening the door. I have no idea if the smile is genuine, but at least it's not a quip about what a whore I am.

As soon as the door closes behind me, the room explodes with laughter. I wipe away the stray tear that has finally broken free and quickly slip my shoes on.

I know my feet are going to hurt from walking home in these heels, but that pain is nothing compared to how beaten up I feel on the inside.

FOUR

Heath

I wake up with a start, although I'm not sure why. There are no alarms going off. Everything sounds quiet in the building. Jaxon isn't even here, so it's not his snoring.

Doesn't matter. Once I'm awake, that's it for the day, so I might as well get moving.

Rolling myself out of bed, I stretch my back and neck muscles that have cramped up during the night before heading to the communal bathroom for my morning piss.

It's quiet in the hall, probably because I'm the only one awake. It's early Sunday morning, after all, and everyone is likely sleeping off the effects of a post-game frat party I didn't go to.

Jaxon seems to think I'm a morning person, and there may be some truth to that, although I never noticed until I moved in with him. I don't seem to have the same issue gaining consciousness in the morning as my roommate. He's like a zombie until he's had at least two cups of coffee. But he's also wide awake at midnight, when I can't keep my eyes open.

Okay yeah. Maybe I am a morning person.

I'm grateful for the early start today, though, because I have some major studying to do. As a senior with a double major in business and finance, my classes are starting to get tough. Business law, in particular, is kicking my ass, and is probably more than I wanted to know anyway. I only decided on these majors so if—I mean, *when*—I get into the pros, I don't have to rely on someone else to manage my affairs. Sure, I'll still have to hire an agent and all. Playing football requires more than forty hours a week of work, and I'll need someone to carry the brunt of the load that comes with having that much money. But I at least want to be able to read over my own contracts and have a basic understanding of what they mean. Too many people have gotten screwed over by someone who either didn't care or didn't know what they were doing. I refuse to be the next sucker. So, no easy degree for me.

Besides, it's only an extra four classes to go from one major to two. Might as well take advantage of it.

Pulling on jeans, because around here, sixty-something temperatures are on the chilly side, I wash my face, brush my teeth, and slap on some deodorant. I'll probably have the whole library to myself, but there's no reason to leave a lingering trail of funk behind me after I finish.

Once I'm fully dressed, I grab all my stuff and head out the door, opting to drive instead of walk. Southeast San Antonio is a big campus, and I'm feeling lazy today. Besides, I'm pretty sure there is a box of protein bars in the center console for breakfast.

The drive to the library isn't normally more than five minutes. It would take me twenty if I was hiking it. Plus, I was right… there is food in my car, which is great. That means I'll be able to last at least an extra hour with my nose in a book before needing to inhale more calories.

As I turn down the main road, headed to my stop, a tiny blonde woman catches my attention. Her head is down, arms wrapped around her waist, as she walks. She's only wearing a short skirt and an oversized shirt, so she's probably cold. I wish there was something I could do, but I've learned that in this day and age, women don't take too kindly to strange men offering them rides. I get it. I have three sisters. I'd be furious if one of them climbed in the car with some random dude just to make it to their destination on time.

And realistically, it's cool outside, not freezing. Whoever she is, she might be uncomfortable, but she's not in any danger from hypothermia.

My truck drives past her and I happen to glance over just as she looks up.

Lauren? What is she doing out this early?

She's not dressed for practice which can only mean she's doing the walk of shame. I'm not necessarily surprised by that realization.

Lauren has always been a flirt. Over exaggeratingly so. It grates on my nerves because she comes off as shallow and like a party girl. Is she those things? No idea. But she certainly doesn't let anyone close enough to find out, and she's the exact kind of girl I've always been warned to avoid. When Jaxon and Annika got together, I tried to brush aside my biases. I really did. Our two best friends were going through a terrible time with the trial, so we all stuck kind of close together. We were like the four musketeers. Except two of the musketeers could never figure out how to get along and ended up hating each other. Hate might be a little too strong. Consider it a personality conflict.

Still, she's Annika's best friend and I feel bad that she's obviously cold. Plus, if listening to my sisters' bitch about how uncomfortable women's shoes are, Lauren's feet have to be covered in blisters with the weird strappy heels she's tromping around in.

Irritated with myself for caring so much, I sigh and pull over to the side. As I wait for her to walk by, I roll down the passenger side window. A frigid wind blows in. Somehow the temperature seems to have dropped in the last few minutes.

"Lauren," I call out when she's finally close enough to hear me.

She whips around, a look of horror on her face. I don't know if it's because it's me or because she got caught wearing hooker clothes on an early Sunday morning. From the way her shoulders slump as she sees my face, I assume she's more worried about being caught.

She straightens up quickly though, putting on a brave face that isn't quite as effective with all the makeup smudges.

"Heath," she deadpans. "What brings you out so early in the morning?"

"Studying," I respond with my own nonchalance. "I'd ask the same of you, but I think it's pretty clear you're finally getting home for the night."

She winces and looks down at the ground, avoiding my eyes.

Shit. Now I feel bad. Whatever happened apparently didn't end well if she's not tossing barbs back my direction. I may not like her, but I don't want to kick her when she's down either.

"Hop in," I say with a kinder tone.

Lauren glances back up, looking startled at my offer. "What?"

"It's freezing. You're not dressed for this weather. So, hop in."

She narrows her eyes. I know she's trying to decide which is more important—her pride or her physical comfort.

"No ulterior motives," I promise. "I'm heading toward your dorm anyway. It's no problem." I'm not really going that way, but it won't hurt me to make sure my roommate is with Annika. Maybe she and I can double team Jaxon and get him to make an appointment for a checkup.

Lauren bites her bottom lip as she considers my offer for a few seconds but finally concedes and opens the truck door. The wind blows even stronger now, and I realize I may have underestimated today's weather.

"Close that door, quick. Shit, it's chilly out there."

She does as I ask and slams the door quickly, immediately rubbing her hands together while I roll up the power window. "I know. I had no idea a cold front was coming in. Maybe they'll freeze to death at the Riverwalk," she grumbles under her breath. I have no idea who she's referring to and I have a suspicion I wasn't supposed to hear that part anyway.

Her legs are covered in goosebumps, so I crank up the heater and wait until she's buckled in before pulling away from the curb. I expect Lauren to start lobbing insults or small digs my way, but she doesn't. Instead, she stares blankly out the passenger window until finally leaning her head against the glass.

This isn't like her. Something is off and it makes me nervous.

"Wanna talk about it?" I offer, hoping she'll open up. After the last year, I'm somewhat hypersensitive to the skyrocketing statistics of on-campus sexual assault. The way she's acting has me wondering if I need to put aside my regular feelings about her personality to help her and maybe beat someone's ass.

She doesn't answer me, but when I glance away from the road and look at her momentarily, I think I see her wipe away a stray tear.

Okay, enough. I can't just let this go. I know she doesn't like letting people in, but if she's been assaulted, we need to go to the police, the hospital, and possibly back from wherever she came from this morning so I can shove someone's head into a wall.

"Lauren, you need to tell me what's going on," I demand, trying to also remain sensitive to the fact that she may be scared right now. My heart is beating faster than it should, and I can feel the rage building. "If you've been hurt, or, or worse, we have a small window of time to gather evidence. I know it's hard, but we'll get through this…"

Her head whips over, eyes wide, immediately putting her hand on my arm to stop my ramble. "Ohmygod, no, Heath! No! No, nothing like that."

Thankfully, we're at a red light so I can look at her, trying to read her.

"Are you sure? No judgment, Lauren. You know that. Something like that is not your fault."

For maybe the first time ever, she smiles at me. A real, genuine smile of appreciation for my concern. Well, she also smiled at me when we were introduced. It was downhill after that.

"No really, Heath. I understand why you went there, after what the four of us have been through. But I promise you last night was consensual."

I take a deep breath, trying to get my blood pressure to normalize. Watching Annika pull her life back together during a very public trial was brutal. She wasn't just put through the wringer because of the rape. Dating a celebrity's son meant her name was a loosely guarded secret. There was very little protection of her privacy. She handled it better than most people I know would have, but it was still hard and required a lot of understanding on all our parts. A few nights during the trial, I slept on the floor next to her bedroom door while Jaxon slept next to her to help her feel safe and ensure no one was going to get her in the middle of the night.

Only the four of us knew about those nights. Lauren and I were back on campus in the middle of the summer for our respective training camps, so it's not like anyone important was around to see. But even if Annika had lived in the dorm during the trial instead of temporarily sharing an apartment with Jaxon, I still would have done it. Jaxon is like a brother to me. If it hurts him, it hurts me. And those few weeks definitely hurt us all.

Lauren takes a deep breath and leans back against the window. Something about her demeanor still isn't sitting right with me.

"So, if it was consensual, what's wrong? Was it not good?"

A quiet giggle escapes her mouth, which makes me feel a little better. She flips her hair over her shoulder, and I see some of the brash, opinionated Lauren finally rearing its ornery head.

"You know what? No. No, it was not good. In fact, it was terrible," she rants, hands waving around. "What is the matter with these guys? Do they not understand that not wanting a relationship doesn't give you permission to not put in your best effort? There is an expectation for you to bring your A-game. That wasn't even a C-game. Hell, that wasn't even a middle school game."

She notices when I grimace and the look on her face changes from rage to amusement.

"That wasn't quite the right analogy was it?"

I shake my head, my own laugh bursting out. "Be careful saying that kind of stuff about kids in public. It would be hard to cartwheel with an ankle monitor after you get arrested."

"No kidding. I can't believe I said that." She sighs and the mood takes a downward turn again. I can't figure out why I'm still unnerved about it. I should be thanking my lucky stars that she's quiet. It's still too early in the morning for her normal energy. Those are the keywords though, aren't they? Normal energy. This isn't her M.O. The vibe she's giving off is one that feels an awful lot like defeat.

"Are you sure you don't want to talk about it?" I offer. "I get that your pissed he was terrible in the sack. But you seem sad. That's not a bad lay. That's something else."

Lauren shakes her head with a sad smile. "It's okay. Just a misunderstanding of what the morning after is supposed to mean."

Unless she's looking at the tick in my jaw, she has no way of knowing she just pressed my other trigger button. I've never told her I have three sisters or that protecting them from the douchebags of the world isn't always successful and it's almost as painful for me as it is for them.

There's no chance to ask anything else, though, not that it's my place. As soon as I pull up into the no parking zone in front of her dorm, she jumps out of the car with a "Thanks for the ride, Heath."

Throwing the gear shift into park and turning on my hazard lights, I climb out of the vehicle and chase her to catch up. "Hang on," I call. "I'm coming, too."

Lauren stops and turns around, the furrow in her brow a little more pronounced since it makes the smudged mascara darken the creases around her eyes. "I'm fine, Heath. You don't have to walk me in."

"No," I huff a small laugh. "I'm trying to track down

my roomie. I figure he's here."

Understanding dawns on her and she waves for me to keep following. She pulls open the door and I grab it over her head for her to walk through. The same dude that is always at the reception desk is still sitting there, feet propped up on the counter. He lowers the magazine in front of his face for a brief second to nod once at us and goes back to his reading. I have no idea what that guy's job actually entails, but he's been here every time I've stepped through that door.

Lauren and Annika are on the bottom floor this year, thank God. I got suckered into helping them move out last year and back in this year. It was a hell of a lot easier to carry all their crap when I wasn't navigating a flight of stairs. It also means we just have to turn the corner and walk a few doors down to reach their room.

Grabbing her key from her clutch, Lauren lets us in. Not all that surprising, the room looks like a tornado hit. Clothes and shoes and rogue textbooks are thrown everywhere. It makes my Type A personality itch.

Also not surprising is Annika sitting at one of the desks, a book open in front of her. She looks up with a smile on her face, not appearing at all like she just woke up, except for the weird plaid pajama dress thing she's wearing. But again, not a surprise. I've always known Annika is a morning person. Her waking him up first thing was literally the only complaint Jaxon had when they moved in together for the summer.

Now he complains about the fact that she doesn't wake him up in the morning, because he has to get dressed and truck it across campus to the dining hall to get breakfast instead of sitting in his boxers eating something she's already made.

His life is so hard sometimes.

"Hey," Annika says quietly, as to not stir Mr. Sleeping Beauty. "I didn't expect to see you home for a few hours."

Lauren's back stiffens slightly but she says nothing and keeps walking across the room dodging piles of crap as she goes. I assume headed for some warmer clothes. Pulling open the top drawer of her dresser, she pulls out a medication bottle and pops a pill in her mouth. Well, that's weird. And again, none of my business.

"And I didn't expect you to bring someone home with you. Certainly not this guy," Annika says with a smile. She's been witness to our butting heads enough times to know Lauren and I being together is unusual. "Good morning, Germaine. You're up early."

Crossing my arms, I lean against the wall by her desk, trying to keep my voice down. "Looks like I had the same idea you did. I'm heading to the library. Care to join me or would you rather study in those…" I give her a quick once-over, "…grammy jammies?"

She laughs and swats at me. "Shut up. It felt like winter in here when I got up."

I shoot my eyebrows up playfully. "I don't even want to know what you were sleeping in if you were cold with that man-sized heating pad lying next to you all night." I gesture over to the lump on her bed. Jaxon hasn't even moved since we walked in. I can still hear him snoring.

She blushes and scoffs. "Heath Germaine! It's not like that. We don't always have sex."

"I know," I say mustering up the seriousness I don't want to bring into the conversation, but feel I have to. Now seems to be the perfect time. "Which is why I'm a little worried about him."

Annika's face falls, and I know she's thinking the same thing I am. Something is wrong with Jaxon's health, and without him taking charge of the situation, we don't know how to help him.

"I don't think I need to be here for this part of the conversation," Lauren whispers. "But I do need to wash last night off me, so I'm going to shower." Sure enough, she's popped her hair up in a bun thing and is holding a ton of stuff—clothes, a towel, a bag with giant shampoo bottles. I thought it was bad sharing a communal bathroom with a bunch of guys. At least all I take to the shower with me is a towel and a bottle of three-in-one soap.

Once the door closes behind her, Annika turns back to

me. "I'm worried, Heath. How is he doing in practice?"

Moving closer so we can keep speaking in hushed tones, I give her the honest answer. The one neither of us wants. "He's dragging, A. He's grumpy. He's breathing heavier. He's slow, which I know is normal for him, but slower than usual." I wink at her, acknowledging my attempt at humor to diffuse the seriousness of the situation. It doesn't work. She's biting her lip, obviously as worried as I am. "Something's not right, but he gets mad when I bring it up."

"You don't think he already knows do you? And that he doesn't want to tell us that... that..."

"Don't even say it," I interrupt her. "We're not putting those words out in the universe. I don't think he's gotten checked out yet. In fact, I'm almost positive. We just need him to make an appointment to see his doctor. I'm afraid he's going to collapse on the field."

Annika nods in agreement. "I keep trying to bring it up, but he just changes the topic, you know?"

I nod, because I do know. For as much as he bitches about his dad not wanting to talk about certain things, Jaxon himself sure has mastered the art of deflection.

Right on cue, the man in question rolls over, making Annika and I freeze like deer in headlights, waiting to see if he's awake now or if we're safe to keep talking. After a few seconds of holding our breath, he finally starts snoring again.

"Let's just keep working on him," I suggest. "It's his life and all, but he can't just shove his head in the sand and pretend he doesn't have a real reason to get himself checked out. But maybe when you get on the field and see it firsthand, he'll finally listen to us."

Annika nods in agreement. Getting into the athletic training program is a huge honor, but she still has a few weeks of classroom time before she gets out to the practice field. "I would be a shitty girlfriend if I just let him ignore this and then he ..." She stops herself from finishing the sentence which I'm grateful for. I'm worried, yes, but I don't want to think about the worst-case scenario. Not yet, at least.

Putting my hand on her shoulder, I squeeze, hoping to convey my support. She pats my hand and smiles half-heartedly. It's scary knowing the statistics of adults who have a second bout of cancer after beating it as a kid. In this case, ignorance really does sound blissful.

"Anyway, I'm gonna head out and hit the library before people start waking up and take all the good tables," I announce.

Annika shakes her head. "Yes. Because there is such a huge demand for the library at eight-oh-seven on a Sunday morning."

"The one time I agree with you is the one time it'll bite me in the ass, and you know it." We both chuckle quietly because she knows I'm right.

"Good luck getting through to that guy." I gesture to Jaxon, whose mouth is hanging wide open as he snores. "I can see how concerned he is that we're worried about him." If I had time and Annika would let me, I'd put a bug in his mouth right now. Unfortunately, Annika is one of those good girlfriends who protect their boyfriend from harmless pranks.

"I can see the wheels turning in your brain, Heath. Don't even think about dropping something in his mouth."

Like I said… overprotective.

I turn toward the door and then spin back as a thought occurs to me. "Oh. You may want to check on Lauren, too." Annika cocks her head in question. "I don't know what happened with the guy she was with last night. But whatever it was, wasn't good." Annika stiffens slightly, and I know where her mind went. Same place all our minds still go, no matter how much we try not to. "Nothing to worry about, except I think maybe the guy was just trying to get in her pants and she thought there was something more to it. She was pretty upset in the car."

"Shit," Annika mumbles and drops her chin to her chest. "I was afraid that was going to happen. Something about that guy sat wrong with me." Looking back up, she takes a deep breath. "I'll talk to her. Thanks for the heads up."

Nodding in response, I finally head out to the library.

I've got a best friend who is avoiding the fact that he could have cancer again, a friend who still has nightmares sometimes from an attack, and a frenemy who got tricked by some douchebag guy just so he could get in her pants.

For someone who is trying hard to reach my goals in the very near future, I've sure got a lot of emotional people in my life making me lose focus.

FIVE

Lauren

'm restless.

I'm sure it's because my mind is spinning and my emotions are on the brink of disaster, which I'm trying hard to hide behind nonchalance. No one wants to hang out with the girl who is distraught over the guy who tricked her into having sex with him. Not even me. I'm hardly the last person who has gone through this. It happens. It's life. It's also my own damn fault.

I got so caught up in the excitement that someone liked me, someone as amazing as Con, that I fell for the whole thing. Really, I have no one to blame except myself. It's not like this hasn't happened to me before. I should have learned my lesson the first time. *Stupid, stupid, stupid.*

But I didn't learn the first time, so all I want to do now is wallow in my hurt for the rest of the weekend. Not so much that anyone knows I'm wallowing. For whatever reason, those deeper, darker emotions seem personal to me. I don't like sharing them. It makes me feel vulnerable. I hate that. I'd rather lie here on my bed, mindlessly scrolling through Pinterest and pretend I'm just a slacker with my studies, all the while knowing I'm just struggling to focus and keep myself from spiraling under the weight of sadness.

Every time I opened up my business ethics textbooks and try to concentrate on my assigned reading, my mind wanders back to Con—the conversations we had at the gym; the fun we had last night; the less than stellar sex; the humiliation of this morning; the worry about what practice is going to be like for the next several weeks.

I finally gave up and have been pinning some new outfits on my page instead. Fashion will never make me feel the way people do. Unless parachute pants make a comeback, of course. That could potentially send me into a deep depression along with much of the fashion-loving world.

"Let's go out dancing tonight."

I almost drop my phone on my face in surprise. Turning to Annika, I half expect her to be suffering from a high fever that makes her delusional, or her skin to be turning green, because something is obviously wrong with her. Offering to go dancing is not normal behavior. "Are you feeling okay?"

She rolls her eyes at me. "I'm fine."

"Are you sure? In over two years of living together, you have never once said you wanted to go dancing. In fact, normally I have to threaten you with the silent treatment to get you to go out anywhere with me."

She shrugs sheepishly, and I know something's up. "I'm not a huge party animal. You know that. I just think it would be fun tonight. To get out and just… relax."

"Liar." I sit straight up in bed, dropping my phone down next to me. "Something's up. What is it?"

"You tell me." Holding my gaze, we end up in a staring contest. Now I know for sure she has ulterior motives, and I have a bad feeling it has to do with my walk of shame this morning.

The guilt of hiding this wretched love life of mine makes me the first to look away, but if she knows enough that she wants to take me to a club to make me feel better, there's no telling what else she'll figure out if she looks at me long enough. Annika is one of only two people who can read me like a book sometimes. The other one, thankfully, doesn't live here.

Lying back down, I pull Pinterest up again and continue my hunt for some kick-ass knee-high boots. Boots and I have a great relationship. I love them by wearing them with pride, and in return, they love me back by making my legs look longer. They are the true loves of my life. "I went out last night, so I'm just tired," I lie, making it a point to not look at her.

Annika huffs and mutters something about "that damn Aerosmith t-shirt" and grabs her own phone, typing something out. Good. She better stop harping on the love of my life, Steven Tyler. Wearing his picture on my chest always makes me feel better. Although, admittedly, I thought it would be harder than that to throw her off the trail of my heartbreak.

"Hello?" a familiar voice says through the speaker of her cell and my head whips over, eyes wide. Son of a bitch! She's not off the trail! She's going to tag team me!

"Hey Kiersten, it's Annika."

"You bitch!" I yell and sit back up on the bed, the wide neck I cut out years ago falling off my shoulder. If there's one person who knows me well enough to get inside my brain from hundreds of miles away, it's my best friend, Kiersten, which is why I haven't called her yet. I don't want her picking through my thoughts and emotions. They're too fresh.

Completely unaffected by my name-calling and continual grumbling, Annika continues being the traitor she is and feeds Kiersten more information. "Something's wrong with Lauren, and I think it's about a guy."

"How did you get Kiersten's phone number? I never gave it to you for a reason."

Annika rolls her eyes which she seems to do a lot with me these days. "I've had it since freshman year. Someone has to make sure you ladies are safe when you go out on the town."

Guilt runs through me. I know she doesn't mean to make me feel that way. But I have never forgiven myself for not tracking her down and instead, assuming she went home with someone the night she was raped. I'm not sure I ever will. It broke her. Hell, it broke me. It's not something I would ever wish on my worst enemy, but to see your best friend go through it because you weren't living up to the girl code of watching her back? That's not something I think I'll ever get over. Yes, Annika is fine now, but she still carries the scars. She always will. So will those of us closest to her.

"Ohmygod, Annika," Kiersten says through the phone, probably feeling the same guilt I do. "I'm so sorry about that night—"

"Stop!" Annika holds up her hand like Kiersten can actually see her. "We're not talking about that night. I'm fine. Trial's over. He's in prison. Moving on to current problems—Lauren got home early this morning in yesterday's clothes and makeup, and now, she doesn't want to go dancing tonight."

I narrow my eyes at her. The other person who can read me like a book doesn't even have to be in the same room to do it. She just has to have my traitorous roommate give her enough information to put two and two together.

"Lauren, what's going on?" Kiersten's tone leaves no room for argument. Either she's already figured things out, or she suspects enough to not let it go until we talk it out.

While Kiersten's concern is appreciated, she already knows too much about me. Which means, she's going to figure out all the sordid details of last night, and I'm not ready to talk about it. Hell, I don't even want to *think* about it. I just want to lick my wounds in peace.

"Nothing happened," I say with as much normalcy as I can muster. It's worth a shot. "I went out last night, so I'm tired. That's all."

"She did the walk of shame this morning and Heath brought her home. Said she was acting strange in the car."

"I was not!"

Annika ignores me and keeps talking as if I'm not sitting right here. "They don't even like each other, Kiersten. If Heath is worried, something is definitely wrong."

I shake my head, pissed that this conversation is even

happening. I understand Annika's good intentions, but I'll talk about this when I'm ready. Or never.

The room stays silent for a few moments, just long enough for me to steel myself before Kiersten says exactly what I expected her to say.

"Lauren. Honey. This isn't Blake Salado again."

Just the sound of his name feels like a spike right through my heart.

"Wait." Annika shakes her head. "Who is Blake Salado?"

No one says a word until Kiersten asks, "It's not my story to tell. But I think she should know, don't you?"

"Sure. Why the hell not?" I say with a humorless huff. Then, I close my eyes and try to block out the memories as Kiersten tells Annika the story of the asshole who took my virginity in someone's master bedroom at a high school party. Blake Salado was the super cute basketball player. He was tall and trim. Had brown curly hair. And his smile was an open invitation to anyone to strike up a conversation. He wasn't the hottest guy in school, but he was the boy next door and he charmed me. He charmed everyone.

Blake and I had been dating for weeks and were falling in love. Or so I thought. But as soon as his orgasm was over, and my hymen was forever broken, he got dressed, went back down to the party and walked up to his friends sing-songing, "I got some puuuuuuusssy. I got some puuuuuuuussy." I heard all about it at school on Monday. That, and how someone's parents were pissed when they got home and found my blood on their sheets. As if I wasn't humiliated enough, the evidence of my virginal status was one of the high points of the story that went around the school.

Blake never spoke to me again. Not even to say sorry when his friends started heckling me in the hallways about the different ways my flexibility could be used to their advantage.

The harassment didn't last long, fortunately. High schoolers have the attention span of gnats and some other scandal came along to delight their love of drama. But the scar on my soul was permanent. I fell into the downward spiral of closet drinking and self-loathing. I cried nightly and rarely slept. I lost weight I didn't have to lose and stopped going to practice. No longer was I the girl who had dreams of finding the love of her life. From that point on, I was the girl who wasn't worth more than a roll in the hay. The guys in the hall made sure I was fully aware of that fact.

Kiersten was the only person who made an effort to pull me out of my funk. She ratted me out to my parents about the vodka under my bed. She fed me tater tots and Diet Coke for lunch every day. And after a couple of weeks of moping around, she convinced me to go back to practice and gave me advice on how to ignore anyone who tried to throw my mistake in my face.

It took time, but I finally pulled myself out of the depression I had fallen into. It's also when I started taking meds. The drugs don't stop my anxiety which can spiral into more if I'm not careful, but it gives me a boost so I can rearrange my thoughts to get back on track.

From then on, I decided there would be no dating anyone who had an affiliation with my school because no guy at my alma mater deserved my attention. In fact, there was no dating at all. One-night stands became my norm. No strings. No emotions. No hurt. It helped me take my power back and perfect my give-no-fucks attitude. By the time I stepped foot on my college campus, I was stronger and more sure of myself. No one could bring me down. Sex couldn't be used as a weapon against me and neither could ugly words. I was free to enjoy life behind my false bravado and keep those more intimate feelings to myself.

Unfortunately, the only one from my old life who knows how bad off I was is the one person Annika has decided to rally. There's no getting away with small talk now, no matter how hard it hurts.

"You're stronger now, babe," Kiersten continues, even though I don't want to hear this right now. "So, you liked him, and he wasn't honest about what the night meant. It sucks so bad, and I know it's triggering some of that old stuff."

I chance a glance at Annika who looks devastated to hear this. As soon as she sees me looking, she starts to stand up.

Holding my hand out, I stop her. "Do not come over here and try to hug me right now, or I will break your arms before they wrap around me."

Annika's mouth drops open while Kiersten laughs. "So. Feisty," Annika mutters, but sits her ass back down.

"That's how you know she's going to be okay. If she's back to being bitchy, it means she's already starting to move on," Kiersten announces through her giggles and then gets serious again. "I know this hurts, Lauren. But I have to ask. You haven't stopped taking your meds, right?"

"No," I mumble and pick at my fingernail.

"Then you just need to get out of your head. Go out tonight with your friends. Dance it off. Stand in the middle of the dance floor, make 'come hither' eyes at all the hotties, and then tell them to scram before your bodybuilder girlfriend rips their balls off. Take back your control again. Hell, take it back again tomorrow. And the next night. And the next. Whatever it takes to make you feel strong. And whatever you do, next time you see him, if he says anything, tell him the same thing you finally told Blake Salado. Remember what that was?"

"Your athletic prowess doesn't extend into the bedroom, and you're bragging to people about it?" I say in my best Kiersten voice.

"Exactly. It worked right? He got stuck in a dry spell for at least a year after that," she says with a laugh. When her giggles finally subside, she asks, "Are you going to be okay? And don't bullshit me Lauren or Annika will let me know, and then I'll be knocking on your door."

Suddenly feeling pissed off again, I exclaim, "Yeah! What the hell is this double-teaming me about? Since when do you guys work together to make me feel emotions and shit?"

Annika gives me a look that says she wasn't born yesterday. "You always feel emotions and shit. You just don't like letting us help you through them."

I hate that she's right. But in a weird way, I do love that it's working. I'll never admit it, though. I need to have some sort of pride, even if it's in front of the best friends I have.

Taking a deep breath, I shake my arms out and stretch my neck. Kiersten is right. I'm strong. I have value. I have worth as a person. So, what if Con doesn't see that? That's his loss and not at all my problem. Or at least that's what I'll keep telling myself until I believe it.

"Okay fine. I'll go out tonight."

"Yay!" Annika yells, a huge smile on her face.

Crinkling my nose, I look at her and deadpan, "Seriously. You need to calm down. This role reversal thing is weirding me out."

"Me, too," she announces. "You know how much I hate clubs. But if it helps you get over this douchebag, I'll do it."

I point right in Annika's face. "I knew you didn't really want to go."

"Of course not. But it's too late now. Jaxon is picking us up at eight-thirty. And I'm pretty sure Heath is coming too."

I groan. Great. Just great. The one time I need to be away from everyone I know so I can reset my façade, the one person on campus who saw me at my worst is going to be there.

Why can't I catch a freaking break?

SIX
Heath

really didn't want to come out tonight. It's not that I'm a homebody or anything. I enjoy a good kegger as much as the next guy. Clubs just aren't my thing. They're loud. They're crowded. And people act like idiots. It all feels very meat market to me.

Sometimes I wish I could enjoy the occasional hook-up with a stranger. I am in college and the best athlete here. Hell, I'm probably the best athlete in the state if you take out the pro teams. Even then, I'm probably better than half those guys. That's not arrogance. It's what I'm banking on to relieve some of the financial stress off my parents in the future. That goal always leads back to football, which is why I'm very, very careful with anything that remotely comes to sex.

I always have been, but last year, that point was driven home when one of our star linebackers found out shortly before he was drafted that a failing condom meant his life was about to change in more ways than one. The ink was barely dry on his new contract, and he was already saddled with a fiancée and baby on the way. He remained tight-lipped about his new family, but we all knew he didn't have a girlfriend. And he still ended up with a wife.

That's not going to happen to me. Yes, I could easily take advantage of my super athletic status and how it just happens to come with a few perks of the female variety. Yes, it would be nice to have the stress relief that goes with meaningless sex with someone who could care less about anything more than bragging rights for banging a football star. But not at the expense of my current sanity, and certainly not at the expense of my future. Next time I'm with someone it's going to be because we're going to build a future together. Clubs like this are not the place to pick up women like that, even if I was looking.

A hot piece of ass ogling me from the dance floor is a prime example of someone I try to avoid. She's been watching me for a while now. Her skintight tank top shows off a very voluptuous chest. Just a small tug and a couple of inches separate my eyes from her peaked nipples. That part I can already see. Gyrating to the music, she makes no secret that she's dancing just for me. The intense stare in my direction isn't hard to read. What is hard to read, however, is if she's the kind of girl who wants to trap me or the kind of girl who wants to get to know me. And that's why I haven't reciprocated.

So, I'm sitting alone at a table off to the side of the bar. Being here is giving me a headache already. The beat is thrumming so loud, you can't hear anything unless you yell. Thank God my friends are on the dance floor so I'm not having to strain to hear them talk.

This is where Annika wanted to come, though, for reasons I can't figure out. She's been avoiding loud, crowded businesses like this since last year. Maybe coming here is part of her healing or something. Maybe her therapist suggested she take this last step. Who knows? I won't ask because it's not my business. We all have our demons, so it doesn't matter anyway. She's my friend. If this is where she wants to be, I'm here.

It's odd, I know. For as irritated as I am about being here, there is no way I wouldn't join my friends. Not because it's fun. It's much more calculated than that. We've fallen into this weird "safety in numbers" thing and now, it feels like the norm to tag along wherever the girls want to go. Lauren and Annika don't go out to bars or clubs without us guys anymore. Ever. Even if they're having a girls' night with ten other people, we're on the other side of the room, doing our own thing but always on watch. Ridiculous, maybe, but you can't unlearn the kind of lesson we all learned last year. And frankly, we care about our friends too much to not keep an eye on each other.

Yes, even Lauren.

I look over at the dance floor again to check on her. She's moving to the music like she owns the place. Her small hips sway seductively as the tiny skirt she's wearing rides up even higher. Any more movement and she'll be flashing the room. Fingers crossed she's not going commando. Not that I would mind getting a sneak peek.

Lauren thinks I don't like her, but that's not it at all. I just don't… well, gravitate toward her. I tolerate her flirty and inappropriate comments. I appreciate her love for Annika. And I have mad respect for her sport and the work she does to compete. She's just not someone I enjoy shooting the shit with. I've tried many times to figure out if it's just a personality conflict or if it's because I always feel like she's hiding something. Or because she comes across as exactly the kind of girl I try to avoid. I just can't figure out which one of those possibilities is the truth.

Shaking my head, I sip my water and continue watching her move. If nothing else, she is a hot little number. Her body is totally cut. Every time she raises her arms, her shirt rides up and I get a glimpse of her abs. I'd be lying if I said the six-pack she's sporting wasn't a total turn-on. Not at all like the other girl who is making her sexual prowess obvious. No, Lauren is more subtle. She cares less about other patrons noticing her and more about finding a good beat. Interesting. I would have thought she'd be more responsive to having an audience.

As I watch her dance, Lauren is approached by some guy. He's short, barely taller than her. I snicker to myself. We've never been at a club together, but Lauren is usually pretty picky about who she flirts with. This poor sucker is about to make a fool of himself.

Without bothering to turn around and get a good look at who she's gyrating against, she smiles and backs up into him, trying to find their groove. Hmm. It seems her standards may have changed. She raises her arms, exposing that tight stomach again. I watch as she practically melts into him and he leans down to say something in her ear.

That's when her demeanor does a complete one-eighty. She stiffens and her face takes on a pained look. I immediately sit up straight, paying closer attention.

Lauren shrugs the guy off her, face scrunching up like she's disgusted, or distressed. I can't put my finger on it, because it changes so fast into a look of anger. Still on alert, I scrutinize the scene as it unfolds. I want to race out there and squash whoever the asshole is like a bug, but I know Lauren won't appreciate it. She likes being invincible to people. That much, I've figured out on my own. So, I'll let her fight her own battle. But if it looks like she's about to lose, she won't be able to stop me from getting involved.

She pushes the guy away, then storms off the dance floor and heads straight to the bar. The stiffness of her body tells me she's still agitated, but in true Lauren fashion, she's holding her head high.

As she waits for the bartender to notice her, she glances around the room, her eye catching something, and that's when I see the look on her face again. I don't see any tears from here, but she looks dejected. And she keeps trying to ignore whatever has her attention but can't seem to stop from taking quick looks to the same side of the room.

Turning my head to try and figure out what's going on, it suddenly all makes sense. At a different table is a group of guys. All of them are what I would consider to be pint-sized. All of them are laughing. And all of them are looking right at Lauren as they do it.

My heart pounds as I start to put two and two together. Picking her up on the side of the road this morning, her crying in my car, pushing the guy that's now laughing with his friends. It all makes sense.

"Son of a bitch," I huff.

Annika didn't want to come out tonight for fun. She wanted to help Lauren feel better because some douchebag screwed her over. Unfortunately, I think the douchebag showed up to ruin the good time.

Scanning the room, I see Jaxon and Annika getting way too close on the dance floor for my viewing pleasure. Which also means Annika doesn't realize her best friend is being harassed by what is probably the entire male gymnastics team. That's a reasonable assumption to make about a group of unusually short guys all hanging out together. Regardless, I'm not going to sit here and watch this shit go down.

Decision made, I down the rest of my drink, stand up, and walk straight to Lauren. Her expression changes as I approach, probably trying to put a strong front on. It quickly changes to one of confusion when I keep walking, backing her into the bar as I put my arms around her and rest my hands on the smooth wood, caging her in.

It's quieter over here so there's no reason to yell in her ear. Still, I want to make a statement to the assholes across the room, so I lean down anyway.

"Is that the dickwad that fucked you over this morning and made you walk home in the cold?" My big body covers hers from their view like I want.

"What?" I hear the confusion in her voice. I've never gotten this close to her before, so I know it's going to take a second for her to catch on to my game.

"The guy you pushed away on the dance floor."

"You saw that?"

"I did," I admit. "And it pissed me off. So, tell me, is that the guy?"

She shakes her head, her blonde hair brushing up against my cheek. I think I've just found something to put on my very short "like" list—her hair smells like some kind of tea tree oil. The minty kind. I like it.

"But it's one of the guys over there?"

Lauren stiffens, and I know I've assessed this situation out correctly. She doesn't even have to answer me. Her body language confirms it all.

"Which one?" I growl, halfway hoping she doesn't tell me. I'm fired up enough, I'm liable to get myself in trouble.

Lauren pushes me back so I can look down on her face. She's got long lashes. Much longer than I remember. And her blue eyes are looking up at me through them.

Huh. That's thing number three for my list. If she didn't have such a hard personality to deal with, I might be able to go for a girl like Lauren. I might even break my one-night rule.

But now isn't the time to worry about this weird turn of events. She had a rough last night, an even rougher morning, and now those idiots are trying to make her tonight even worse. I'm not having it.

"What are you doing?" she questions softly, the most demure look I've ever seen on her face.

"I'm helping you take your power back."

My words seem to startle her, and I wonder if I've read the situation wrong.

"But you don't even like me."

I hold her gaze trying to decide how to answer. I thought her knowing that she wasn't my favorite person wasn't a big deal. I'm not her favorite person either. But her questioning my motives stings in a way I didn't expect. Not because I want us to be best friends, but because she doesn't even trust me enough to trust my intentions. Now isn't that just a kick in the gut for a guy who prides himself on his integrity and character.

"First of all, I never said that." Out loud anyway. Semantics. Whatever. "Second, like you or not, I respect you as a woman," I explain. "That douchebag treated you like dirt this morning and he's treating you like dirt again. I know guys like him and he gets off on it because it makes him feel good about himself." Leaning closer, I add, "But it makes you feel like shit. That's not okay. So, let's have some fun. Turn the tables on him."

She cocks her head and narrows her eyes at me. But she's also sporting the same kind of devious smirk I am. I lift one eyebrow at her in silent question. Finally, she nods once.

Smiling, I grab her hand. "Follow my lead," I say, guiding her back out to the dance floor.

As much as I hate techno music, I admit it's easy to find a beat. And Lauren has good rhythm so within seconds we're moving to the tempo. She's tiny—easily a foot shorter than me—and it almost feels like I'm surrounding her on all sides. Like she's completely safe within the concave form of my body.

Putting my hands on her hips, I guide her back toward me more. "Relax," I say into her ear when she tenses. "He's watching, so at least pretend you're enjoying this."

I feel her laugh as she leans into me. It's odd how much I enjoy the feel of her small body. I'm trying not to think too hard about it, though. Dancing with Lauren isn't about lust or feelings. It's about unraveling some idiot's campaign to ruin her reputation and focus. I can't put my finger on the whys of it, but I get this weird feeling that his treatment of her is partly about sabotage. It wouldn't be the first time a college athlete tried to knock their teammate off their game. I can't figure out why Lauren failing would benefit him, but I don't follow her sport. Maybe there's some co-ed event I know nothing about.

We stay tangled up together for a couple of songs before deciding it's time for another drink. Like the gentleman I am, I spring for her cocktail and another bottle of water for me. The season is just beginning. I don't need unnecessary calories.

The table we vacated earlier is miraculously still empty, so we head back that direction. And I just happen to see one of the douchebags walking our way as we do.

"Don't say a word," I instruct Lauren quietly. "Trust me on this."

I sound all caveman and overprotective, but I've been stressed lately and could use an outlet. Nothing would make me happier than throwing down with this guy. I won't because the last thing I need is an ass chewing from Coach or a court date interfering with a game. But I can still push this guy's buttons and defend myself if he snaps.

Lauren peeks up at me with a question in her eyes before looking over and realizing we're about to have company. Her expression changes, and if I'm not mistaken, she's less concerned about what he might do and more interested to see what *I* might do. Sliding into the booth, I sit next to her and put my arm around her shoulder. My eyes flick up to the guy who is now just feet from our table, daring him to take this any further.

He does. Just like I knew he would. Guys like him don't enjoy missing out on something good. And if I'm having a good time with Lauren, then in his mind, I've taken his toy. He may as well pee a circle around her. It's pathetic.

Taking a drink of my water, I keep my eyes trained on his, even as he speaks.

"Enjoying my sloppy seconds?"

Lauren jolts just slightly at the dig. Not enough for this guy to see, but enough for me know she feels like she's been slapped. I hold myself back from reacting, though. That's what he wants. I'd rather play with him for a bit, so I finish my drink and slowly lower the bottle to the table before speaking.

"Seriously, Danny Zuko?" I spout, referring to his black jeans, white t-shirt, and black leather jacket. All he needs is to slick back his hair and he'd be in full on Travolta mode. "What is this, a shitty 70's movie?" His eyes widen slightly before tugging down the jacket he thought made him look good until now. "You need to show a little more respect for women than they did back in those days."

His eyes narrow and I know he's about to spout off again. "She needs to deserve any kind of respect for me to do that. Fucking on a first date doesn't exactly qualify."

I throw the meanest glare I can conjure at him, which isn't hard since I'm already just about done with this conversation. "I'll let that slide this time because we're here on our first date and unlike some of us, I'm a gentleman and wouldn't even consider treating a woman like trash over what she does with her own body. But if you don't want any trouble, I suggest you go crawling back to your tiny little friends over there and head home." I gesture toward the table of guys who are no longer laughing. In fact, they all look either mystified by this turn of events or slightly nervous. Except one guy. The redhead seems to be enjoying his friends' nerves. Not sure what that's about. I could be reading him wrong. I may have to ask Lauren about it. If she has just one ally, I'd feel better.

"Who's gonna make me?"

I guess I'll have to bring my question up later because this prick wants to keep going. Fine by me. I get run over by three hundred some odd pounds of offensive tackle regularly. What's he gonna do? Head-butt my knee?

Sliding out of the booth, I stand up in front of him making sure I reach my full height, which is at least a dozen inches over him. Drawing on my most intimidating glare, I make sure he knows he doesn't stand a chance against me. "I don't care what your opinion is. I like Lauren. And I don't like the way you're talking to her or about her."

The air around us changes to one of nervous anticipation, and I know the other patrons are paying close attention to our conversation. Body language doesn't lie and mine says if he pushes me, this will be over before the bouncer even knows what happened.

Finally, he takes a step back, tugging down his jacket again. He glances at Lauren once and then back at me, probably not sure how he lost control of the situation so easily.

"This isn't over," he threatens, but it falls flat.

An amused chuckle bursts out of me. I shake my head at him, clearly displaying my disappointment with his tired act. "Again, welcome to a new millennium. That Neanderthal shit is boring. Just go home and leave her alone."

His nostrils flare, but he turns and storms off, signaling to his friends who all follow him out the door.

Sitting back down, I exhale and turn to my fake date. "You okay?"

She's smiling, but it's not reaching her eyes. She still looks sad. I hate that.

"Yeah. I feel like *West Side Story* was about to break out in front of me." I chuckle, but I'm also acutely aware of how much the humor feels like a classic defense mechanism. "It's almost flattering to have two men fake fighting over me."

"That wasn't fake. And I take it you didn't know they were going to be here tonight?"

She shakes her head and absentmindedly plays with her straw. "I thought they were going into the city. If I'd known they were going to be in town, I would have put up more resistance when Annika made me get dressed."

"Ah-ha. I knew something was off with her wanting to go clubbing."

This time when Lauren smiles, it's real. "It took me a while to figure it out, too."

We sit in silence for a few minutes, neither of us moving to the other side of the booth, or even away from each other. Our thighs are still touching, and I must admit, I don't hate it.

"But really," Lauren continues a few minutes later. "Why did you do it?"

"What? Shut that guy down?"

She nods, biting her lip. I've never seen her do that. Maybe I haven't been watching her closely enough, but it could also be because she's never been this real with me before. Like her guard finally came down just a bit.

I take a breath and think about how to answer without giving too much away. But I also don't want to insult her by insinuating it wasn't to help her out. It was. There's just more to it for me.

"I don't like guys like that," I finally decide on, figuring it's a safe enough answer. "I know you said last night was consensual and all, and I'm not judging you for that." She looks down at the table, and I nudge her shoulder with mine. "I'm serious. You're a grown-ass woman. Sleep with who you want."

Her eyes shift back up to mine, and she nods for me to continue.

"I just think when a guy is trying to get in someone's pants, he needs to be honest. Tricking someone into something, that's not cool. It's not right. It's unethical, and I'll call someone out every. Damn. Time." I slam my finger on the table accentuating each word. I can feel myself getting fired up again, so I opt to take another swig of my drink, then crush the now empty bottle.

Lauren doesn't say anything, so I look over at her. She's smiling. The same kind of cocky Lauren smile I'm used to and usually don't like, but there's something more genuine behind it this time. Understanding, maybe?

"Sounds like this is personal to you."

I nod because there's no sense in lying to her. "I've got three little sisters."

"Let me guess." She pushes her watered-down beverage away and leans her forearms on the table. "At least one of them isn't so little anymore, is she?"

"Nope."

"And somewhere in the back of your mind, you wish the guy she'd gotten involved with had been the one challenging you tonight?"

It appears Lauren is quicker than I give her credit for. I blow out a deep breath and push back the memories. "Probably good it wasn't him. I'm not sure I would have stopped at just words."

I get lost in my thoughts of hearing my sister's cries over the phone when she realized she'd been used and tossed away. We've always been close, and I felt so helpless in that moment. It was shortly into my sophomore year and there was nothing I could do to fix it for her. I couldn't go home and beat the guy's ass—partially because he was a minor and that wouldn't look good on my record. Partially because I'm at least half a day's drive from home. The guilt of not doing more to protect her from the assholes of the world still eats at me. I'd always made sure any of the guys around me knew she was off-limits when I was in high school. I should have known it would take just a year away for them to forget all the threats I promised.

"Hey." This time Lauren nudges my shoulder. "You know she's going to be okay, right? We women are stronger than we look. It's a shitty thing to happen, but it does. All the damn time."

"None of you should have to deal with shit like that," I

practically growl. I get distracted by our friends who are finally making their way back to the booth. They've missed all the drama tonight, too wrapped up in each other. Good for them. They deserve to not have to worry about this mess.

"Of course, we shouldn't. But welcome to the world of being a woman," she mutters and then pastes a bright smile on her face when Annika sits down, Jaxon headed toward the bar.

"Hey guys," Annika yells, ears probably still ringing from how much louder the dance floor is than this corner booth. "Are you having a good time?"

Lauren and I look at each other and smirk, silently communicating our amusement. I'm not sure "good time" is what either of us is thinking right now. But it's also not horrible hanging out together.

Annika looks back and forth at us. "What? I feel like I missed something."

Jaxon walks up and drops another bottle of water in front of me before sitting down next to his girl.

"Not sure you missed anything as much as your besties may have just found some common ground." Lauren lifts her watered-down glass to toast my plastic bottle. "To the shitty world of womanhood."

Raising my bottle, I echo, "To the shitty world of womanhood," and tap our beverages together with a *thunk*.

SEVEN

Lauren

Reaching forward, I stretch my arms out as far as I can on the floor in front of me and roll my hips until my legs have shifted into a full straddle split. I point my toes for three seconds, then flex my feet all the way, then back to a point. Depending on how I move my feet, different parts of my legs stretch and strain. It's painful, but in a weird, good way. Like when you wiggle a loose tooth. It hurts, but not bad enough to stop.

Taking a deep breath, I pull myself back into the sitting position, staying in my straddle, but moving my arms in giant circles before leaning to the right and grabbing my toes.

I like the fuzzy socks I'm wearing today. They're ultra-soft and striped with bold colors. They give me comfort like a fluffy blanket. And they typically stay in my drawer all year until winter. That's my favorite part. They remind me we're having a reprieve from the normal Texas humidity and getting a blast of cooler temps. It'll be short-lived, I know, but I'm not complaining about it while it's here.

"I heard what happened."

I look up and see Ellery next to me reaching for her own foot as she stretches. Everyone else is sitting in circles together, chatting and laughing. Probably over whatever antics they were up to this weekend. I don't normally participate, content to stretch on my own. Not that anyone on the team usually seeks me out. In their eyes, I'm basically a reserve team member. Which is why it's a surprise to see Ellery sitting next to me.

Reaching for my left foot so she and I are facing each other, I play dumb. "A lot of things happened. Which one are you referring to?" I say it quietly enough no one can hear us. The last thing I want is for her to mention anything about Con and someone to eavesdrop. I'm sure the rumor mill already has enough to talk about after Sunday morning.

Ellery keeps her body folded over but looks around quickly before whispering, "That you slept with Con."

I'm not surprised the news was passed around so quickly. With that many witnesses, it was inevitable. I'm sure my "night" with Heath has also been shared with interest and delight. Somehow, though, I doubt the almost beat-down Con got at the hands of Southeast Texas State's most eligible athlete has been talked about. Funny how that works around here.

Putting a disinterested expression on my face, I look up at Ellery. "So?" Twisting my body, I reach out to the middle again, stretching my arms as far as I can in front of me, lengthening my spine.

"So?" She mimics, sporting a look of horror and her stretch somehow gets deeper as she tries to get closer to me. "So, everyone knows you had sex with Con. Doesn't it bother you that, that… he told people?" Ellery whispers that last part like she is shocked and appalled on my behalf. Clearly, she has her own issues when it comes to sex, but I do appreciate she is worried for my virtue instead of trying to make me feel bad. Maybe I underestimated her before. Maybe she's not as much like everyone else as I thought.

"It's just sex, Ellery," I lie, because there is no way I'm letting my guard down in this gym. Even for someone who comes across as loyal and kind as Ellery. "Everyone has it."

I sit straight up, put my legs together, one knee bent, and position myself to push into a backbend, but Ellery's expression stops me. Relaxing my posture, I lean in closer to her this time. "Ellery."

"Hmm." She doesn't look at me, but even at this angle I can tell her face is as red as a tomato.

"Ellery, you've had sex, right?"

She whips her head over to look at me, eyes wide, mouth sputtering. "Of course... why would... I..." Her breathing picks up and she can't get her sentence out.

It appears I've touched a nerve and she may hyperventilate if I don't backpedal a bit. Holding my hand up, I stop her from speaking. "Ellery. Stop. You're going to pass out."

She's still breathing heavy, but at least she's not trying to talk through it now.

"It's okay not to have sex, Ellery." Her eyes widen, but she doesn't say anything else. "Your body, your choice. If your choice is to stay a virgin, there is nothing wrong with that. I actually find it admirable."

Ellery blinks a couple of times in disbelief. I know people think I'm a loose cannon sometimes, but geez. Do they think I'm out trying to convince everyone to join me on the promiscuous dark side?

"I... I thought you'd make fun of me."

"Why?"

She shrugs. "Because everyone else does."

People are such dicks. It's one thing to talk about me and try to make me feel shitty about myself. I'm sure there's some psychological diagnosis on why I make sure to be an easy target for hate. Something about always dodging barbs means I'm never surprised when a new one is lobbed my way. It sucks and gives me anxiety, but I'm used to it. It's a different level of low, however, to attack someone like Ellery who never says a mean word about anyone and is sweet as can be.

"Your body is yours, Ellery. If someone wants to make you feel bad about your choices, fuck 'em. They don't have to live with your decisions. You do." Having given the only advice I have on how to deal with shitty people, I push into my backbend and straighten my legs, stretching my shoulders as far as I can get them to go. I don't mind chatting with Ellery, but I'm done with this particular conversation. It's putting me in a bad mood, and I need to focus my energy on nailing my landing, not worrying about brushing off any snide comments I'm sure to hear for the next three hours.

Thankfully, Coach stays out of what he calls "immature drama" and is ready to get started.

"Let's go!" He yells with a clap of his hands. "Guys, Team A, let's get the vault set up. Team B, head to pommel. Ladies, Team A starts at bars. Team B, head to floor."

Easy to do since I'm already here, so I take my sweet time pushing my legs to the sky and myself into a handstand, watching as my fingers flex on the floor, the only part of my body touching the ground as I adjust my balance. Slowly, I straddle my legs, keeping my knees tight and toes pointed. Leaning forward slightly, I rotate my shoulders and lower my body into a solid planche position, holding it for a few seconds. When my upper body muscles begin to ache, I shift my hips and rotate again until I'm holding myself off the floor in a straddle sit.

Feeling sufficiently warmed up and knowing my coach isn't going to wait much longer for us to start tumbling, I push up and trot over to the edge of the floor to strip out of my sweats. The air feels frigid against my skin considering I've been snuggled in my favorite oversized Aerosmith sweatshirt and fuzzy socks for the last hour. I'm sure my nipples are poking through my sports bra and brightly on display, even though I opted for black which conceals. Just what I need—more reason for some of these assholes to chide me.

Fortunately, except for a few glares and disgusted glances down at my chest, floor warm-ups are relatively uneventful.

Round off,
    back handspring,
        back handspring,

back handspring,
back handspring,
rebound,
back in line.
Round off,
back handspring,
back handspring,
back tuck,
rebound,
back in line.
Round off,
back handspring,
back handspring,
back layout with a full twist,
rebound,
back in line.

Four or five rounds of skills, each building on the next to get our minds and bodies ready to throw the hard skills. The ones we must perfect to win.

Ellery is up first with a triple full she's been working on. She's got the skill itself down but wants to make the landing more solid to match the feel of her music.

Cassidy Graham is next with a double back as an extra warm-up. She's taking a few extras since her skill is so much more difficult. Not that she has anything to worry about. She's been chunking that double back with a double full for at least three years.

My turn. Stepping into the corner, I take a couple of deep breaths, focus on my goal and launch.

Five running steps,
Hurdle,
round off,
flip flop,
PUNCH...

Pulling my arms in, I twist as I turn in the air, landing my double full plus half just slightly too far back. It's enough that I have to take a huge step backward instead of forward like I need for the punch front.

Dammit!

Jogging my way back in line, I don't look at my coach. It was my first attempt. I've got time before he starts getting frustrated with me. I just need to remember to open my eyes and look for the ceiling until muscle memory kicks in and my body naturally holds tight until it's time to release...

"Hey, Lauren."

Con's voice catches me off guard. I didn't realize we were on speaking terms, nor do I know if I want to be. I'm not sure what the protocol is on conversing with the guy who had sub-par sex with you, then kicked you out of his room after forcing you to get dressed in front of his friends. What I do know, however, is it was fun and somewhat empowering to watch him squirm last night. I'm not going to undo all that by giving him the satisfaction of knowing how earlier yesterday made me feel.

"Um... hey?" I make sure to put extra confusion in my voice, like speaking during practice isn't something we've been doing for months.

At the sound of the pound of the springboard, Con looks off that direction. He's not ending the conversation. It's obvious he has something to say, but he's having a hard time looking me in the eye. Good. He should be having some guilt over treating me like dirt.

After a few seconds of silence, he takes a breath and turns toward me. "Who was that guy you were with last night?"

Ah. So that's what this is about. It has nothing to do with humiliating me and making me the laughingstock of the team I've worked so hard to be part of. No, this is about jealousy. Or more accurately, being a sore loser.

Playing dumb to his real intentions, I look to the side, pretending to be confused by his question. "You mean Heath? The guy I'm dating?"

"You're dating him?" Con asks it a little too quickly and with a little too much surprise, completely losing the air of cool he was going for. I won't make that same mistake. As much as I hate playing games like this, indifference is the only way to get guys like Con off your radar.

Weakness equals prey to assholes like him.

"We were on a date. Heath told you as much."

Con looks away again and fidgets more, seemingly oblivious to the whispers around us. I notice them, but not in a "I wonder what they're saying" kind of way. It's more like a hum of bitchiness that I'm ignoring.

"Anyway, it's almost my turn." I begin to walk away, when Con turns quickly and grabs my arm.

"I just don't understand how you ended up dating him after leaving my bed that same morning."

Slowly, I look down at my arm and then back up at him. I'm not sure when we went from him treating me like a plaything to feeling like he can grab me whenever he wants, but now I'm pissed. I may struggle with knowing my own value, but even I know I'm worth more than being manhandled.

Seething, I yank my arm out of his grasp, barely noticing that the hum of bitchiness has stopped. If it weren't for the sounds of the springs in the equipment and the pounding of bodies tumbling, the room would be silent.

Regardless of who can hear me, I'm not one to back down in a situation like this one. Not only did Con trick me, but he also discarded me, he grabbed me, and now he's declaring some sort of possession? Oh. Hell. No.

"I happened to run into Heath on my way back to my dorm. Unlike some people I know, he was gentlemanly enough to make sure I got home okay. And on the way, we hit it off and decided to go out. Even better, we had a great time at the club and plan to do it again. But I don't think that's any of your business, is it, considering you… what was it you told Heath? Oh yeah. You won't respect me until I'm respectable."

"Lauren!" Coach yells, tearing me away from my confrontation. "Whenever you're done chitchatting and would like to join us, you've got a skill to perfect."

I know Coach is using sarcasm to deflect his annoyance, but I'm so angry at Con I don't even care. Instead, I stalk over to the corner of the floor, trying to see through the red haze of anger as I focus. Then I launch.

Five running steps,
   hurdle,
      round off,
         back handspring,
          PUNCH,

Pulling my arms in tight, I twist my body and release when I see the ceiling for the second time, landing with just enough forward momentum to punch again, tucking my body and flipping forward. I land with my arms in the air—completing my connection element for the first time.

"Whoo!!" Coach yells across the gym, clapping his hands. "Atta girl, Lauren! You got it now!"

I feel the tiniest bit of vindication over sticking the landing as I strut off the floor, not even looking in Con's direction. If I can stay this pissed off at him all the time, I might knock Cassidy out of the running for that finals spot after all.

EIGHT

Heath

Business economics is my least favorite class this semester. Possibly of my entire college career so far. Unfortunately, it's also required for my degree... one I hope I don't actually have to use in the future.

Sure, I need all this information and understanding to make sure I can negotiate my own contracts and manage my own finances, but if the worst happens and I don't make the NFL cut, I'll get stuck working in an industry I hate.

That's not going to happen, though. I refuse to think I could get this close to my dream, only to have it snatched away. I will make it into the pros. I *will*. And when I do, I need to be prepared to alleviate the financial stress off my parents, while planning on my own long-term future. So here I sit, reading about the global economy and how it works with, and for, various organizations.

It's boring as hell.

The good news about this class being reading-intensive is it gives me a chance to ice the knee I tweaked in practice. I was pissed when I felt the strain after a particularly hard hit between me and a freshman running back. That kid is big and *fast*. And he's barely nineteen. I'll be keeping a closer eye on him. Not only for practice purposes but because he's up and coming. The pain in my knee is proof of that.

Fortunately, it's only a small injury and should only take a day or two to heal. Until then, ice and tape will be my best friends.

And reading-intensive classes like this one.

Drumming my fingers to the music coming through my favorite Beats headphones, I almost miss the sound of pounding. I'm not sure if I'm hearing things, but I know for sure it's not my music, so I slide the headset back to figure it out. That's when I hear it again.

"Heath!" It sounds like Lauren yelling. "Heath! I need you! Open the door!"

More banging.

Tossing my book aside, I hobble to the door, leg wobbly from my knee being numb. That's not important though. Whatever is causing Lauren to panic has me on edge already. Is it possible to have PTSD from someone else's trauma? Because my heart rate sure does pick up quickly these days when Lauren sounds alarmed.

I fling open the door, ready to jump into action.

"What..." I'm quickly distracted by her scantily clad body so my thoughts change gears. "... in the world are you wearing?"

"I just got done with practice," she says by way of explanation and pushes her way past me into the room, dropping her bag and sweatshirt on the floor in a heap. "I need to talk to you."

Shutting the door behind her, I opt to address the issue glaring me in the face first. "No really. Why don't you have any clothes on?"

"I always wear this to practice. Focus! I need you to be my boyfriend."

I hold my hand up to stop her. "We'll get back to that weird statement in a second. I'm still trying to understand why you're practically naked in my dorm room."

Practically naked and asking for me to be her boyfriend. Because boyfriends and girlfriends do some very naughty things when they are practically naked and that's all I can think of at the moment, which is not ideal while I'm trying to figure out what the hell she's talking about.

Lauren huffs like I'm exhausting and puts her hands on her hips. The movement only puts her body more on display, nipples clearly feeling the effects of the cooler temperatures outside. It's not helpful for my focus at all.

"This is what I wear to practice every day, Heath."

Not sure what I feel about her dressing like this in front of that Conrad-shithead and his equally disgusting buddies. Not that it's my business. "It's in the fifties outside, which we're not at all equipped for being that we live in South Texas, and you don't have a car. I assume that means you walked here."

"I ran. I needed the extra work out and didn't want to use a treadmill when I have places to be. Come on, Heath," she whines, frustrated that we're still on the topic of her spandex. "I need your help."

Rubbing my hand down my face, I take a second to stop thinking of her stripping that sports bra off and tossing it across the room. Instead, I remind myself that she didn't come over here offering a one-night stand. That would have been a whole different conversation and admittedly, one I would have highly considered jumping all over. I don't trust many women, but Lauren is an athlete. The last thing she wants is to get trapped herself.

But she didn't offer sex. She asked me to be her boyfriend.

I don't get it.

Limping my way back to my chair, I sit and toss the ice pack back on my injury. "Let's start this conversation over. I feel there's a punchline I'm missing."

She makes herself comfortable by grabbing Jaxon's chair and pulling it toward me, straddling it and leaning her arms on the back. "Con started talking to me at practice today."

I grimace, partially from the pressure of ice on my knee; partially from hearing that she had to interact with that guy again. "Do I need to kick his ass this time?"

"No. Although maybe eventually. He was all mad I

was with you last night and gripped my arm kind of tight when I tried to walk away." The nonchalant way she says he grabbed her and hurt her pisses me off. But not nearly as much as just knowing he put his hands on her at all. Even a gentle touch would send me into a weird rage. But this is so much worse.

"What?" She can see the menace in my eyes because immediately her hands go up like she's trying to calm a caged animal.

"Before you get all ragey, I shut him down. Don't worry about that." Fat chance of that happening. "And after I told him to leave me alone, I cranked out the double full and a half with the front salto."

Now she's completely lost me. "I have no idea what any of that means."

"It means," she says excitedly, "that I need to keep all this rage, at least until that pass becomes second nature. Which is why I need you to be my boyfriend."

"Still lost." And I am. She keeps saying these things that should have meaning, but I feel like I'm missing a huge part of the puzzle. At least I'm not about to fly off the handle and squish that shorty on her team anymore.

Lauren rolls her eyes like she shouldn't have to explain this to me. It's one of her signature moves that used to piss me off. But I feel like we've turned a corner in our relationship, or whatever you call this, and it doesn't seem to bother me anymore. Maybe she should wear tiny shorts around me more often. It obviously puts me in a better mood.

"Let me see if I can dumb this down."

I quirk an eyebrow at her.

"Poor choice of words," she responds quickly. "What I mean is I'm going to try to explain this without having to start all the way at the beginning. I've been working on this skill I'm required to have for my floor routine, and it hasn't been going well. I just can't get enough power behind it to land how I need."

That part, I understand. Her sport may be different than mine, but the fact remains if you don't have enough power behind your movements, ultimately what you're trying to do will fail.

"Today, when Con grabbed me…" I see red again, but she continues like it's no big deal. "… I was so angry, ya know? Not that he grabbed me, although that was part of it. But more because he was upset that I was dating you."

"Dating me?" I interrupt. "I didn't realize our love affair extended beyond Sunday night clubbing while that fucking Danny Zuko wannabe was watching."

"Neither did I. Until I realized exactly how upset the idea of us being together made him. Like I was the one who had thrown him out on his ass, not the other way around."

Once again, I'm beyond unimpressed with this guy's lack of chivalry.

"When I figured it out, I may have embellished our relationship level a wee bit."

Now it's coming together. She needs to keep up the charade to keep him off her back. I nod in understanding. "That's fine. I'll back you up if he asks me. Although I doubt he'd be so stupid to confront me about it."

Lauren snorts a laugh. "I wouldn't. You didn't see how shell-shocked he was. Like he was being disrespected. And then for him to grab me?" She clenches her eyes shut, and I know she's trying to get her emotions under control. "It made me so angry. I went out on that floor and channeled all that anger and chunked my skill better than I ever have. Did the entire connection including the front salto, just like I've been trying to for weeks."

"Atta girl!" I smack her lightly on the leg. I can't visualize what exactly she did, but the smile on her face indicates it was a win for her. "All you needed was some rage to give you a little extra power."

She nods excitedly. "Which is why you need to be my boyfriend."

There goes my understanding. "You've lost me again."

"I need the rage to power my skill. Con's reaction to you gives me rage. Therefore, I need you to be my boyfriend so Con stays upset and I stay ragey."

"So, you want him to keep assaulting you?"

"No." She rolls her eyes again and then looks at me like the cat that ate the canary—all mischievous and sly. And totally off her rocker. "I just need you to show up at a meet and maybe be seen around campus with me, so it gets back to him. I'm telling you, the look of disbelief on his face that I could forget him so easily was empowering. It pulled me right out of my mood and put me back on track."

I laugh at the ridiculousness of it all. "Girl, you are crazy. You don't actually need me to execute this charade. Just let him believe I'm your boyfriend and you're golden. Pretend to text me or something." Using my good leg to pull the rolling chair forward, I move myself closer to the mini-fridge to switch out ice packs.

"Are you injured?"

The abrupt change in topic jars me. "What?"

Gesturing to the ice in my hands, she says," Your knee. Is it busted?"

"Oh. No. Just tweaked."

"What'd the trainer say?"

Only a true athlete knows the trainer's word is basically law when it comes to injuries. I appreciate that I don't have to explain not going to a doctor.

"Just that. It's a tweak. It'll take a day or two to heal, but nothing I can't play on."

Lauren nods and smiles. "Good. Tape it up nice and tight, and if it feels off, don't push it."

Spoken like someone who knows what it's like to push through those minor injuries we athletes refer to as inconveniences. Another interesting tidbit about the woman I'm starting to be less annoyed by.

Flashing her an ornery smirk, I settle the fresh icepack on my knee. "What's this? Are you... worried about me?"

Pursing her lips, Lauren makes sure I know she's not falling for it. "Of course. I'd hate to see the team lose their top spot in the standings. I've got money on your next game."

Her snark makes me laugh out loud. I don't know how I never noticed Lauren's wit. She's pretty funny when she wants to be. Maybe it's because I was never paying close enough attention. Or maybe it's because we didn't get to know each other until we were thrust into a stressful situation. Regardless, I've added yet another thing to my list of positive attributes.

"Anyway, back to our new relationship."

And the con list grows again.

"I don't understand why you need me for this ruse," I say and then hiss when the ice shifts and a particularly cold spot settles in.

"Because while this is a large school, it's a small campus. Everyone knows everyone, especially you. If people see us together, word will get back to him."

"Who cares what he thinks? You can still hate him and use the rage."

Her face falls and I have a strange constriction in my chest over the idea of disappointing her.

"You're right. I can figure out how to stay pissed. I mean, I have to look at him every day, right?" She laughs lightly, but there's no humor behind it. All the bravado she had a second ago is suddenly gone. It's the same look she had on her face when I picked her up on the side of the road a few days ago. There's something else going on, some other reason she's trying to hang close to me. What is it?

Standing up, Lauren grabs her sweatshirt off the floor, where she dropped it as she came in.

"Lauren, wait."

She doesn't. Instead, she yanks it on and pulls the hood over her head.

"Lauren."

Again, no response, except to grab her backpack and swivel toward the door. I have a feeling if I don't make a move now, I'll never figure out why this is so important to her. Nor will I ever figure out why it's so important to me to have that information.

Ignoring the pain in my knee, I launch myself off the chair and follow her across the room.

"Lauren, you came to me for help, remember? Talk to me."

She pauses with her hand on the doorknob but says

nothing.

"Explain it to me," I say gently. "Please? Why is it so important to you? We don't even like each other."

Lauren bristles but doesn't turn around. "You're wrong, Heath. I've never not liked you. I just didn't do anything to change your mind when you made your decision about me. The same kind of opinion Con made."

With that, she pulls the door open, leaving it ajar while I watch her walk away, stunned by her own words, and my own pre-judgments.

NINE

Lauren

I didn't mean to run out on Heath like I did. Even at that moment, I knew how irrational it seemed. I'm not even sure how it happened. One minute we were joking around and the next I realized our camaraderie at the club was about Heath's own issues with jerky men and had nothing to do with actually caring about me. After such a huge blow to my ego and being hyperaware of people looking at me, I had finally felt safe from the judgy eyes. The ringleader had been put in his place and everyone else would follow suit.

But when Heath made it clear he had no interest in helping me beyond that, it hit me all at once that he isn't my friend. One short-lived prank-like night doesn't change that fact.

Almost immediately, I felt the walls I've spent the last several years building start to crumble at that realization. I was going to spiral if I didn't shift my thought process and staring at the man who used me to help settle his own agenda about his sister was making it worse.

So, I booked it out of there with a parting shot and never looked back. I also never set anyone straight about the true nature of my and Heath's relationship, or lack thereof.

Assumptions swirled around me, and I just let them and spent the time focusing on my goals.

The ruse worked for a while. For a couple of weeks, my responses to Con's inquiries were limited to one- and two-word answers that he didn't question. Mostly it consisted of phrases like, "Buzz off." At least when my coach was listening. I added a little more sailor to my verbiage when no one of authority was around.

It worked because Con didn't have any reason to doubt Heath and I were together. He never came right out and asked, and I never corrected his assumptions, so the sham remained in place. That is, until Con started to realize he hadn't seen us together since that one night. No one had. And that's when things started to fall apart, just as I had predicted in Heath Germaine's dorm room.

The first indicator the jig was up was when Con stopped me on my way out of the gym and said, "I haven't seen you and Heath together in a while. Are you still dating, or did he get tired of you already?"

I rolled my eyes and very calmly responded with, "Contrary to what your ego likes to think, I don't plan ways to flaunt my dating relationships in your direction."

It was all lies. I had tried very hard to flaunt it, but Heath wasn't willing to play the game with me, and there was nothing I could do about it.

After that, Con was onto me and it became clear he was once again on a mission. The goal? Prove that Heath had used me and tossed me away just like Con had.

Why? Who knows? I'm not even sure I want to know. But that was several days ago and the subtle taunts and under the breath comments are back. It has been very disappointing, to say the least. Hurtful and degrading at most.

I try to blow it off and not let the disgusting comments bother me. Logically, I know this is nothing more than petty, childish bullying and possibly some inter-squad sabotage, although I still can't figure out that particular angle. And it helps that Ellery continues to seek me out and stays kind. One semi-friend is better than none, right?

For someone like me, though, who already struggles

with anxiety and depression, it's hard to let the opinions of others roll off my back. I tend to hyperfocus on the negative, which can cause me to spiral and I never want to go back to that horrible place again. It's why I created the false bravado I've mastered—so no one can see the pain underneath. It's also why I wanted Heath to play along and give everyone a bit of a show. If Con were to continue making assumptions, I wouldn't have to be on my guard as much. I would be "protected." I could concentrate on important things in the gym and not be thrown off my game.

But no. Just as I anticipated, the insults are back. And the snickers. And the whispers.

Fortunately, my ability to complete my skills hasn't suffered. I'm not sure why, but I suppose my rage and snark hung around long enough for muscle memory to finally take over.

Today's the day I get to finally show off everything I've mastered. And I'm pumped.

Every year we have two intra-squad meets. We're divided into "teams" of four people and compete against each other. It's a good way to prep ourselves for the upcoming season and the stressors that come with staying focused when all eyes are on you.

This first meet is also the only time the gym is open to spectators. Most of our practices are closed to the public. But today, there are bleachers set up against the far wall for anyone interested in seeing a preview of sorts.

Glancing over at the stands, I concentrate on the task at hand and absentmindedly chalk up my hands for my first event—uneven bars. It's not my favorite, but I've been working on some fun release moves I can't wait to show off. Especially since Annika and Jaxon are here watching. It's not the first meet they've ever attended, but every single time they act shocked by what I can do. It may be the only time I ever impress them.

Coach gives the signal that the meet is beginning, and I step up to the mat. I've been paired with Ellery, Cassidy, and Layla Overton. I'm the weakest competitor on this event, so I'm up first.

Saluting the judge, or who most people refer to as the athletic director, I step forward until I'm in my spot.

Acutely aware that all eyes are on me, including eyes that would love nothing more than to see me fail spectacularly, I push back the nerves that are sitting squarely in my stomach and turn it into excitement. Feet together, I take a deep breath to focus my thoughts, reach my arms back, swing them forward and jump.

The second my hands grip the low bar, my body takes over, every move second nature. Gliding my legs out, kipping up to a handstand, back hip circle to another handstand where I carefully step onto the bar and jump to grip the one above me.

I concentrate on letting my muscles do what it's been trained to do—point, straighten, stretch, release, re-grip. Moves I've been working on for months come like second nature. I love the way it feels like I'm in flight. Like I'm defying gravity. It's an almost magical feeling.

In the groove now, I swing forward, let go and flip my body around, add a half twist and reach for the bar to re-grip, my body bent in a piked gienger. Just as my fingers brush across the bar, I realize I'm too far back by a fraction of an inch. My fingers grip as hard as they can, but it's no use. Down I go, landing face down on the mat with an "oomph".

I hear a collective gasp from people on the bleachers. My teammates, on the other hand, don't even flinch. Falling is part of our sport, and this wasn't an injury fall anyway. Just a frustrating one.

Popping back up, I take a moment to chalk up my hands again before kipping back onto the low bar and finishing my routine.

In what seems like a matter of seconds, I'm spinning around the bar again doing giants, building power for my dismount.

At the exact right moment, I release my hands, tuck my knees in and double back my way through the air, landing on my feet and taking two giant steps back. Finally balanced, I raise my hands and "finish."

My score isn't going to be good with that big of a fall and two huge steps at the end, but like I said, bars isn't my strength.

A few minutes later the score is finally tallied.

8.75.

I'm disappointed in myself but also not surprised at the result. The fall alone was a huge mistake, but it also meant not completing a mandatory skill. I knew the point hit would be big.

Ellery nudges me as I pack my grips and wristbands into the small carry bag and shove it all in my duffel.

"You okay? That was a hard fall."

Being third up, she's adjusting her grips and waiting for her turn. She should be concentrating on her own skills as she waits, but instead, she's checking on me. I'm not sure if I'm endeared or annoyed.

"I'm good. I landed straight so it didn't hurt."

She nods her approval and turns her attention back to our teammate who just completed a full twisting Pak Salto. She makes it look easy. Everyone here does. Sometimes I wonder if I'm the only one who struggles and why that is. Am I not naturally a gymnast and it's only because of how hard I work that I can power through my skills? Or is everyone in the same boat, they just pretend better?

I have way too much time to think self-deprecating thoughts like this. Only four competitors on bars means wait time until everyone is done on all the different events that take longer. And being that I was first, the extra three minutes of doing nothing isn't helpful. Even wrapping my ankle for extra support is such a mindless activity and doesn't keep my thoughts from reeling.

This is what I was afraid would happen—that the dark place I pulled myself out of in high school would settle in again, only to have to claw my way back out. Sure, I put up a good front. Good enough that most people can't see through the mask, but I know. I know I'm mentally struggling. I know I'm not performing at my best. I know I'm holding onto to my anxiety, terrified it's going to spill over the edge of my tightly controlled emotions and end up in an anxiety attack for everyone to see.

I can function on a daily basis. I go to class, I go to the gym, I go out with friends. I do all the things a normal, functioning person does. I just do it while always being aware of what others around me are thinking. Always questioning whether or not something I've done will be used against me. It's not paranoia. It's a constant understanding that the other shoe can drop at any moment, and I need to be prepared.

Finally, finally, we're given the signal to rotate to the next station, and I can't wait.

Floor exercise is my favorite. It's my jam. It's where I shine.

Dropping our stuff in the designated spot, we get in a line for a couple of quick tumbling passes to warm up. I'm thrilled to be going last on this event, which gives me extra time to mentally go through my whole routine again. That's the other good thing about gymnastics. When I can get myself focused on a routine, nothing else bleeds into my thoughts.

As I do a few quick stretches, I look over into the stands, hoping Annika is still here. She's heard me talk about this routine enough. I want to make sure she gets to see what the big deal is.

And that's when I see him.

His huge frame and broad shoulders. His dark skin and eyes that seem to see things others don't. His large hands, clasped together as he rests his elbows on his knees, leaning forward to watch. I can't tell for sure, but I think he's watching… me. I can't look away, so shocked that he came.

What is he doing here? He didn't think it was necessary to be seen around me. Now, I'm confused and trying not to lose focus.

Unfortunately, I'm not the only one who notices the star football player in the bleachers.

"I see I'm not the only one looking for another dip in your pool."

I vaguely acknowledge the sound of Ellery's floor music beginning. Con, however, I hear loud and clear, his words like a punch to my gut. By the chuckles coming from a couple of his friends, I'm not the only one who is listening to him instead of focusing on the task at hand.

"You should be concentrating, Con. You only have one shot on vault."

"I'm not worried," he says with overwhelming arrogance. "One vault is all I need to clinch my all-around spot." One day that ego is going to come crashing down. I personally can't wait to see it. "Besides, watching you squirm is more fun. And seeing the guy you've been pretending to date sitting right there, flirting with another woman," I quickly look over and sure enough, some beautiful brunette is getting awfully chummy with Heath, "... it's too good of an opportunity to pass up."

Applause breaks out as Ellery finishes up her routine. She runs off the floor, straight to me, and I give her a quick, congratulatory hug.

"What's going on, guys?" she asks, getting between Con and I. Man, I'm starting to love her.

"Nothing," Con answers with a smirk. "Nothing at all."

He saunters away and Ellery looks at me quizzically.

"You don't want to know," I grumble and strip my warm-up pants off, folding them on top of my duffle and pick up my water bottle. That old familiar feeling of anger courses through me again.

Why the fuck does Con care so much about who I date? He doesn't want me. He doesn't respect me. He clearly doesn't like me. But what the hell have I done that makes him so vicious? It makes no sense at all. It's infuriating, and I'll be damned if a guy like Con is going to jack with my mental health for shits and giggles.

Glancing back over at Heath, he's ignoring the co-ed next to him. Even from here, I can tell his eyes are focused on me, which means he witnessed that entire exchange, and he doesn't look happy about it.

Before I can stop myself and while having some sort of out of body experience, which is the only way I can explain why I even think this next move is a good idea, I raise my hands up and flash Heath a heart sign.

"Give me a fucking break," Con grumbles behind me with a condescending laugh.

Low and behold, that wasn't the dumbest thing I've done all day after all. Not when Heath responds by bringing his first two fingers to his mouth, kissing them, then pointing those fingers at me like he's tossing me his kiss.

Ellery gasps. "I thought you were just pretending to date him to get Con off your back," she whispers.

I shrug and then glance over my shoulder to see a furious Con, eyes blazing. I just roll mine in response, like he's not worth my time. Because he's not. In my head, I know this. But I admit it feels good to put him in his place. Especially since he's up on vault and now his mojo is thrown off.

Sauntering onto the runway, I watch as Con gets in place, salutes the judge, and runs at full speed toward the apparatus. As soon as his feet hit the springboard, I know he's screwed up. The sound of the springs was just... off somehow. And if the sound is off, it means his hit was off. And that means a domino effect of everything else.

In less than two seconds, his skill is complete, and he's landed safely, but with two giant jump steps forward. That's going to be a huge deduction and could potentially cost him the all-around spot. Today isn't decision day of course, but if someone outshines Con, a mistake like that landing will be taken into consideration.

I can't help the smirk that crosses my face. Sucks for him.

Returning my focus back to the task at hand, I avoid watching Layla as she finishes her floor routine, instead bending forward to stretch my hamstrings. Just one more competitor to go before it's my turn, and I have a feeling I'm going to shine.

TEN

Heath

I don't know why Jaxon and I agreed to go out for seafood after the meet. It's tasty and all, but we burn too many calories to eat eight shrimp for dinner. So, I ordered five servings. This meal is going to cost me my entire week's allotment of food money, and I'll probably still leave here hungry. Looks like the dining hall will be the only place I can eat this week since it's included in my scholarship. Fingers crossed they have steak night again. Hell, I wouldn't mind if steak night ended up being tonight after we're done here. Damn tiny fish.

I would have suggested something else a little more filling, but Lauren wanted to celebrate her success at the meet, and I didn't have it in me to bring her down. Not with the excitement she had after some amazing routines. Even that big fall off the bars didn't faze her. Of course, it was overshadowed by that stunt with the tiny douche. I don't know for sure, but I have a feeling she's the reason he choked on vault. I may not know a lot about gymnastics, but I know the goal isn't to take all those steps at the end of a skill, and after what she told me a couple of weeks ago, I doubt it was coincidence it happened right after I blew her a kiss.

Yeah, that was weird. I'm not even sure why I respond-ed like that when she flashed a heart sign my direction. It was this strange automatic reaction I had. But something in her eyes told me she was really pissed off by something he said for her to risk blowing her own cover. She didn't know how I would react to the impromptu gesture, but I couldn't *not* play along. Even from a distance, I knew he was back to harassing her again.

I'm glad I responded the way that I did. Especially after seeing the floor exercise she was so excited to nail. I'm still not sure how those two things connect—Conrad Turner and success on her floor exercise—but, hey, I have lucky socks I wear during the season. I have no room to judge anyone else's process or superstitions. I do have one question, though.

"What was that thing you did?" I ask, as I dunk one of my last remaining shrimp in some red sauce. I could prob-ably eat forty more and still not be full.

"Which thing?" Lauren doesn't look up from her fish, probably starving as well from the meet. I knew gymnasts were hardcore, but today's the first time I've actually gone to watch what they do live and in person. I thought I was a badass. It's no wonder Lauren's got a six-pack.

Trying to explain what I'm thinking of, I say, "You were on the floor and did a flip or something. Then you jumped up in the air in like a cheerleader straddle and belly flopped on the floor."

Lauren laughs around her bite of fish, and finishes swallowing before she answers. "That wasn't a belly flop."

"Faceplant. Whatever."

She giggles again, this time with our friends joining in, but how the hell else can I explain it?

"It's a Shushunova."

"Shoesha-what?"

"Shushunova. You don't land on your face. You land in a front support. It's almost like ending in a pushup or a plank."

"Well, whatever it is, it looks like it hurt."

Lauren drops her fork on her empty plate. "Not at all.

I'm not doing it on concrete. That floor is made of ply-wood and springs. There's a lot of give."

Looking up at her, I raise an eyebrow playfully. "So, you cheat."

"Hey," she counters, "I didn't design the thing. Don't hate the player." Leaning forward, her normally cool-as-a-cucumber mask falls briefly, and her tone is suddenly full of excitement. "Wanna know something cool?"

Something about the way her eyes and her smile are lighting up has me absolutely wanting to know something cool. I nod.

"I wasn't supposed to do the Shushunova. It just sort of… happened."

Annika looks over quickly, putting her glass down as she swallows a drink of her Diet Coke. "What do you mean? How can you accidentally do something like that?"

"You know how Con has been making my life…" Lauren stares up at the ceiling, probably trying to find another word for living hell. "…difficult?"

Not the description I would have gone with, but it's not my story so we'll go with that.

"Yes," I say at the same time Annika responds with "no." We look at each other momentarily, but Lauren distracts us as she continues.

"He was pulling the same bullshit before my routine. I know you saw it, Heath."

I can feel myself getting pissed again. I wasn't for sure but figured that's what was going on and didn't like watching it as it happened. It wasn't the time or place for an-other showdown, however. Still, I don't like hearing about it after the fact either. Something about Lauren has been making me feel protective lately. It's part of the reason I didn't want to get involved with this situation. I don't need the distraction.

But time and distance didn't do a damn thing to change the way it all makes me feel, so I've concluded it's easier to roll with it. "Sure did. Took everything in me not to go down there and step on him."

"Wait," Annika interrupts. "You saw what? And why

do you care? I'm so confused."

Lauren pats her arm. "Don't worry about it. I'm fine. It doesn't matter."

"It does matter," Annika argues, eyes practically blazing with anger. "What he did to you before, that's not okay."

Lauren puts her trademark "nothing bothers me" smile on her face and I suddenly realize it's her go-to move when an issue is too painful, and she wants someone to back off. "You're right. But I'm fine."

Annika opens her mouth to speak, still looking furious.

"Anyway, after you blew that kiss…"

"What?" This time Annika and Jaxon both chime in, each of them looking like they're missing a big piece of this puzzle. We ignore them and Lauren continues like she didn't hear their reaction.

"…I was raging. Not at you," she clarifies, to which I nod in understanding. "Just at the whole situation. You know how you get so angry, you're practically seeing red, and if you don't hurry up and channel it into something productive, you just might lose your mind?" She knows I do. We've talked about it a couple of times. "That's how it felt right before I did my routine. He just makes me… Grrrrr!"

Lauren grits her teeth and clenches her fists together, getting upset all over again. I reach over and put my hand on hers. It's the first time I've ever done that voluntarily, and I'm shocked by how good it feels. Her hand is warm but not soft. Her fingers have obviously been banged up and scarred from the intensity of her sport. But it's not a turn-off. Quite the opposite. It's kind of a turn-*on* to know she puts her all into being an athlete. Into her team. Into her individual accomplishments in the gym.

She takes a couple of breaths and finally looks up at me. Smiling shyly, she pulls her hand away. I miss the contact, but she's calm now. She doesn't need me anymore.

Sitting up straight, the indifferent, flirty Lauren returns to finish her story, still ignoring a gaping Annika who looks like she has a million questions about what's going on here.

Get in line, Annika.

"Anyway, in laymen's terms, my anger combined with the adrenaline of it being an actual meet with scoring made me over-rotate my front salto. So, I just sort of added the Shushunova at the last second to make it look like I did it on purpose."

"You just… added that face-plant thing," I joke, fascinated that she was able to get her body to randomly do some extra skill without even thinking about it. I suppose I do the same thing when I'm on the field, but I've never had to "land" anything when I do it. Just fall the right way.

Lauren giggles lightly. "What else was I going to do? Take a bunch of giant steps and throw myself out of bounds? It was just as easy to change direction. Plus, I upped my point value. Coach was pumped about it!"

The three of us just look at her, thoroughly confused.

She glances around at us and rolls her eyes. "I really need a friend who follows gymnastics."

"You have a friend who follows gymnastics," Annika says flatly. "But right now, that friend is not focused on the gymnastics part of the conversation. She's sitting here confused about what the hell is going on with you two." She points back and forth at Lauren and me, lips pursed in annoyance.

Lauren and I look up at each other, neither of us speaking. I wish I knew what she was thinking because I don't know what to say. The short answer is nothing. Nothing is happening. The four of us are hanging out together, which isn't unusual.

There's a longer answer here, though. I just don't know how to explain it. Probably because I don't understand it myself.

Lauren beats me to it before I can even try. "There's nothing going on… exactly. Con is a dick, which you already know," Annika nods in understanding, "so Heath set him straight one night."

"You didn't tell me this." Jaxon wipes his hands on a napkin, suddenly interested in the conversation. Likely his concern is less about gymnastics team drama and more about me and my single-minded focus on football. Me getting involved in a situation like this isn't something I would normally do. I shrug and toss a hushpuppy in my mouth, content with letting Lauren continue.

"It wasn't a big deal," she says, downplaying how stressful it was for her. "No punches were thrown. No security was called. Just some words tossed around and letting the asshole come to his own conclusions."

"Is that why you threw that finger-heart-thingy up in the air at the meet?" Annika asks. "Are you letting Con believe you guys are together, so he'll back off?"

This time it's Lauren who shrugs. "That's the basics of it, yes."

"But… why? I thought you didn't care what anyone thinks? Is he making life that difficult for you?"

Annika asks the question that's been haunting me for a few weeks now. Lauren goes on to explain the whole anger creating power thing she keeps using as her reasoning. I get it. I just don't buy it. Maybe it's because I caught her in a vulnerable position on her walk of shame, but ever since that morning, I see her differently. It's like she has a wall around her that I never saw before until one of the bricks came loose, and now, I know everything is not as it seems with her. She's more fragile than she lets on. That part is very clear.

"I'm just able to focus so much better now. Plus, as long as Con thinks Heath and I are together, he's off his game, which is just bonus fun for me," Lauren concludes with a smile on her face.

Annika and Jaxon, however, aren't smiling. Jaxon looks more confused than ever, but Annika looks equally worried.

"I never know what to expect from you," Annika finally says, shaking her head, "but this has got to be the weirdest thing you've ever told me." She's obviously decided not to say what makes her concerned, instead focusing on us. "You two don't even like each other." Jaxon seems to agree and doesn't that make me just feel like shit, since I'm the one solely responsible for why people assume we're enemies.

Lauren, on the other hand, does what she does best—rolls her eyes. "I never didn't like Heath. It just took him some time to get used to me, so I made myself scarce around him," she explains like I'm not sitting right across from her, feeling guilty over how dismissive I've been to her and how it took a guy treating her like a toy to be fought over for me to care. What kind of man am I if I can't look past a personality conflict to treat someone like a human being? A shitty one.

Lauren doesn't seem to notice or care about my internal conflict, though. She's still too excited about her success.

"It doesn't matter anyway. Heath and I found some common ground, so we're okay now. Right, Heath?"

She's smiling as she steers the conversation back to the results of the meet, but the look on her face is still hiding something. Disappointment or sadness or discouragement. I can't tell, probably because it's in such stark contrast to her words and lingering adrenaline. But it's there. Deep down and for whatever reason that I can't seem to put a finger on right now, I want to fix it. I don't want her to struggle with it. I don't want her to have to deal with guys like Conrad and his gang of wannabes and be forced to put up a front just to survive while doing something she loves. I want her to feel strong, and if I need to be the backbone for her until she can do it on her own, that's what I want to be for her.

I can almost feel the words as they bubble up, but I can't stop them when I blurt out, "I'll be your boyfriend."

The three people I spend most of my free time with stop their conversation that has since turned to the merits of leftover seafood to stare at me. Jaxon and Annika look equally shell-shocked and confused.

A smile slowly stretches across Lauren's face and it makes me feel like I'm doing the right thing. "Really?"

"Yeah." I clear my throat, feeling oddly shy about having this conversation in front of my friends. "It keeps that dick off your back, but it benefits me, too. If I'm officially off the market, then I can focus too. Not spend all my time fighting off football groupies."

Lauren cocks an eyebrow at me, so I turn to Jaxon for confirmation.

"You know what I'm talking about. You're there."

Jaxon shrugs. "Yeah. I mean, it's not every day, but I can see how letting the rumor mill do its thing might help eliminate some of those issues. Hell, that girl today was obnoxious. I could go without chicks like her hanging around."

Annika swats him gently. "That's not very nice. She was just being flirty."

Jaxon gives her a disbelieving look. "That wasn't flirty, babe. She was making her intentions very clear. You didn't give her your numbers, did you?"

"Hell, no," I practically shout. "I have a girlfriend, re-member?"

I wink at Lauren as I toss the last of my food in my mouth. Annika mutters something like, "So weird."

It is. But oddly, I don't care. Having a fake girlfriend is going to benefit both of us.

ELEVEN

Lauren

"Dating" Heath is no hardship, but I wasn't expecting to enjoy it as much as I do either. The only things I knew about him is he's Jaxon's friend, he's a business major of some sort, and his football stats. That's it.

Sure, I had assumed he was a good guy, being that he went above and beyond for our friends over the summer when things were at their roughest, but was that because he's like that in general or because he cares about Jaxon? I didn't know.

Until now.

When he finally came around to my way of thinking, I expected him to walk me to a couple of classes or put his arm around me at a couple of football parties.

What I never expected was him to search me out and sit with me in the dining hall. Or walk me back to my dorm from gymnastics practice. Or to hold my hand on the way to class. But he does almost daily. Quite frankly, Heath Germaine has taken this whole fake boyfriend thing more seriously than I expected. Not that I have any complaints. It's been fun getting to know him. He's not quiet, per se, but he kind of fits the mold of the strong, silent type. He's an observer, always watching what people around him are doing. It doesn't come across as paranoia. It's more like an interest in people and what they're up to.

One of the biggest benefits to this change in situation, however, has been how my issues have changed at practice. Con and the other guys have been laying off me since the meet a couple of weeks ago and the subsequent public outing of my relationship. It's been nice to not have a giant target on my back in the one place I love the most. Well, maybe the target is still there, but it's much, much smaller now. I feel like I can breathe again.

The other nice part of practice has nothing to do with Heath and everything to do with all the hard work I've been putting in. After the accidental addition of my Shushunova, Coach made it clear I'm a contender for one of our floor-exercise spots. It's not a guarantee, and I need to make that a permanent addition to my routine, but for a walk-on athlete, it's still a dream come true. And that little bit of extra confidence has been as effective as the rage was at getting things accomplished. Maybe even more so.

Confidence, however, is something Ellery seems to be lacking lately in her own skills.

"I just want to make it on bars. I'm not asking to vie for the all-around title," she whines to me for the millionth time. She is seriously stressed out over the intra-squad meet coming up next month. "I know I'm not as good as Cassidy and Layla, but at least give me a shot to show I can medal on bars. Have you seen my piked Deltchev? I've almost got it nailed. That's huge," she says, referring to the release move she's been working on for weeks now.

"Coach still has one more meet to decide, Ellery," I remind her. "You don't need to stress about it yet."

It's still odd having conversations with her. This is our third year of being on the team together and the first time we've become sort of friends. Maybe because this is the first year I haven't just been the outsider, I've been the target. Maybe Ellery has truly seen some of the shitty behavior people around here pull. Or maybe she finally stepped away from the crowd to actually get to know me and likes what she's learned. Either way, it's been okay having someone to hang out with in the gym. Even if the conversation is as simple as, "Can I borrow your grip tape? Mine just ran out."

She lets out a heavy sigh. "I know I've got time, I'm just nervous. You know how cutthroat people can be."

I snort a laugh as we push open the heavy gym doors and step out into the chilly evening air. "Oh yeah. I'm shocked my jugular is still intact sometimes."

She stops short and the look on her face entirely changes from one of frustration to one of delight. Gesturing with her head to something behind me, she says, "You seem to have made it through okay." She gives me a small wink, and I look over to see my "boyfriend" leaning against the wall.

His strong, denim-clad leg is bent, foot propped up on the wall behind him with his hands shoved in his pockets. His broad shoulders and large frame relax like he's deep in thought. His dark skin camouflages him in the last remaining shadows that are cast across the building. He's beautiful. And I'm not the only one who notices.

Ellery giggles next to me and says, "See ya later, Lauren," before heading the opposite direction, leaving me alone with Heath.

I shouldn't feel giddy about him being here. I shouldn't have butterflies in my stomach when he hears us and looks up. But I do. And it takes everything in me to remember this isn't real. He's not really looking at me with heat in his eyes. He's playing a role. A very convincing role, but that's all it is, regardless.

"Hi." I stroll toward him, shoving my own hands in the front pocket of my hoodie.

"Done already? I wasn't expecting you for another fifteen minutes or so."

"And yet, you're standing out here waiting for me?" I tease.

He flashes me a small smile that doesn't quite reach his eyes and before he confirms it, I already know he needed some time alone. "I was just thinking. No big deal."

Heath pushes off the wall and we slowly walk toward the dorm, neither of us in a hurry. Normally, I would be booking it across campus. Rarely do I slow down. But something about his mood makes me feel like he needs this—fresh air, and maybe even a friend. Plus, I've come to enjoy our walks. It's my favorite part of the day.

"It sounds like a big deal. Anything I can help you with?" I offer.

He ponders my question, probably deciding how much he wants to tell me. We've had some decent conversations over the last couple of weeks, but this one already feels more personal than, "How did your economics test go?" and, "Did you finish watching all those game tapes?" We're close enough now not to avoid each other, but I'm not sure we could consider ourselves good friends.

"Are you close with your family?" he finally asks. That's not at all what I expected him to say, but it gives me a little insight as to what's got him needing time alone. Apparently, it has nothing to do with life on campus.

"No. Well, yes. I mean…" I fumble over my words, not exactly sure how to explain my weird family. "I guess it depends on your definition of closeness. Do I go home for the holidays and talk to my mother on the phone once a week? Sure. Do my sister and I make contact outside of those holiday visits? No."

"How come?"

Now it's my turn to think about how to answer. "I don't know. We don't have much in common, I guess. She's kind of self-absorbed by nature, and I've been told I can be stubborn." He chuckles next to me, but I can't blame him. I'm not exactly stealthy when I dig my heels into the ground. That's how I got a fake boyfriend, after all. "I guess once I get tired of being treated like I'm insignificant, I shut people out. Not on purpose, necessarily. Maybe more out of self-preservation."

"She's really that bad?"

I shrug. "She's not as bad as my teammates. But she's made it clear over the years that my choices are my problem. And she's passive-aggressive with her comments. The small pokes and prods sting after a while. Waterboarding is illegal for a reason. I feel like sometimes she gives me the emotional version of that."

Heath looks like he wants to say something. Maybe try to make me feel better about the fact that my sister and I will never be close. Or maybe to tell me that she's the one missing out. Not that I need his reassurance. When I was a kid, I always thought the TV shows with close-knit families were purely fiction for our entertainment purposes. It never occurred to me that real families like that exist. Obviously, they don't all push through conflict in twenty-two minutes plus two commercial breaks, but there are people out there who are close with their parents and call their siblings their best friends. It's kind of mind-boggling to think about.

I suspect Heath has one of those families. And I have a feeling something happened with them tonight. I don't want to come right out and ask, though.

"I take it you're close with yours?"

"Oh yeah," he replies with no hesitation at all. "I talked to them earlier. I wish I lived closer."

"Where do they live?"

"Lubbock."

"Wow. I had no idea you hailed from West Texas. That's quite a hike if you want to go home for a weekend."

He nods. "I don't have time to go home for weekends anyway. But yeah, it would be nice if I at least had the option."

"Maybe. Or maybe it would make you more frustrated if you were closer but couldn't take advantage of it because of your football schedule."

He considers me for a minute as we stroll. The air around us is crisp, but not really cold for a November evening. It feels good on my skin, which is still warm from exercise. This time of year is my favorite for that reason— the reprieve from the scorching heat, but not cool enough that you run the risk of hyperthermia from walking out of practice sweaty.

"They're struggling, ya know?"

Heath's comment confuses me. "Who is?"

"My parents," he says quietly, and I wonder if he's afraid he's already said too much. I don't push him, though. I don't like it when people try to force me to talk about certain things, so I don't want to do it to him. Instead, I remain quiet, giving him an opening if he wants one. Apparently, he does. "I just worry about them."

I wasn't going to push, but I feel like he needs someone to vent to.

"How come?"

Heath heaves a sigh. "I have three little sisters—Jackie, Maggie, and Amy. All of them are teenagers which means all of them have upcoming proms and college and probably weddings in the future. I hate that my mom and dad have to work so hard to pay for everything. They should be looking at retirement, not picking up more hours."

My dorm comes into view, the lobby seeming extra illuminated as the sun goes down. I feel like some of Heath's stress has also been illuminated as well.

"Can I ask you something personal?"

He looks at me for a long minute before finally nodding.

"Is that why you worry so much about staying focused on football? Because you want to get into the pros to take care of your family?"

Looking up at the sky, he sighs before answering. "That obvious, huh?"

"No. But you aren't the only one that can figure people out."

"It just seems like there is so much on the line sometimes. Jackie was telling me tonight about her prom coming up and how she needs a dress and a hair appointment and a mani/pedi… her list just kept going and I kept thinking, *they can't afford that. Dad's gonna have to work twenty extra hours to make enough money to pay for all that*." Heath shakes his head in discouragement. "Sometimes I wish my sisters would stop growing up for just a couple more years until I sign a contract and get my first paycheck."

We come to a stop at the bottom of the entryway stairs.

Our walk may be over, but it feels too abrupt to end this conversation right now.

"I know I don't have the closest family, but I used to watch a lot of family sitcoms when I was a kid."

Heath chuckles. I like the sound. It's soft and deep and reverberates throughout my body. "And what life lessons did you learn from the magic of television?"

"That most parents, the good ones, don't want their kids worrying about how the bills are going to get paid. That's not your job."

"It feels like it, though. I have the means to make their life so much easier."

"I know. And you will. In two years or less, depending on if you get invited to the combine this year or wait until next." I put my hand on his arm, hoping to convey my understanding for the pressure he's under. "Do your parents know how much you want to help them?"

Just as I suspect, he shakes his head.

"That's what I thought. Which means you have two years to keep your eyes on the prize and work for your goal. If they don't know you plan to support them when you go pro, they're going to be surprised either way. And if it doesn't happen, well, they won't be disappointed about something they never knew."

Heath nods, and I hope that means he agrees with me. But I can tell he's still in his head trying to come up with the best game plans to take care of everyone. I hate that he's put so much pressure on himself. But it's also endearing to see how much he cares. How much he wants to make things easier for his family. I don't know if mine would care if I had to work overtime regularly to make ends meet for my kids. It's a sobering—and sad—thought.

"Well," he finally says abruptly, making it clear this topic is finished. "I have a paper to write for my eight-a.m. class, so I better head back to my dorm."

"Thanks for walking me home. I like talking to you."

His dark eyes flash up to mine and there's a look in them I can't decipher. It almost seems to be one of surprise. "You're welcome. I enjoy talking to you, too."

I look at the ground and turn quickly, trying to hide the fact that I'm biting back a smile. I think that's as close as I'll ever come to Heath Germaine admitting that he may have been wrong about his initial assessment of me.

Trotting up the stairs, I use my key fob to unclick the door and yank it open into what feels like a sauna. "Ugh," I say to myself. "Who the hell runs the HVAC around here, and why do they think it's a blizzard outside?"

What's-his-name who sits at the desk doing who knows what just glances up at me, unconcerned if I belong in the building or not. *Glad to know our safety is the top priority around here.* I shake my head.

It takes just a few seconds to get into my room and realize I'm all alone. I'm sure Annika is with Jaxon somewhere. The two of them are inseparable. It's only a matter of time before they get engaged, which makes me happy for her. She deserves someone great like Jaxon.

Me? Not sure I'll ever be so lucky to find a great guy. Girls like me are the last to be chosen. Like in elementary P.E. class when two people pick teams and everyone crosses their fingers, praying they aren't the last ones standing against the wall.

No. No! Those self-deprecating thoughts aren't welcome right now. I had a great practice and a great walk home, and it's not about being wanted by a man. My future is dictated by whether or not I want him.

Or at least that's what I'll keep telling myself until I really feel that way.

Blowing my bangs out of my face, I know the quickest way to derail the negative self-talk is with some good conversation. I grab my phone out of my pocket and dial. Flopping on my bed, I listen to it ring once... twice...

"Hey!" Kiersten's voice already puts me in a good mood.

"Hey. What's going on?"

"I am getting ready for a date."

My eyes widen. Hook-ups we're used to. But a date? That's extremely rare. "Like with dinner and a movie and everything?"

She laughs through the line, and I can tell she's excited about this new experience. "More like dinner and dancing…"

"Of course."

"… but yes! His name is Chad and he's super cute. Came into the bar last week and hung out at the end until closing time. He's so nice."

"That's so great, Kiersten," I gush. "Is he hot? Tell me he's hot."

Another laugh. Man, she's really into this guy. "Hot in a boy-next-door kind of way."

"Oooh. That's the best kind."

"I know," she says with a sigh. "I don't want to jinx it, but I like him so much. We've hooked up a few times, and I wasn't expecting more than that. It's kind of nice being appreciated for more than just my skills in bed, ya know?"

No, actually I don't know because I haven't found anyone who likes me for more than that yet. Case in point… Con. I don't say that though. I know she would immediately start wanting to psychoanalyze me, and I don't want to ruin her date.

"Totally get it. I hope it works out. If you like him this much, he must be a great guy."

"He is." I can practically see the dreamy look on her face. "But enough about me. How's it going there? Still kicking ass and taking names in the gym?"

"Every day. My routine is coming along, and if I keep perfecting it, I should be a shoo-in for a Nationals spot."

There's a click on the line before she yells, "That's so great! I knew you just had to get over that mental plateau."

"Did you put me on speaker?"

"Yeah sorry. I'm finishing up my makeup."

"No worries," I grunt as I push myself off the bed. "I know you're getting ready to go, but I want to know when you're planning to visit again."

"Um… I was thinking like next month? Before your season officially starts and your weekends are always booked? So, I guess maybe the week before finals."

I snort a laugh because if anyone is going to take a long

weekend break in the middle of a college student's busiest time of the semester, it's Kiersten.

"I'll check my schedule and let you know. I haven't even looked at it yet." I use one hand to shimmy out of my pants and hoodie, leaving me in my skimpy work-out clothes. Gathering my shower supplies, I use my chin to hold my phone in place. "I should know by next week, and we can make plans."

"Sounds good. And by then, I should have more news about Chaaaaad," she singsongs making me laugh.

"I hope so. And if not, we'll make a voodoo doll and stick pins in all the right places."

"Deal," she says with a laugh. "Anyway, I gotta run. I'm supposed to meet him downstairs in five."

"Cool. Call me later."

"Adios, chica."

We disconnect, and I toss my phone aside, heading for the shower we share with our suitemate, who always steals my shampoo. Jokes on her! I keep it in my room now.

I hate that Kiersten lives so far away, but I love that even when she's not here, she's always got my back. It's nice to have solid friends.

If only I could say that about my teammates.

TWELVE
Heath

I'm sweaty. My muscles hurt. And I'm in desperate need of a shower. After an hour of weight training, I'm spent.

It's not just my body. My head is starting to hurt, too, because of a tiny blonde gymnast who won't leave my thoughts. I can't get my conversation with Lauren out of my mind. I was just babbling when I walked her home yesterday, processing my thoughts out loud and all that. I didn't expect her to do more than listen at the most. Honestly, I thought she was pretending to be paying attention, not actually hearing what I was saying. But she cared about the pressure I feel and felt compelled to give me what essentially amounts to words of wisdom. My already changing perception about her shifted once again, and I'm not sure what to do with that.

"How you feeling? You ready for this weekend's game?" Jaxon claps me on the back as we start the walk across campus like we do almost every day at this time.

"Yeah. I feel okay." Not totally true, but not a lie either. I just don't feel like having another in-depth conversation today. Not with my thoughts and feelings all tangled up like they are. "I need to study the game tapes a little more, but physically I feel good. Ready."

"It's New Mexico State," he scoffs. "I think you can relax a bit. They're not much competition."

I disagree. I can never relax regardless of who we play. "They won a bid for a bowl game, Jax. We didn't."

"They barely got that spot because of a fucking field goal and an alumni association that has been vocal for the last several years about not being picked. I think you're good."

I grunt my response because he doesn't understand. It must be nice to not have to worry about the future and the where money is going to come from to take care of your loved ones. Or to not be concerned if a dream job falls apart, you'll end up doing something you hate because it's the only thing you know, and no one ever pulls out of the financial holes they're in.

Those are all things I worry about daily. Things my roommate will never have to even think about.

Not that Jax necessarily has it easy. He wasn't born with a silver spoon in his mouth, or anything. When he decided to go to med school, his dad wasn't happy which caused a bunch of tension. Tension I heard about almost daily. But once they hashed it out, the plan was set in motion. All Jaxon has to do now is pull the grades and ace his MCAT. His name alone will help make him a contender for enrollment almost anywhere he wants to go, and the finances will be taken care of by his dear-old-NFL-legend dad.

I don't hold any of it against him. Jaxon is the best guy I know. But I admit to feeling a little envious sometimes. I just have to keep my eye on my own prize and that means never relaxing. Never discounting a team we're up against. Never acting like a game doesn't matter. They all matter. Until that pro contract is notarized and my signing bonus is safely tucked away in the bank, every move I make counts for or against me.

"How are you feeling anyway?" I know I'm deflecting, but I need to get my brain off my family and the upcoming game. Spinning this conversation back onto Jaxon's issues seems like the best way to do that. "You still feeling run down?"

He bristles, and I know this is going to be a short-lived discussion. "I'm good."

"Jax—"

"Nope. Not talking about this. Like I've told you and my girlfriend almost daily, I'm fine." His jaw clenches in anger which should deter me. It doesn't. He's not taking this as seriously as he should.

"Dude, we're worried about you. I've seen the statistics."

"As have I," he says angrily. "It's not that. Leave it alone."

"Fine," I grumble, irritated that he's not taking his health seriously and yet irritated at myself for acting like a fucking helicopter parent. I can't let it go, though. We're not talking about a fucking common cold. We're talking about making sure he doesn't have cancer again. I don't think it's that—at least I hope not—but with his history, he doesn't have the luxury of powering through illness. Hell, I don't have the luxury of standing back while he tries. "You better figure out something before Thanksgiving next week, though. Your dad is gonna be all over your ass if you're still dragging like this."

He harrumphs and I know he realizes I have a very good point. Doesn't stop him from being an ass though.

"Since you seem to want to talk about uncomfortable topics, how about you tell me what's going on with you and Lauren?"

I look at him quizzically. "What do you mean? You were there. You know exactly what's going on."

Jaxon shakes his head, a shit-eating grin on his face. "Nu-uh. Having a fake girlfriend..." he lowers his voice, which I appreciate, "... means being seen at a party here and there. Maybe sitting at the same table at the library. It doesn't mean walking her home from practice every day and going out of your way to study in the same dorm room, where there are no witnesses to your interaction."

I shrug, trying to buy myself some time. How do I explain something I don't even understand myself?

"Hanging out is nothing new."

"Hanging out without Annika and me as a buffer is new."

He's right. And I know what he's getting at. Sighing, I decide to lay it on the line. Hell, maybe he can help me sort my shit out. "I don't know, man. She needed my help and it's not like it's a hardship to study in the same room as her. I have my Beats on anyway."

"Nope. I'm not buying it. I think you decided you don't hate her anymore because you think she's hot and want to bang her."

I shove him, hard enough that he steps off the sidewalk.

"Hey!" he protests. "These are my new kicks. I don't want to muddy them up yet."

"Since when you do say the word 'kicks'?"

"Since I got them." He inspects his shoes closely for wear which is so weird. Jaxon is hardly the most pretentious guy I know. "They're the same ones I got Caleb for his birthday. He seemed to like that we have the same shoes."

Grateful for the change in topic, I take quick advantage of distracting him from my faux relationship. "I didn't realize it was his birthday. How's he doing, anyway?"

Satisfied his precious sneakers are fine and forgetting about Lauren just as I hoped he would, Jax begins walking next to me again, content to open up about the teenager he thought was his long-lost brother. Even though the genetic link isn't there as originally suspected, Jaxon continues to have a relationship with the guy. "The usual. A little dorky. A little odd. Trying to find himself and maybe a girlfriend. Still on the hunt for his birth dad, but I doubt he's ever going to find him at this point."

"Sucks. Did you ever tell your parents the DNA test didn't match?"

"I told my mom." I raise my eyebrows. This is news to me. "At first, I wasn't going to, but I figured it probably sucked to walk around thinking your late husband had a baby with someone else while you were married. I didn't want her having to deal with that."

I nod because I'd probably do the same thing if it were my mom. "Was she glad to hear it?"

"Indifferent mostly. I guess she let those issues go a long time ago. No idea if she told my dad. She probably did because I told her I'm still going to continue having a big brother relationship with Caleb, and I don't want anyone to ever mention he isn't actually a Bryant or there will be hell to pay."

My eyes widen. "No shit? You said that to your mama? Did she slap you silly?"

He chuckles, knowing full well my own mother would have. In fact, she did the one time in high school I dropped an f-bomb in anger after missing a tackle that cost us a game. Turns out that loss wasn't the worst thing to happen to me that day. The wrath of my mother was.

"No. She actually agreed and said it was a no brainer. Then grumbled something about sounding like another Hart man she used to know. I don't even want to know what that was about."

I bark a laugh. "I'm sure it has something to do with the great Jason Hart—the husband, father, and role model we all know and adore."

Jaxon rolls his eyes but he's more amused than anything. His dad is a fantastic guy, if you take out the part about him driving Jaxon up the wall half the time, but that label has become a running joke between my best friend and me.

"Now you know why I didn't ask what she meant. But I do want to ask you a question."

"What's up?"

"Why'd you shove me when I said you wanted to bang Lauren?"

Dammit. I was hoping we were beyond that conversation. "I didn't."

He comes to a halt, which makes me stop and look at him. "What?"

Squinting his eyes, he studies me for an uncomfortably long moment. It's bordering on creepy.

"Seriously, Jaxon. Why are you looking at me like

that?"

"I'm trying to figure out why you're lying to me about Lauren, and why your attitude regarding her has suddenly done a one-eighty. You've hated her for at least a year."

How the hell did this conversation suddenly come back to me? It was so much more tolerable when we were talking about Jaxon's problems. Frustrated with his assessment and maybe with my own previous actions, I throw my arms out. "Why does everyone keep insisting I hate Lauren?"

"Because you do."

"I do not. I never did."

"You have a funny way of showing it."

With a deep sigh, I shake my head. I wish I was disgusted by his assessment, but mostly, I'm upset that my actions are what led everyone to this conclusion. I'm especially upset it led Lauren to believe the same thing. It was never my intention for her to feel that way.

As if I'm not experiencing enough guilt, Jaxon starts ticking off evidence on his fingers. "Ignoring her when she comes in a room…"

"I don't do that."

"… not going with us to her gymnastics meets on campus…"

"I went to the last one."

"… shaking your head when she's talking, and you don't think anyone is looking at you…"

"Whoa." My hackles rise. "I do not do that."

"You *do* do it. You may not realize it, but we've all seen it more than once. Even Annika has mentioned it a couple of times. She knows Lauren pretty well and thinks it hurts Lauren's feelings more than you realize."

I sigh in resignation. I've never been one to hide my feelings all that well, and if everyone in my social circle has noticed, it means I've been doing a shit job of controlling my expressions, too.

"It's not that I don't like her. Lauren is just… energetic. And she never wears clothes."

Jaxon laughs. "She's an athlete, dude. You rarely have

a shirt on during practice either."

"It's not just that, though."

"Then what is it?"

"I guess I just assumed her energy and the way she flaunts her body is because she's flaky and a bit of a party girl."

"So, you just saw what was on the surface and didn't bother to get to know her."

Guilt and shame punch me in the gut. As much as I want to deny it, he's right and we both know it. I shake my head to clear my mind of the sudden influx of negative emotion. "I just try to stay away from those kinds of girls because I've got too much to lose if I get involved with the wrong one. I was trying to steer clear of her. But lately, I've just seen a different side to her. Like she has more depth than I thought."

"You mean, you finally pulled your head out of your ass and got to know who she really is, not just the shield she puts up."

I grimace. "Yeah, I figured out the other day that she has a lot of defense mechanisms."

"Good." He claps me on the back again. "So how are you going to fix it now that you understand you've been a total douchebag and hurt her feelings?"

"You mean being her fake boyfriend so those jackasses she trains with stay off her case isn't enough?"

"I admit, that's pretty classy of you. But no. I'm thinking something more along the lines of an apology."

He's right. I still don't know much about Lauren, but I get the impression she hasn't always had it easy. Not being close with her family, not having a big friend circle, making poor choices in dates... I can only imagine that my carelessness around her hasn't helped her at all.

"Yeah, I know."

Pulling out my phone, I decide now is as good a time as any. Shooting off a quick text, I feel good about my plan, ready to get this all sorted out.

"What are you doing?"

Shoving my phone back in my pocket, I don't answer

him. This is between Lauren and me. Somehow, I don't think she'd appreciate me drawing this kind of attention to her and her feelings.

"Nothing. But I just realized I need to be somewhere. We need to book it."

I take off in a jog so I can hit the shower before I head to the women's dorm, with Jaxon yelling behind me.

"Oh, come on, man. We just got out of practice. No more exercise."

I turn so I'm running backward as I yell back at him. "I bet your doctor could tell you why a little jog makes you so tired."

He flips me the bird, which I expected and doesn't offend me at all. If he wants to be an asshole and let this all play out, I can be an asshole and harass him about it. I've got three sisters. I practically have a degree in pestering.

I don't have time to worry about him anymore, though. I've got somewhere to be and a sudden urgency to get there. No time like the present to make things right with someone you've wronged.

THIRTEEN

Lauren

Popping my earbuds in, I crank up the volume on my phone. Nothing like a little Aerosmith to get my blood pumping so I can wake up for some last-minute studying. It's not late or anything, but some of the conditioning at practice wiped me out and I haven't caught my second wind for the evening yet. I could easily take an overnight nap if I'm not careful.

"What's this?" I ask myself as I notice a missed text from Heath.

Heath: We need to talk. I'm heading your way in twenty.

That was fifteen minutes ago. Weird. I wonder what he wants to talk about. I can feel my anxiety kick up a notch, automatically assuming it's something negative. Have we been outed? Is he done with this pretend relationship and wants to pretend break up? Did I say something that made him mad?

Stop, Lauren! Relax. Deep breaths. He's a guy, so he's not going to be wordy on text. It's probably nothing. No reason to worry yet. Just breathe... two... three... four...

My spiked heart rate begins to slow, which is good and yet adrenaline would have given me that extra energy I need to stay awake.

Yeah. We're just going to have to stick with Steven Tyler for adrenaline. At least that way, my thoughts won't spiral.

Hitting play, the familiar opening notes to "Love in an Elevator" fill my head and my anxiety is quickly eased once again. Closing my eyes, I let the music flow and my body move with it. Before long, I'm fully engrossed in the words and lovin' it up til I hit the floor. It grounds me and makes me feel strong. Empowered.

Ironic considering the lyrics but come on. It's Steven Tyler. 1980's him can basically do no wrong.

Swaying to the music, I raise my arms in the air and spin around, jumping back with fright when I catch a person in my room.

"Ohmygod!" Hand clutched to my chest, I try to control my breathing. "What the fuck, Heath?"

He's got a shit-eating grin on his face, arms crossed as he leans against my closet. He mouths something that I don't catch, electric guitar and bass still pounding through me.

Pulling my earbuds out, I stop the music. "What was that? I couldn't hear you over my rock and roll idol."

"I said, are you having fun?"

I toss my phone aside and plop down on my bed. "I was until you scared the shit out of me."

Heath grabs the desk chair and rolls it closer to me, straddling it backward when he sits. "What are you listening to that has you acting like a back-up dancer?"

I throw my hands out and furrow my brow like the answer is obvious. "Aerosmith, of course."

"Oooh," he says with a laugh. "Of course. I should've known you were a fan."

"They're only the greatest band ever."

"They're pretty good."

"Pretty good? That's like saying Robert De Niro is a decent actor."

"My mistake," he says with a laugh. It's odd seeing him enjoy this conversation and my weird obsession. "Ever see them live?"

"Of course! Twice. It's ridiculous how agile they still are. If I'm only half that active when I'm in my 70's, I'll be happy."

"What's your favorite song?"

I open my mouth to answer him, but I stumble over my words before saying anything. Partially because I'm not understanding his interest. With the exception of the other day when he was processing some family stuff, this may be the longest conversation we've ever had. And he's the one who started it. Not to mention, it's almost an impossible question to answer. There are so many fantastic songs to choose from.

"That's like asking me who my favorite niece or nephew is. Is my favorite something newer like 'Living on the Edge', which is arguably still pretty old, but not compared to 'Dream On' which released in the 70's? I don't know how to answer that. Wait!"

He looks at me expectantly, which is new. Usually, by this point in one of my rants, he's rolling his eyes and tuning me out, maybe leaving the room. Not this time. His eyes are locked on mine like he's interested in what I have to say. More weirdness. I'm starting to wonder if he's sick.

"'Janie's Got a Gun'." I throw my head back and blow out a breath. "Man, that song hits me every single time. And did you know Steven Tyler founded two different Janie's House locations to help abused women and teenagers because of that song?"

His eyebrows raise in surprise. "I didn't know that. That's cool."

"I know, right?" Realizing I have a wide smile on my face, I'm suddenly feeling self-conscious. Sure, Aerosmith as a band is legendary, but my fangirling is a little over the top sometimes. I make a mental note not to mention the ratty concert tee I wear to bed most nights.

Clearing my throat, I try to regain some of my confidence. "So anyway, what's up?"

Now it's Heath's turn to look a little self-conscious. This entire exchange has been confusing. It's not our normal mode of operation, and it's starting to freak me out a bit.

Finally, he speaks. "I owe you an apology."

I blink rapidly, sure I've misheard him. "I... what?"

His lips tilt up on the side like he's fighting a smile at my confusion. "I'm sorry."

Sitting up, I crisscross my legs and straighten my back to stretch it out a bit. "For what?"

Heath sighs and rubs the top of his nose, fidgeting while he gathers his thoughts. I let him because whatever he's apologizing for seems to be bothering him. It has me on high alert that maybe there's something I don't know about.

"I never win at poker."

Okay, now, I'm really confused. What does a card game have to do with his apology? "You lost me."

"I know. I'm trying to get to my point so you can understand, but I'm already doing a shit job. Let me try again." He takes a deep breath and looks me right in the eye. "I'm not good at hiding my emotions. I never have been. My mother has always said I should stay far away from Vegas because my biggest tell is my expressions."

"Ah. I understand the poker reference now."

He chuckles before continuing. "As you know from our conversation yesterday, a lot of the pressure I feel is from my family and wanting to help them."

"It's an admirable desire."

"It is. But it never goes away. I'm constantly thinking about it and worrying about them. So, I made a commitment to myself years ago that nothing is going to get in my way of getting that pro contract. Nothing."

"Right. I knew that. But what does this have to do with me?"

He grimaces, and I know he's getting to the heart of the matter and it makes him uncomfortable. "I was warned a long time ago about the groupie element when it comes to this business. It's always there. High school had it, too.

But it's different now. The stakes are higher, and there are women out there who will try to hook-up with a star player, specifically so they can get knocked up and trick him into supporting her for the next eighteen years."

Suddenly, I understand how this relates to me, and I don't like it. It feels like a slap to the face. Not that I didn't already know Heath dismissed me like someone who wasn't worth his time, but to know he thought I was a cleat chaser doesn't feel good at all.

"You thought I was going to take advantage of our mutual friends to try and trap you."

He shifts uncomfortably which I'm glad about. If he's going to be a judgmental asshole, he should feel bad about it.

"It's not that I thought you would do that…"

"It's not?" I deadpan.

"No. It's more that I didn't know you well enough to make that determination, so I just sort of… steered clear of you."

I look down at my clasped hands, unsure what to say. This is what I wanted, right? This is why I don't get close to anyone and opt to be who I want without regard to anyone else, isn't it? Because if I don't get close to them and don't care about them, conversations like this can't happen.

But I did get close to Heath. Not bestie close or anything, but he's seen me more intimately than most people. He's seen me do the walk of shame. He's seen me humiliated. Hell, he's even seen me cry, but I'd never admit to him that those were actual tears that spilled while he drove me home.

And right now, he's seeing me disappointed, sad, and somewhat regretful for letting him partway in, to begin with.

"I'm sorry, Lauren." His voice is soft, probably because he knows how much this hurts me. "I finally realized that you and I are more alike than I knew."

This makes me look back up at him quizzically. How in the world are we alike? Besides the obvious differences—

race, gender, height, weight—we also have completely different personalities. It's a wonder anyone has bought our fake relationship just because we're such opposites.

"How so?"

"I hold myself back from getting to know people—women, in particular—as a form of self-protection. Keep my eye on the prize and my mind fully engaged on the goal. Don't let anything get in my way. But you..." He licks his lips, again, probably stalling for time to think. "You don't let anyone get to know you, the real you, as a self-defense mechanism. Like armor. It keeps you from having to feel rejection, right?"

I look away quickly, not wanting him to look me in the eye anymore. I don't know how he was able to figure out my vulnerabilities, but he did. It terrifies me that he can use them against me now.

Still, he's not done.

"I'm sorry I acted the way I did, rolling my eyes and not being friendly. I've never hated you. I was trying to protect myself, and in the process, I hurt you."

"You didn't hurt me," I argue. "Very little hurts me, Heath, and rolling your eyes isn't even close to being that big of a deal."

"Maybe not. But I also didn't make you feel any better about yourself."

I scoff, trying desperately to put my emotional armor back on before I burst into tears from being overwhelmed. "Don't give yourself so much credit. It's not your job to make me feel better about myself. I feel just fine."

"I said that wrong. I meant I should have been nicer and gotten to know you for who you are, not who I assumed you were. I'm sorry."

Standing up quickly, I walk over to the dresser, realizing I haven't taken my meds yet. It's not ideal to take them in front of Heath, and I hope he doesn't ask about it, but it's a chance I have to take. Today is obviously not the day I need to miss a pill. "Stop saying you're sorry. I forgive you, okay? You used to think I was a whore. You've changed your mind, and I'm not as trashy as you thought.

The end." Popping the tiny pill in my mouth, I swallow quickly but continue facing that direction.

I hear him stand up, but his footsteps make almost no sound until he's right behind me.

"But that's not the end, Lauren. It's not just that I've changed my mind. It's that I like you."

His words make it hard to breathe right. I don't understand why he's saying all these things. I like it better when he thought I was tough as nails and only traded quips. I don't like that he sees past that to what makes me tick. It's unnerving.

"I'm not trying to make you uncomfortable."

I bark out a humorless laugh and cross my arms over my chest, still refusing to turn around.

"I'm trying to make this right," he continues, despite my obvious attempts at ignoring him. "I fell into the habit of being that guy who makes judgments about others without cause, and I don't want to be him. Especially not with my fake girlfriend."

Try as I might, I have to bite a smile back at that one.

"I'm asking you to forgive me for being an asshole. And I'm asking to maybe spend some time together, without the buffer of our friends."

I snort a laugh. "They spend too much time sucking face anyway."

He chuckles and I kind of want to kick myself for having such a big reaction to an apology. It took some guts for him to lay it all on the line and be so honest about what he perceives as mistakes. If he's not going to be the guy that makes judgments, I don't want to be the girl who's known for her drama. Although at this particular moment, we're both doing a shit job of being better people.

Turning around, I take a cleansing breath. "You are forgiven for being an asshole. If you'll forgive me for this melodramatic outburst."

Heath furrows his brow. "That was melodramatic? I was raised with three sisters. You have to do worse than that before I start to wonder about your stability."

I smack him playfully on the arm, grateful for his ability to see past my over-the-top display of emotion. He easily blocks my attack, laughing as he does.

"Listen, I brought my books in case you might want to study together?"

It comes out as a question to which I have no hesitation.

"Sure. I was getting ready to start anyway. But I have one condition."

He narrows his eyes, unsure how this is going to go. "What's that?"

"Steven Tyler has to join us."

"I figured that one out already," he says with a laugh and turns to grab his backpack while I settle back onto my bed. It appears my second wind has hit, and it has nothing to do with my favorite band and more to do with my favorite football player.

FOURTEEN

Heath

I don't normally get to take naps. There's too much activity in the dorm, too much studying to do, too much, well… everything. But today is different. Thanksgiving is just a few days away and almost everyone has cleared out already, even my roommate. It's peaceful.

Don't get me wrong, Jaxon is fantastic to live with. I just rest better when part of me is not waiting for him to come through that door, Annika in tow. So, I'm taking advantage of the quiet and lack of action to rest. Or trying to. If only the ice pack under my arm wasn't so uncomfortable to lay on.

A hard hit in yesterday's game has me still feeling the pain today. A helmet right under my pit could have been worse, but a deep bruise somewhere in my ribs isn't something to joke about. A couple of Tylenol and rest will hopefully help it heal quickly.

And, of course, my phone dings with a new text message. I could ignore it, but I know how it goes. One ding means more are coming. It's like Murphy's law. So much for my nap.

Taking a deep breath, I brace myself for the pain, then push into a sitting position and grab my phone. Surprisingly, it's not Jaxon texting me about how his pops is driving him crazy. That was my first assumption, mostly because he deserves for his dad to be up his ass right now.

No, the message is from Lauren.

Lauren: Awesome game yesterday! How're your ribs? That was a nasty hit.

My fingers flying to respond, I find myself smiling at her reaching out.

Me: I didn't realize the game was televised. That's cool.

Was it? I wouldn't know. I was in the stands.

Nothing like a live game to build my team spirit!

I furrow my brow. She was here? On campus? I guess a lot of people decided to stay for the game, but why is she texting me now? Isn't she headed home?

Wait... are you texting me while driving? If so, you better stop!

Too much traffic out there!

cue eye roll because it's your favorite response from me

Relax, Dad. I'm in my dorm room.

I thought you were going home for the holidays? What happened?

Short answer - They're letting us stay through tomorrow for an extra practice.

What's the long answer?

I'm avoiding spending time with my family as much as possible.

That makes much more sense.

So what are you doing now?

I told you. Sitting in my dorm.

Wanna do something?

Come over so we can go somewhere.

No way. You come here.

My dorm doesn't smell like boy funk.

I can't help the laugh that comes out of me. She may be a snarky little shit, but Lauren can be funny sometimes.

Fine. Give me twenty. I need to finish
                    icing this bruise.

Perfect. I need to do my hair anyway.

I find myself smiling again... this time even bigger. Looks like my nap can wait. I've got a real date with my fake girlfriend. Now I just have to come up with something good to do.

• • •

Thirty minutes later, the door swings open and an angry scowl greets me.

"You're late." The words are barely out of Lauren's mouth when she turns away from me, leaving the door open so I can follow her.

I'm not surprised she's calling me out. What I am surprised by is her outfit. Skinny jeans, a tight white sweater, hair down around her shoulders, and the one item I have a hard time resisting...

"You're wearing heels."

Tossing her newly curled blonde hair over her shoulder, she smirks. "I wear heels a lot when I'm not in work-out clothes. Short girl problems."

"And yet, you're still so tiny I could put you in my pocket." I get close to her and purposely look down on her to accentuate exactly how close to the ground she is.

Lauren purses her lips and puts her hands on her hips. "You're not original, you know. That joke is old and tired."

"Who says I'm joking? I kind of like the idea of carrying you around."

"Since when have you been a caveman?" She pushes

me back through the door, which let's face it, is me just humoring her. We both know if I stood still, we wouldn't be going anywhere. As we hit the hallway, she locks the door behind her.

"I just think you're kind of cute."

She gives me a flirty grin, one that I can see is full of disbelief. "Oh yeah? Since when have you wanted in my pants?"

So, she wants to go there? Two can play at that game. I shrug, pretending to be nonchalant. "Since always."

In true Lauren fashion, she cocks her eyebrow at me playfully but deflects. My apology the other day was necessary and genuine, but I'm a strong believer that actions speak louder than words. Based on her reaction, I have a feeling she feels the same way, and it's going to take me being consistent with my friendship before she'll believe me. Going out tonight will hopefully be a good start.

"Where are we going anyway?" she asks as we pass by what's-his-name at the front desk. Today's magazine of choice? *GQ*. I can't help but wonder if he pays for all these magazines or if he steals them out of the trash by the mailroom.

Reaching my arm out from behind her, I push the door open. "I hadn't really thought about it. Wanted to see if you had anything in mind first."

"Geez, you don't date much do you?"

"What? I didn't want to be presumptuous. I assumed you wanted to go dancing but you have more experience than me with the clubs around here. Anywhere I'd choose would probably be only sub-par."

We reach my truck, which is illegally parked in the fire zone. I've got my hazards on, and there're so few people on campus, I'm not worried anyway.

As I open the door for her, Lauren climbs in. It hits me that the last time she was in my truck, she was upset and freezing while doing the walk of shame. And I wasn't exactly a gentleman by pulling over to the side of the road, yelling "Hop in" and barely speaking to her on the ride home. No wonder she's only tentatively accepting my apology. I can only hope she isn't having the same memory flashback I am.

Once I make my way around the front, climb in, and get myself situated, I turn to look at her. "Well?"

"Well what?"

"Where are we going?"

She crinkles her nose a bit, so I know she has no idea how I'm going to react to her suggestion. "Would it be weird to do something cliché like dinner and a movie? But not in that order?"

Chuckling, I crank the engine now that I have a general idea of where we're headed. "A little weird coming from you, but totally doable. Not feeling up to the crowds tonight?"

"No, it's not that. I tend to stay pretty energetic most of the time. Stop laughing…" I can't help the chuckle since she's already called me out. She smacks me lightly. "I said no laughing."

Raising one hand defensively I mutter, "Sorry."

"I think my energy is directly related with how much I have to do, for whatever reason. And with my normal routine slowing down for the upcoming holiday, I feel like my body is, too."

"I get that. Like if you stop moving, you're suddenly tired."

"Exactly. It took everything in me to roll off my bed and get ready to leave."

Glancing over at her, I appreciate the effort she put in for me. "It was worth it. You look really pretty."

I catch a glimpse of the blush that graces her cheeks before I turn my eyes back to the road. I've never seen that happen to her before. Like she's not used to the compliments and is flattered in a way she's not quite comfortable with. It's a more innocent side to Lauren that she's never let me see before.

Clearing my throat, I bring us back into the moment. "So, dinner and a movie, not in that order?"

"Right."

"That makes it easy. What movie do you want to see? I

don't think any of the Thanksgiving blockbusters are coming out for a couple of days."

She huffs. "They're not. I already looked. But there is a new Dwayne Johnson action movie I haven't seen yet."

It's been so long since I've paid attention to pop culture, it takes me a minute to recall the one she's talking about. "The one with Jack Black? They're like in a video game or something?"

She nods vigorously. She may not have as much energy as normal, but there's still no stopping Lauren from getting excited over the things she likes. "That's the one."

"Wait," I furrow my brow. "Didn't that come out a couple of years ago?"

"The last one in the series did. I guess they keep doing well enough in the box office, they keep making more."

"Good enough for me."

Heading my truck in the direction of the movie theater, I press the gas pedal. We've got a movie to enjoy and I don't want to waste a minute sitting in this old truck.

• • •

"Mmmmmm." The moan that comes out of Lauren's mouth has me watching her intently and shifting in my seat as my jeans tighten. Who knew watching someone eat a greasy burger could be so erotic? I sure as hell never got hard eating at Cactus Burger with Jaxon. But with Lauren—well, this is something different altogether.

Lauren's eyes roll in the back of her head and her tongue snakes out to lick the grease off the side of her lips.

My thoughts and hormones are a muddled mess from the snapshots in my brain of her splayed out on my bed, her tongue and mouth caressing my dick the same way they're currently caressing that burger. My mouth goes dry, and I'm unable to put coherent thoughts together.

"This is the best burger I've ever had." Finally, she opens her eyes. As she looks at me, confusion crosses her face. "What? Why are you looking at me like that?"

"Huh?" That's as good as it's going to get from me right now.

She grabs a napkin and begins wiping her mouth. "Do I have something on my face?"

I groan as the image of what I'd love to see on her face assaults me. I try to look away but can't, and as if she can read my thoughts, suddenly a shit-eating grin crosses her face.

"I'm making sex noises, aren't I?"

I nod, my mouth still dry from slow recovery time.

"It's giving you good visual images, isn't it?"

Clearing my throat, I croak out a, "Sorry."

"Don't be," she says as she wipes more grease off her face. "This burger is practically orgasmic, so it's justified."

Of course, I choose that exact moment to try and swallow the water I'm drinking to help me out of my lust-filled thoughts. Nothing like choking on my drink to bring me back to the here and now.

Lauren doesn't even lend a helping hand. Probably too entertained by my reaction to her. I've heard women say sex makes them feel powerful, but I've never understood it until this moment, because it's painfully obvious that the thoughts of her orgasm face have rendered me almost totally defenseless.

"I don't usually eat like this during the season," she finally adds, once I'm not hacking up a lung. "Sometimes, I forget how good a burger can be compared to baked chicken."

I understand how she feels. I doubt this is lean beef, which is an infrequent indulgence this time of year. I made an exception today in the name of chivalry. Besides, it's not like I'm trying to lose weight.

She's right about one thing, though. Cactus Burgers has the best hamburgers in town. There is a possibility I would've been making sex noises too, if I'd taken a bite before she did.

Finally feeling confident that I've pulled myself together, I try speaking again. "How'd you like the movie, anyway?" I ask, as I pop an illegal fry in my mouth. And by illegal, I mean Coach would give me shit if he saw how many carbs I'd already eaten today. Protein is one thing. Veggies are another. Bad carbs? Not in the quantities we had today. Lauren may be tiny, but she eats like a grown-ass man. Somehow, I think her metabolism can take it.

"Ohmygod it was so funny," she exclaims, still holding tightly to her prize meal. "I swear Jack Black can play any character. He's so fucking talented."

"He should have this character down pat with as many times as he's played it. How many movies have they made in this series so far?"

She doesn't respond so I look up at her. She's just staring.

"What?"

"Have you never seen the other ones?"

I shrug noncommittally.

Lauren leans forward like she's telling me something very important. "Well, no wonder you don't get it. Every movie in this series, he plays a different character."

"Really?" I don't know that I understand what she's talking about or even care that much, but she's excited, so who am I to shut her down?

"Hell yeah! He played a sorority girl one time, once he was an old man. In the last one, he was a kid." Pointing a fry at me, she adds, "That one was hysterical. I knew boys were obsessed with their penises but had no idea how big they are from an eight-year-old boy's perspective." I clear my throat, thankful that I'm able to ward off more choking. She's on a roll tonight. "We should rent it some time since you don't seem to get out much."

"My time is limited, so watching movies is pretty rare for me."

She takes another bite, talking around it. "I can see that. You're stretched pretty thin."

"I'm surprised you have as much time on your hands as you do. You're an athlete, so you know how it feels like a full-time job sometimes. Twenty hours a week of practice, plus classes, plus team events and parties. I'm not sure if I came here for an education or the team half the time."

She keeps eating but doesn't respond. It's not that she doesn't agree with me, it's more like she doesn't feel the same, which is weird. If anyone should understand, I would think it would be her. But the more I learn about Lauren, the more I learn that what one would assume would be her normal is usually not.

Taking a chance, I ask a question that can go either way.

"Don't you feel like it's a full-time job sometimes?"

She shrugs and keeps eating. Now I know she's in avoidance mode again.

"Lauren." She peeks up through her lashes, still chowing down like it's her last meal. Or maybe like it's her first real one in months. "I said something wrong, but I don't know what."

She takes one more giant bite and puts her burger down, wiping her hands on a napkin as she chews. It's a stall tactic I've come to learn well with her lately. But I can wait her out.

When she finally realizes I'm not going to let it go, she swallows and leans in. "You didn't say anything wrong. I'm just not invited to most of the team events, so I tend to have a lot of free time on my hands."

That makes no sense to me. "But team events mean the team is there. The whole team."

One shoulder comes up in a half shrug. "Not in my world it doesn't."

"So, it's not just that group of guys that are so horrible?"

She shakes her head slowly. "Not even close. The girls are vicious. But to a degree, I get it. Competition spots are limited. It's every man for himself for the most part."

I shake my own head, trying to wrap my brain around this new information. More pieces of the puzzle that is Lauren Bagley are starting to come together. "But wait. Gymnastics is a team sport."

"To a degree, yes. But only if each individual does well. There's not a collective team effort except for everyone to get the best scores they possibly can. Like in football, if you're about to get tackled and you can, you toss the ball to someone else so they can keep going. Every point is earned by eleven people. In gymnastics, every point is earned by one person at a time."

I take a minute to consider her comments. Team sports all have the same concept—if you aren't the best, you're replaced.

"I can see the wheels turning in your brain," she jokes, finally settling back in her seat now that most of her food is gone.

I snatch one of her fries off her plate. "I'm trying to figure out the difference between losing my spot and you losing yours."

"Consider it this way—in football, everyone has their spot, and there are tons of them. Offense, defense, special teams, kicker. Yes, you have to maintain your level of performance, but everyone has a role. You are either a starter or second string or practice team. Your job is outlined for you.

"In gymnastics, however, we're constantly vying for our spot. All season long. And there aren't many of them. We have sixteen spots total, but twelve of them will be used up by our top three competitors trying to win all-around. That leaves four spots for thirteen of us. If I get chosen and I screw up, I'm sitting out the next meet. If I fall, I'm out. If I don't complete my skill, I'm out. It's a precise sport anyway, but one tiny bobble means the difference between me suiting up or sitting in the stands."

This surprises me. I knew everyone on the team didn't compete every time, but I had no idea the chances of actually performing were that slim. "This is why you were so freaked out about that skill you were trying to perfect."

She shrugs, palms up like I finally understand her point.

"Oh wow. And I thought I felt pressure."

"It's just a different kind of pressure. Once college is over, my gymnastics career is over, too. This is the end of the road, so at least I'm not always thinking about the draft. That would suck having my future in limbo."

I grunt my response. She's not wrong. It's my daily

struggle. "Sure, it does. But don't you get lonely some-times? Not have any teammates that are real... I don't know... like a team?"

The look on her face only lasts for a second, but it says it all. This is why she pushes people away. This is why she's brash and aggressive. Is all that part of what makes her who she is? Absolutely. But they're the only sides any-one is allowed to see because trusting people doesn't typi-cally go her way. And yes, I got all that out of one fleeting expression. But as she bites her lip, I can tell she's trying to battle her way through it with me. She needs to test me and see if I'm like the very few people she's let in, or if I'm like all the others.

Lauren straightens her spine and looks me dead in the eye. "It's lonely every single day. But they won't drive me away from the sport I love."

I refuse to look away, not because I'm trying to have a power struggle with her, but because I want her to know her feelings don't make me uncomfortable. I like her. And maybe if I'm lucky, this new friendship, not the fake rela-tionship but the real, developing friendship will turn into something deeper. She needs to know I can handle all the different sides to her.

Satisfied that this is the beginning of something good, I nod once and in return, I get a shy smile.

"So uh, I guess I'm skipping the next team party so we can watch that movie, huh?"

Her grin widens, and I feel like I've passed the test.

Bring it on, Lauren, I think to myself. Because I play to ace them all.

FIFTEEN

Lauren

The few days I was at home for Thanksgiving weren't bad, per se. They weren't good either, but I try to remind myself it could have been worse. I got to see Kiersten. I got to watch football. I indulged in pumpkin pie. All good things that I'm focusing on.

Except the pie. We're at the very beginning of the competition season. I should have skipped dessert and have been regretting it since I got back into the gym.

The whole week was made more bearable by the constant stream of texts between Heath and me. It started with a quick check-in to make sure we got home okay on our prospective drives. Then morphed into him checking up on me, knowing it can go either way with my sister. Soon, we found ourselves just chatting about everything and nothing for five days straight. It was nice. And it made the attraction on Heath I had been successfully avoiding develop into a small crush.

Small? Maybe medium-sized is a better description. Regardless, it's a little too many feelings for my liking.

Although I can't deny that Heath seems to be trying to make good on his apology. He's kind. He initiates conversation and actually listens when I talk. He pays for my meals when we go out.

Yes, I know those should be a given with any relationship at this stage, but we're still not "in a relationship," so it all feels above and beyond to me. Especially when he does things like text me that he'll be late to my meet because of a last-minute meeting his coach called regarding tomorrow's game. I find it to be very considerate of him to let me know.

So, I remain cautiously optimistic that maybe Heath is truly one of the good guys.

I know quite a few men, however, who are very obviously *not* the good guys. The leader of the assholes being one of them and speaking of the devil—Con's heading my way.

Clasping my hands behind my back, I bend over and stretch my shoulders. I'm hoping this position deters him from trying to talk to me.

"What's up, Lauren?"

Dammit. No such luck.

Standing back up, I swing my arms back and forth a few times. That's my perimeter. As long as he doesn't come any closer, he won't get hit. Reluctantly, I answer him. "Con."

He reclines against the judges' table and crosses his arms and legs. And so, the battle of wits is about to begin.

"Where's your little boyfriend anyway?"

I snort a laugh because that's pretty hilarious coming from him. "He's six feet tall, so Heath's hardly little. And he's at a team meeting because he has a job to do tomorrow. Kind of like we have a job to do today. In about ten minutes. Which means we probably should be concentrating and not shooting the shit, don't ya think?"

His eyes narrow ever so slightly, and I know my brush off isn't going to work this time. He's come prepared to spar with me. I just don't know why. "I'm just trying to have a friendly conversation with my teammate. Nothing wrong with that."

"Well do it over there." I grab my foot and pull it up in front of me until it's above my head, making sure I stay flexible while we wait.

Unfortunately, Con seems to be lacking in the personal boundaries area and comes around to my other side before leaning in and quietly speaking. "Answer me something... did you put out on the first date with him, too? Is that why he sticks around? Because you're an easy lay? Why do you stretch like this when I'm right in front of you? As a reminder of what it's like to be between those very flexible legs?"

Doing my very best to school my features and pretend Con's words don't hit their intended target, I slowly lower my foot back down to the floor, turn directly into Con's line of sight and step forward. Holding eye contact, I keep my voice low and steady. "As fun as you are to talk to, the last time you worried more about my relationship than your routines, you choked on vault." I reach my hand up and fix the shoulder strap of his singlet, then pat his arm condescendingly. "Scholarship renewals are coming up soon. The board wouldn't look too kindly on one of their full-ride recipients not getting an all-around spot, would they?"

I smile menacingly as I watch his jaw tick. It was a low blow and we both know it, but I feel not one ounce of guilt. Don't start shit if you don't want me to finish it. I might cry in the shower later, but Lauren Bagley will not let the likes of Conrad Turner bring her down in this arena. Not when I'm so close to getting what I want.

Pulling himself together, Con tilts his head just a little bit closer and whispers, "Good luck with that front salto. Don't underrotate." He thinks he just gave me a parting shot before walking away, but he didn't. He just fueled my anger. Gave me more power. Underrotating is the last thing I have to worry about now.

"What in the world did he want?" Ellery mutters, as she settles in next to me and strips off her warm-ups. We were grouped together again for our final intra-squad meet, which I'm glad for. It's nice knowing at least one person on my "team" is genuinely cheering for me on the sidelines.

"I don't know. It feels like he's purposely trying to

throw me off my game for some reason."

Ellery thinks for a moment, looking as confused as I feel. "Why would he do that? Whether or not you get a competition spot doesn't affect him at all."

I shake my head and shrug half-heartedly. "Who knows. Some guys are dicks like that. I have more important things to worry about right now." Plus, I'm getting bored of Con and his games. I'd much rather talk with Ellery. "Are you ready for today? Feel good?"

She and I chat about the new skills she's added to her bar routine and how much more confident she feels. Since the last meet, she's upped her game and her difficulty levels are showing because of it. We all know she's a true contender for bars now, not just to get a spot but to medal at Nationals. That's the power of upping the point value of the routines.

Within minutes, the National Anthem is over and we're ready to begin.

Since this is our last meet before competing against other universities, we're in the arena today. It's huge and gives a whole different vibe to the meet. That's the whole point. It's easy to become complacent in the place where we spend twenty hours a week. But this venue can be intimidating, which is to be expected considering it seats twenty thousand and has layout changes. The spring floor is up on a platform for maximum visibility, the apparatus is more spread out to keep events separated, even the air is cooler to accommodate for all the additional body heat. It's intense.

It also means there's no way we can forget how much is on the line. This isn't just messing around in the gym where we practice every day. This is uniforms and sparkly glitter makeup and hair bows. This is the first time we're truly showing off everything we've been working for.

The rush of adrenaline is unreal. I thrive on it. Which is why I'm all the more pissed that I'm simultaneously fighting to keep Con's words out of my head.

"Did you put out on the first date with him, too? Is that why he sticks around?"

Fucking dick. If Con was half as worried about his own shit as he is about everyone else's, he probably would have met that Olympic goal and wouldn't be fighting to remain king of the college circuit.

The meet is in full swing, and I try not to watch too closely as my three teammates go before me. I'm thrilled to be going last on floor exercise. That means Coach considers me the best in my group on this event. But I won't get cocky. I know from experience that it never helps anyone to watch the routines before yours and try to compare. It's the easiest way to psych yourself out. However, I've also seen these routines a million times at practice, so I give myself a few peeks.

As Layla's routine comes to a close, I move myself into position on the platform, awaiting my turn.

And then her score is flashed.

9.725.

It's a good score. But I can do better. I know I can.

Pasting my signature smirk on my face, I salute the judges and strut into position, awaiting the beginning notes of Aerosmith's *Walk this Way*. It was a shocking and delightful surprise when I found this floor exercise music, but it felt a lot like fate. I had to have it. The first time my teammates heard it, I got a lot of snotty looks, but I didn't care. Still don't. It's perfect. Not only do I feel this music deep down in my soul, but it also keeps me energized and excited, and it feels perfectly me.

The beginning beats finally sound, and I launch into a series of twists, turns, and jumps as I dance my way into the corner of the floor, prepping for my first tumbling pass. This one goes first because it's the big one—the one I've been working on for so long. The one that will hopefully cement my spot as a contender and the best person for the competition spot this season.

I take a deep breath in preparation and wait for the timing of the music to be exact in three...two... one... LAUNCH!

Five running steps...

One hurdle step...

Round off…

Back handspring, back handspring…

PUNCH!

I pull my arms tight toward me as I spin in the air, relaxing slightly as my body feels the motion and remembers exactly how to move. I begin to open my arms to land, readying myself to immediately punch into the front salto, but don't get that far.

Instead, my leg lands in a strange position and I feel a *crack* followed by an intense, stabbing pain that shoots up my leg. I try to stop but in a practical sense, my old science teacher was right—a body in motion stays in motion, and mine can't stop with this much power behind it. So, I do the best I can to tuck myself into a ball and complete the front flip, content to land on both my other foot and my rear, my injured leg pointing out in front of me.

With a grimace on my face, I immediately clasp my lower leg, willing the pain to stop. I've never felt anything like this before, and I have no doubt it's broken. The question is where and how badly.

Hopefully, I don't have long to find out though, because this pain is horrific.

Groaning, I squeeze my eyes tightly and roll back and forth, trying to find a position, any position, that lessens the intensity. Nothing works.

My breathing comes out in short gasps as I try not to cry. Coach comes running onto the floor, and for the first time, I'm cursing the springs underneath as the vibrations make me bounce. Not enough for anyone else to notice, but enough for my leg to feel it.

Coach crouches down next to me, gently touching my shoulder. "Lauren? Where is the pain?"

"My leg," I groan. "It's broken."

His attention turns to the lower portion of my body and I realize I'm beginning to shake from the adrenaline and pain. Once again, the movement doesn't help.

The next however long is a blur as more people come to our aid and I'm carried off the platform. It hurts so bad I cry out. I'm quickly loaded into an ambulance and driving to the hospital, still in my red, sparkly leotard. The drive may just be minutes, but it feels like hours and still, I'm feeling no relief. The pain is just as intense as it was when I landed.

"Please help me," I beg as soon as the doors to the ER open and some woman I assume is a nurse runs over to push the gurney. "It hurts so bad."

"I know, honey. We're gonna help."

She's a liar. They don't help. Instead, they move me into an x-ray room first and maneuver my leg onto a table, which causes me to actually scream and practically jump off. Why are they not giving me something for the pain?

"Please, can I have some drugs? Please?" I'm practically clawing at my own arms, praying to pass out if that's what it takes.

"As soon as we can, I promise."

That's not the answer I was looking for and it makes me angry. Unfortunately, my frustration takes a back seat to the millions of knives hacking away at my leg.

The process of x-rays and moving me into a tiny little room takes way too long for my liking and still, no drugs. Something about making sure I don't need emergency surgery first. Again, not the answer I want. But at least the nurse, whose name I still haven't learned, is finally starting an IV. My only complaint is that someone lied when they told me you can't concentrate on more than one kind of pain at once. I can attest to the fact that it doesn't matter how hard I concentrate on that needle, I can still feel my leg.

Finally, *finally* my x-rays are back and confirm what I already knew—tibia fracture. I don't care how bad. I don't care how long it will take to recover. Right now, all I care about is drugs.

"Okay, the doctor has given the go-ahead for pain meds," Nurse Helpful says. "Do you have any drug allergies?"

"No. Nothing." I'm practically panting at this point. "Please hurry."

"Okay," she says as she inserts a needle into a tiny vial.

"I'm going to give you four milligrams of morphine to help control the pain." That sounds a lot better than it turns out to be, because I swear my life must be in slow motion at this point. It's taking forever for this little bit of medicine to get sucked into the syringe. What part of, "I am in horrendous pain and want to die" is she not understanding?

After what seems like three lifetimes, the needle is in my IV and I feel the familiar rush of cold through my veins as the morphine is pushed through. It takes just a few seconds, but my head begins to feel heavy and my leg, while still hurting, is more of an ache than being ripped apart.

I sigh in relief and lean my head back. Better. So much better. I think I'll just rest...

SIXTEEN

Heath

Slamming my truck into park, I race through the parking lot and practically run over the woman who steps out in front of me just as I step onto the sidewalk.

"Oof!" We try to avoid each other at the last second, which only causes us both to lose our balance, so I grab her by the arms, keeping us upright.

"I'm so sorry, Heath. I didn't see you."

"How is she? Is she okay?"

I swear Annika's brow furrows just slightly, but I don't have time to ask about the expression. All I know is what Jaxon texted me.

Lauren fell. She's hurt bad. Heading to the ER.

It was way too cryptic for my liking, and I haven't been able to reach him since, despite my multiple calls.

"She's gonna be okay," Annika responds, shoving her phone in her pocket. "I came out here to call her mom since we can't get reception in there." That explains the lack of response but doesn't ease my immediate concerns. "We're just waiting to see what Lauren wants to do, and if she wants her mom here or not. You never know with her."

All good information, but not what I need right now.

"Okay, but what's wrong?" I demand. "Concussion or

surgical? She didn't break her neck, did she?" I suck in a breath, my hands cradling my head as thoughts of paralysis and brain bleeds go racing through my mind.

"What?" Annika looks confused now. "It's nothing like that. I told Jaxon to text you. What exactly did he say?"

Grabbing my phone, I open up the message and turn it around for her to see.

Annika quickly reads it and rolls her eyes at his lack of information. "No wonder you're freaking out. We probably need to have a sit-down conversation about how to appropriately text during a semi-emergency if we're going to keep hanging out with athletes." Taking a deep breath, she puts her hands up defensively. She almost looks like she's trying to calm a caged animal, which, if I'm being honest, I kind of feel like right now. "First, calm down. There is no life-threatening or life-altering injury."

My body relaxes a bit. I'm still amped up from adrenaline and not knowing what's happening, but at least I have reassurance that whatever it is can be fixed. And that I can punch Jax in the nuts later for not leading with the important parts like, "She's going to be fine."

"We're pretty sure she doesn't need surgery. It's kind of a wait and see for now."

"But what's actually wrong?"

"It happened so fast. You know that floor routine she's been working on?"

I nod because that damn routine seems to be at the center of almost every part of my life these days, or at least two of the most important things—Lauren's stress and my dating life.

"I'm not exactly sure how it happened, but she landed that tumbling pass wrong," Annika continues. "Got all the way to the front flip thing and ended up on her butt, holding her leg."

"Oh shit. Ankle?"

She shakes her head and guides me back through the sliding doors into the building. "Tibia. Early x-rays show it's probably a spiral fracture."

My heart sinks. Having been through my fair share of

injuries, a broken bone never means good things, especially at the beginning of a competition season. It basically kills your chances for meeting your goals or staying relevant in your sport. I can't imagine how heartbroken she must be right now. "That's not good. What is it, six, eight weeks for recovery?"

"Try four to six months minimum." I groan in response. That's even worse than I thought. "Right now, they're just patching her up but want her to follow up with her orthopedic for a second set of x-rays in a few days."

No one even looks twice as Annika leads me through another set of double doors into the back. Nor do they try to stop us when she pushes open a sliding glass door and moves a curtain to the side.

"Knock, knock. How're you feeling?"

"I feel great!"

Stepping all the way in, I find Lauren laying on the bed in a hospital gown, leg propped up and bandaged from her toes to mid-thigh. She's got a huge smile on her face, and if we weren't in a hospital room, I'd assume she'd been hitting the sauce. Especially when she finally notices me and shrieks. Loudly. Not at all the reaction I expect from an athlete who just lost most of her season to a major injury.

"Heath! You're here!" Lauren reaches her arms out to me and moves all her fingers in a very clumsy "come hither" movement. "Come give me a hug my huge, handsome, huge boyfriend who I like way too much, and he doesn't even know it."

Oh yeah. Those are some good meds.

Leaning over, I draw her into a hug, careful not to move her body too much. She may be feeling just dandy right now, but she won't be as soon as the pain killers wear off, and I don't want to create unnecessary movement that agitates it.

"What did they give you anyway?" I say with a chuckle as she holds me tighter than what many would deem appropriate, especially since I can tell that she's naked under this gown. I can feel the skin of her back. It's soft and smooth and not at all what I need to be thinking of right now.

"Morphine. I like it."

Amused, I try to pull away, but she clings to me, so I settle in. If Lauren needs comfort, I'm okay with that. But... wait. This may be more about the drugs again.

"Lauren, honey. Are you sniffing me?"

"You smell so good," she slurs.

Annika snickers from the other side of the room. "And on that note, I'm gonna go find my boyfriend and let him know she's feeling good enough to hit on you."

"I can't hit on someone who's already my boyfriend, Annika, duh," Lauren says with a roll of her eyes, as she finally pulls out of my arms. "Wait. Are you still my boyfriend? You are, right?"

"That's the last I heard of it," I joke, but she just looks at me with a confused expression.

"Is this still a fake relationship?" Lauren's eyes widen and she throws her hand over her mouth in horror. "I have to say that quiet! It's a secret!" she whisper-yells, completely defeating the purpose.

Pulling the chair next to her bed, I take her hand in mine, intertwining our fingers. The higher than normal placement of Annika's eyebrow doesn't go unnoticed by me, but there's a more important woman I need to focus on. Lauren needs to feel comfortable and safe. That's my focus. Everything else can wait.

"It's okay, baby. You can just say I'm your boyfriend." Yes, I know this is the coward's way out, and I should be waiting until Lauren is fully coherent before suggesting that I like her this much and want to date her exclusively, but I can't seem to stop myself.

"For reals?" Lauren says a little too loudly once again.

"Sure."

"Did you hear that Annika?" Lauren's eyes and smile are huge and very drunk. "I have a real boyfriend now!"

"I heard. I'm just as surprised about it as you are." Annika looks like the cat that ate the canary, and I know I'm going to get shit from my friends before we get home.

"Weren't you about to go rip your boyfriend a new

one?" I suggest. Annika doesn't take the bait, though.

"I was, but now I have something much more interesting to talk with him about."

Before Annika can pop off again, the door slides open again and a woman in scrubs walks confidently in the room.

"Nurse!" Lauren squeals. "I'm so glad you're here! This is my boyfriend! My real one. He's not fake at all. See?" She begins squeezing my arm in various places to prove how "real" I am. I really should be recording this right now. Drugged Lauren is a hoot.

The nurse only giggles, probably used to hearing all kinds of crazy things from patients. "I hope your real boyfriend brought his real car because it looks like you're about to be free of this place."

I have no idea how it's possible that Lauren's eyes can widen even more, but they do. "Did you hear that, Heath? I'm getting out of hospital jail!"

"I sure did. I guess that means you have to get dressed, huh?"

"That's going to be a problem," Annika cuts in. "I just realized she was wearing her leotard when she came in. I didn't even think to go grab some clothes."

"That's no problem," the nurse interjects. "We have scrubs she can wear. I already brought them in for her."

Annika clears her throat and I notice her stiffen for just a second. I don't understand what that's about, but the moment is over quickly so it must not be that big of a deal. "Yeah. Great. Thanks. Heath? Do you mind stepping out so we can get her dressed?"

"Yeah," Lauren adds. "You don't want to see my lady parts." She pulls her gown out and peaks down at herself, mumbling. "No one ever does anyway. Stupid gymnast boobs."

I pat her arm and stand up, still entertained. And I thought she had no filter when she was sober. "I'll go sit with Jaxon. Maybe bash him over the head for that message he sent me."

"Good idea," Annika says as we trade places. "And

while you're at it, maybe get him to have some blood work done since he's here anyway."

"I'm on it. Let me know when you're done so I can go get the truck and help you guys out."

"Bye, Heath!" Lauren raises her hand over her head and waves like I'm across town, not six feet away. "Come back soon!"

Shaking my head, I leave and let my two best girl friends handle their business.

It doesn't take long to backtrack and find my way into the waiting room, where I drop down into the chair next to Jaxon's.

"Dude. The next time you send me a message that someone I care about is in the hospital, maybe lead with 'she's not dead.' I fucking freaked out."

He chuckles but he doesn't sound amused. "Yeah, well, I was keeping an eye on Annika so it didn't occur to me that you would assume death when reading a text that said she was hurt."

Something about his demeanor tells me there's more to what he's saying than I'm catching. "What's wrong with Annika?"

Slowly, Jaxon looks over at me, a pained look on his face. "This is the hospital she was brought to last year." He looks down at where he's sitting. "This might actually be the same chair I sat in for like four hours while I waited for an update on her."

I sink further down into my seat, feeling like a dick for giving him a hard time. "Oh, shit man. I didn't realize it was here. Is that why she got freaked out when the nurse brought Lauren scrubs to wear home?"

"Probably. I bet they're similar to the ones Annika came home in."

Rubbing my hands down my face, I briefly worry about my friend and what kinds of memories she's being bombarded with right now. "I'm sorry, man. That sucks."

"Yep. An assault like hers never goes away," he says, leaning his head back on the chair.

"She's doing okay, though, right? Do we need to do

anything? I mean besides keep Lauren high as a fun diversion."

Jaxon smirks. "Nah. She's okay. It just sneaks up on her sometimes when she's not expecting it. You should have felt how tightly she was holding my hand in the car." He absentmindedly begins rubbing his palm. "Once we got back there with Lauren, and Annika realized the place had been renovated, she relaxed a little. It doesn't look the same at all."

I nod because I'm not sure how else to respond. What do you say when your friend will likely be terrorized by memories of her brutal rape for the rest of her life? Nothing. You say nothing. But there're no magic words for it. Just support. And maybe even distraction.

An idea hits me out of nowhere, and it might be a low blow, but I think Annika will forgive me this time.

"You know what would help her?"

"Hmm?"

"Getting a blood draw."

Jaxon furrows his brow. "What are you talking about?"

I punch him lightly on his knee, so he knows how serious I am. "Your girlfriend is worried about you man."

"Oh, Jesus. Not this again…"

"Hear me out," I interrupt, despite the anger that is now radiating off him. "This has been going on for a long time, and it's not going away. I don't have to spout off the statistics of childhood cancer survivors growing up and getting it again. You already know all this, so I get it. I know you're scared. But Jax, so is she." I lean forward and rest my elbows on my knees. "Annika needs you, man. And she's scared something is wrong and that by the time you do something about it, it'll be too late."

Jaxon leans on the armrest, rubbing his bottom lip with his thumb. The gears in his head are turning. I can practically see it. His fear and his understanding of the right thing to do are battling it out in his brain. It's the same look he had when he was about to change his major. The struggle. The concern. The worry. But he ended up making the right choice. I only hope he makes the right one again.

"I just… I don't know if I can do it again, man," he finally says quietly. I barely move and just listen. "My body doesn't feel as strong anymore. And this time, I know what's coming. I know what chemo entails and how bad it makes you feel." He shakes his head and presses his lips together. "I can't do that again. I can't."

Sitting up, I put my hand on his shoulder. "You don't even know what's wrong yet. It could be something completely different. Hell, it could be mono." We both know it's not, or else he'd have some serious explaining to do to his girlfriend. "Don't get ahead of yourself. But if it is that, which would be worse? Treating it at Stage One? Or treating at Stage Four?"

We both know this answer, too. And that the longer he waits, the worse it'll be. But he needs to know he won't be alone, no matter what.

"Just go get the blood draw," I prod gently. "Let them look at your counts. If nothing else, do it so your girlfriend can relax. I'm tired of her getting on my case about not getting on *your* case."

His eyes whip over to mine. "She does that?"

"Hell yeah. She's on that field during practice now. She sees it."

Jax rubs his face and sits up. "Shit, I didn't even think about that." He blows out a deep breath, like a decision has been made. "Okay. Yeah. I'll go do it now while we're still waiting. She needs peace of mind."

We all need answers, but I don't say that. If he wants to use Annika as a crutch so he has the strength to finally face this head-on, so be it.

"You're doing the right thing."

We push ourselves up to standing and Jaxon looks around until he finds what he's looking for. "Looks like the lab is that direction." He points to the posted sign. "I'll go find it and get this done as quickly as possible."

"Take your time. I've got my truck, so I can drive Lauren home. Do you need to call your doctor or something?"

"Yeah, I'll call Dr. Gates on my way. All I need is for him to tell them what to test for. He'll do it. And I'm sure my dad won't mind me using my emergency credit card if the insurance doesn't go through fast enough."

I chuckle. "Knowing your dad, he'll probably fight with insurance to be able to pay for it."

Jaxon snorts a laugh and pulls his phone out. "Ain't that the truth. I'm, uh… I'm gonna go before I lose my nerve."

I nod in support and watch as he walks away. When he's out of sight, I sink down into the chair and put my face in my hands. I'm glad he's finally taking charge of the situation. It's too important to let it slide any longer. But knowing we're about to have answers is a bittersweet pill to swallow. And I'm not sure how any of us will make it through if the worst outcome becomes our reality.

SEVENTEEN

Lauren

I feel foggy. Like I've been on an all-night bender. I don't have a headache or any nausea, but my mouth feels like it's full of cotton.

Moving my head, I lick my lips, trying to rid myself of the feeling. No luck. I'm going to need some water and quickly.

As soon as I push up, I remember why it's such a bad idea to move.

"Ahhh!" I cry out in pain and flop back down, which makes me bounce and cry out again.

Pressing the heels of my hands into my eyes, I take slow breaths as I wait for the initial stabbing pain to ease. And that's when it all comes back to me.

My leg. I broke my fucking leg. Tibia fracture, if I'm remembering correctly. Through the fog, I vaguely remember the words, "Out for four to six months, minimum."

Fuck.

A warm hand brushes the hair out of my face and my eyes flutter open. Heath.

"Don't move, baby," he says gently. *Baby.* I like the sound of that.

Putting a straw up to my lips, he encourages me to

drink. It's just water, but I have no complaints. The cool liquid feels like a much-needed rainstorm in the desert my mouth has become overnight. I'm so parched I'm thinking in prose.

"Here. Eat this." Heath puts the cup down and hands me a cracker.

I grimace at the idea of making my mouth dry again. "I'm not hungry. Just thirsty." I try to push the food away but he's insistent.

"I know, but it's time to take another pain pill and I don't want your stomach to get upset."

It's hard to object to his logic, considering how much it hurt to try and sit up a few seconds ago. Not to mention how gentle he's being as he adjusts the blankets around my leg. He's wearing what looks like pajama bottoms and a white t-shirt. Was he sleeping here with me?

"What time is it, anyway?" I ask, as I slowly chew and swallow my cracker, motioning for another sip of water.

"A little after midnight."

I feel my eyes widen. "Midnight? Holy shit. How long was I out?"

Heath chuckles and places a large pillow I've never seen before under my shoulders to prop me up a bit, then hands me the water. "Not that long, actually. But you were hopped up on morphine for a while. You finally crashed when we gave you a pain pill for the ride home."

My chewing slows down as I think back through my foggy memories. Maybe it was me being hopeful they were dreams and not vague memories of acting like a fool. And declaring my feelings for Heath. And telling everyone he's my fake boyfriend.

I groan and drop my head back. "Tell me I did not squeeze your biceps to prove to the nurse you were real?"

"Oh, you did." He takes the cup from me, and now that I'm coherent and not in danger of spilling everywhere, cracks open a water bottle and hands it to me. "After you told everyone I'm your not-so-fake boyfriend anymore. Here. Take this before the pain comes back."

I look at the huge horse pill he just handed me. "Is it

going to knock me out, so I don't have to think about what an idiot I was? Or… wait…" I stop with the pill halfway to my mouth, giving him the best stern look I have. "You didn't take any videos, did you?"

For a split second, the look on his face has me convinced he did.

"Nah," he finally answers, and I breathe a sigh of relief, swallowing my medication like a good little patient. "You were so busy manhandling me, I couldn't get a hand free to hold the phone steady."

I immediately begin choking on my water. Heath just laughs, the bastard.

"You're such a jerk," I say, as I get the last of the water out of my windpipe. "I could have choked on that pill."

"But you didn't, so just calm your little feisty self down." He hands me another cracker, which I begin nibbling on as I rest, eyes closed, thinking over my new reality.

A lot of today, well, I guess yesterday at this point, seems so long ago. And other parts seem like they just happened. Getting to the hospital and the massive pain I experienced are right at the forefront of my mind. Holy shit, that was horrid. I never want to feel anything like that again. The whole thing just sucks.

The only silver lining I can think of is I don't have to worry about breaking another bone for a while. I won't be working on tumbling passes any time soon.

"He said four to six months of recovery time, didn't he?" I ask, my eyes still closed.

"Minimum. You need to see an orthopedist first to do some more x-rays. Make sure nothing was missed during the first set."

"Shit," I grumble. "That hurt like a bitch. Can't they just treat it using the first set of films?"

"Wish they could, babe." Babe. There's that term of endearment again. It may be the one good thing to come out of this shitty situation. "Sometimes the extent of the injuries don't show up until a few days later. And since yours is a spiral fracture, they want to make extra sure."

I sigh again. This just keeps getting better. Not only am I out for the first part of the season at the very minimum, but they also can't even give me an estimate of when I can get back to practice. I am probably out for the entire season.

Frustrated, I try to keep my voice under control. Heath didn't do this to me. I did it to myself. I pushed too hard. I got too cocky. And it bit me in the ass.

"Do I have an appointment yet?" I ask quietly, not meaning to whisper, but that's what happens when the gravity of your situation hits out of nowhere, and you're suddenly trying to keep yourself under control.

I hear Heath cross the room, the bed moving just slightly as he sits on the floor next to me. He grabs my hand with his and clasps them together. I know he's trying to be supportive of me. If anyone understands how hard this is to accept, it's him. And I'm grateful he's here.

"The training department director put in a call to the orthopedist we work with. His office will call tomorrow with your appointment information."

I nod, my lip trembling and a lone tear sliding down my cheek, the feeling of disappointment too much to bear right now.

Heath wipes the wetness away with his thumb, the movement so gentle, so caring, I turn my head and look at him. It feels like he can read my mind, or at least my emotions, and he understands how major this is. To someone else, it's a broken leg. An inconvenience. An annoyance to be worked around.

To me, it's one of only two shots I had to reach my goal snuffed out faster than I could say "front salto."

"It's not over, Lauren."

"It feels like it is."

"I know it does. But I've already been doing research on different kinds of exercises we can do to keep up your strength and skills." He reaches over and grabs his laptop off the floor, flipping it open to show me a document that looks suspiciously like a workout schedule. "Mostly it's going to be upper body and core work until we're given the go-ahead to add in some glutes. I'll have to research a little more on what kind of exercises won't put too much stress on the break. We may have to stick with scissor-type moves at first."

The way his tone turns from informational to more monotone, I wonder if he's still talking to me, or if he's making mental notes for himself. Regardless, the amount of effort he's put into researching a new workout schedule for me is intense. I'm stunned that he would do all this for me.

"This is amazing, Heath. Thank you. I bet Ellery can help me with some of these. Although I might have to see if Coach can spare someone to spot me." A flash of disappointment crosses his face, which makes no sense. "What?"

He gives a small shrug and sheepishly says, "I was hoping to be the one to help you."

I blink rapidly a few times, speechless at his offer. It's one thing to help me home from the hospital. It's another to hang out with me the first night and help put a plan together for the immediate future. But it's an entirely different issue for him to be planning the next several weeks, if not months, of working out together. Especially since so much of that time would be dedicated to spotting me.

Finding my words, I do what comes naturally—I resist. "You don't have time for that."

"Sure, I do."

"Heath, you have football practice and classes and…"

"And what?" When I don't answer, he continues. "That's all I have. I have to work out anyway. I might as well do it with my girlfriend."

I quirk my lips at his joke. "Don't you mean fake girlfriend?"

Heath clears his throat and shifts around, closing the laptop and placing it on the floor. "I guess you were a little less coherent in the ER than I thought."

I know what he's referring to, but I didn't know he was sincere. "Wait… were you serious?" He just looks at me, giving me a small shrug. "I thought… I mean… weren't you just pacifying me in my time of need and overly euphoric state?"

A grin crosses his face and he chuckles lightly. "Yeah, doped up Lauren is pretty fun."

I try to shove him, but my angle on the bed doesn't allow for much force. Not to mention the fact that he's the size of a Mack truck compared to me.

Clearing his throat again, which I'm starting to realize is synonymous to him feeling nervous, Heath reaches his arm up on my bed and begins playing with my fingers. The feeling is not unwelcoming at all. It's actually really soothing. The deliberateness also seems to emphasize the pending magnitude of this moment. "I know we started this whole relationship to get those assholes off your back and to help keep the groupies off me. Which incidentally, hasn't worked that much."

I giggle because I could have told him that from the beginning. He's smart. He's friendly. He's hot. And he's on his way to getting an NFL contract. Women may say they want a man to pursue them, but we're not stupid either. Heath is a catch. Putting ourselves in his line of sight in the hopes that he notices isn't the worst move.

"I'm glad you find it amusing," he says with a smile. "Anyway, I guess the more we hung out and pretended to enjoy each other, the more I started to enjoy you." He grimaces. "Shit. That sounded bad. I don't mean it like that. I…" He runs his hand down his face in frustration. "I'm totally fucking this up."

Grabbing his fingers, I stop his rant. "You enjoy being with me?" I whisper in disbelief.

He pauses only momentarily before nodding. "Well, yeah. You're so motivated with your goals and willing to do whatever it takes. You understand where I'm coming from with my own ambitions and why I have to stay focused. And you're the one person I know besides Jaxon who doesn't pressure me to do my life any differently."

I furrow my brow. "That can't be true."

"Well, not my family. They're pretty good about letting me do my own thing. But they're not here. People I interact with daily don't seem to understand why I do and don't do certain things. The guys on my team are always asking me to go out with them and encouraging me to get blitzed and chase tail. It sounds fun and all, but I just don't have any interest in going down that road. Not anymore. Maybe after graduation, once I'm under contract I can let loose a little. But for now, I'm just three months away from the most important day in my life." He looks up at me again, his eyes soft with emotion that I never expected to see directed at me. But it is. His words just confirm it. "I want to spend those months with you."

I'm well and truly stunned. Heath Germaine, football god, and campus catch, just declared his feelings for me.

"I... um... I don't know what to say. Are you sure?"

He gives me a shy smile, one that I haven't seen before, and I can't help but think about how intimate it is. It's a side of him he doesn't show people. But he's showing... me.

"I may be a little overzealous," he states playfully. "I don't mean to sound like I'm planning out the few months of our lives, but if you'd be interested, I'd like to try dating. For real, I mean."

"Um..." I gesture down to my injured leg. "That might be kind of hard considering I'm practically immobile right now. The only time we'd be able to spend together is when I'm sitting and you're sitting with me. Or you could walk around, but obviously, I'm not going anywhere."

"Which leaves studying and binge-watching Netflix. And that's why I was talking about the workout schedule."

I bite my bottom lip, still feeling a bit discombobulated from this turn of events. Or it could be the pain pill. Either way, this whole conversation is surreal.

"So basically, it's doing the same things we've been doing, plus a few additional things like you taking care of me."

He nods. "Exactly. Only this time it's bona fide dating. Really getting to know each other. On purpose and not for show."

"I just want to make sure you're aware that I won't be

able to engage in any hanky panky for a while." Looking down at my leg, I sigh. "Maybe a long while."

Heath squeezes my hand, knowing my depressed mood is less about sex and more about everything else. "That works out well then. We have a long while to see what happens, to see where we go emotionally, so you never have to wonder what my true intentions are."

Well, damn. That just may be the sexiest thing anyone has ever said to me.

Taking a deep breath, I try to clear my addled brain. "I think I'd like to try legitimately dating you. Seeing what happens."

I didn't know it was possible for Heath to smile any bigger. But as his lips stretch and he puffs out a breath that I know is either relief or happiness, I see it. It looks like pure joy. And I put it there. How did this even happen?

Suddenly, his expression changes to one that is more heated. His gaze drops to my mouth and I know what he's thinking. Inside, I'm screaming, "Kiss me. Please kiss me!", and everything in me hopes he takes advantage of this moment.

As if he can hear my thoughts, he licks his lips and begins leaning in. Being propped up, I can't meet him in the middle, so I grab his hand tighter, hoping it encourages him to keep going.

Finally, after what feels like hours, we make contact. His lips are soft and smooth as they glide over mine. The tip of his tongue snakes out, requesting entrance. And I wholeheartedly comply.

Heath takes what I offer and tangles his tongue with mine, reaching his free hand up to cup my jaw and tilt my head exactly where he wants it. His kiss is both aggressive and reserved, making his desires clear without pushing too far, the sounds of our breathing the only thing I hear. It's sweet and loving and sexy as hell.

When he finally pulls away, my brain feels like mush, my eyes fluttering as I try to keep them open.

Heath chuckles and kisses the tip of my nose. "I knew I was a decent kisser, but this may be the first time I've rendered a woman practically immobile."

I smile, as I rest back onto my pillow. "Don't get cocky. My verdict on your abilities isn't in yet. We might have to try that a few more times...."

My voice trails off as the pain pill kicks in. I barely feel him pull the covers over me, but register when he kisses my forehead and says, "Go to sleep, Tiny."

"Okay..." is all that comes out before I drift off, everything clearing of my mind except the feeling of a perfect first kiss.

EIGHTEEN
Heath

"What's happening here?" the voice whispers.

"I have no idea. I'm as confused as you are," a second voice says just as quietly.

"He said something at the hospital about honestly dating. I thought he was just placating little miss druggie."

That must be Annika. For whatever reason, my brain is registering she was the only person I know who was in the hospital room during that conversation with Lauren. It makes sense that she would be both there and here. Although, my not-quite-awake brain can't figure out who she's talking to and about what.

"He said that? Is that why he was freaking about her being in the hospital?"

Ah. Got it. That's Jaxon. This realization also makes sense to my foggy brain, which is slowly starting to catch up to where I am and what I'm doing here.

Lauren's room. Taking care of her because she's hurt. Bad.

"Must be. I thought it was sweet but didn't expect to come home to *this*."

"I can hear you, ya know," I grumble and roll over on my back, making sure the covers stay over my lower half to cover my morning wood. Doesn't matter that it's Jaxon's girlfriend, who is off-limits even if I was interested in her. That part of me has a mind of its own.

"Good," Jaxon says at a more normal volume. "Then maybe you can explain what's happening here."

Raising my head up to see what they're going on about, I look through half-lidded eyes at the situation around me.

"Huh. I forgot about that," is my only answer as my head falls back onto the pillow. I'm exhausted.

It was a rough night, which I anticipated but living through it is still hell. Lauren woke up just before four in a lot of pain. Unfortunately, it wasn't time for her meds and the doctor had warned me that with her small stature, the times couldn't be fudged.

So, I did the best I could helping her get in different positions, hoping to relieve some of the pain and discomfort. After much maneuvering, she ended up on her left side, pillow between her legs. It means the break isn't propped up as much as we'd like, but it helped a little.

The other thing that helped was rubbing her head. I don't know if it was from comfort or distraction, but either way it helped her relax enough to power through until I could give her another pain pill. At that point, I practically needed one myself from keeping my arm in a weird position, so a little redecorating was necessary if I was going to keep up the movement until the meds kicked in and she fell back asleep.

And that's how Annika's bed was moved right next to Lauren's and I ended up asleep, holding her hand. Not that I'm going to explain that to my best friend and his girlfriend. I have questions of my own I want answered.

"What time is it, anyway?" I rub my face and take a breath, pushing myself to a sitting position.

"Almost eight."

"Damn," I grumble, swinging my legs onto the floor. "No wonder I'm tired. Did they run the tests?"

Annika makes herself busy pulling things out of drawers as Jaxon pulls out a desk chair to sit in.

"Yep. Took them for fucking ever to let me go. This is

why I didn't want to go in the first place."

"Bullshit," Annika blurts out. "If you had planned ahead weeks ago, the offices would have been open, and they wouldn't have kept you overnight in a hospital while Dr. Bates called in a favor to get the results faster."

Jaxon opens his mouth to respond but catches the look on my face first and wisely thinks better than to argue with her. I'm on her side with this one, and he knows it. But I still want to know, no... *need* to know what's going on.

"But they let you come home. That's a good thing, right? They didn't have to admit you so that means everything is manageable?"

Jaxon nods, a small smile crossing his face. "Yeah. I'm in the clear."

I clench my fists and raise them up in victory. This is the best news I've had all week. "That's fucking awesome, man. What a relief."

Annika shuts the drawer and turns around. "Wait. You're not totally in the clear. Your iron levels are low. Too low. We still have to get those under control."

"Your iron?" I ask, confused. I wasn't expecting that.

"Yeah, just another lovely long-term side effect of having leukemia and a bone marrow transplant. Isn't it great surviving cancer just to deal with this shit for the rest of my life?"

I hold up my hands and cock my head. "I mean, you're not dead."

"I know." Jax runs a hand down his face, probably exhausted from pulling an all-nighter like mine. "Trust me, I'm grateful that's all this is. It's just irritating sometimes, and I'm exhausted so I'm not in the best mood."

"Understandable. So, what do we do now? Anything?"

"He got a prescription for some super-powered iron pills we have to pick up later today," Annika says running her hands through Jaxon's hair. He looks like he's about to fall asleep from the ministration. "And he's on a strict diet to load up on more iron-rich foods and avoid food that blocks iron absorption."

"I have to avoid cheese, man," he whines. "What kind

of diet makes a man not eat cheese?"

"The kind that is going to help you feel better and not collapse on the field in front of your girlfriend," Annika chides, to which Jaxon smirks.

He grabs her hand and kisses her knuckles as she gazes at him. Sometimes they're like a fucking Hallmark movie and make me want to puke. Other times, like when he's dodged a huge life-altering bullet, I have no choice but to recognize she's the best thing that's ever happened to him.

"Why don't you go take a shower so we can head back to my place, babe? I'm so ready for a nap."

"Now how did I know you guys were going to commandeer our room?" I remark as I stretch my arms over my head, relieving some of the tension in my shoulders. "Damn good thing I swung by and got some clothes for myself."

Annika smirks and heads to the en-suite bathroom. But, of course, she can't leave without taking one last dig at me. "Sure. That's why you got clothes. It has nothing to do with the fact that suddenly there is a queen-sized sleeping space in my room partially occupied by you."

And, of course, she closes the door before I can defend myself. Not that I'm going to. What's happening between Lauren and me is between us. That doesn't stop Jaxon from staring me down as soon as his girlfriend is out of eyesight, though.

"Did they give you a list of foods or something?" I ask, hoping he'll take the bait. "Anything in particular we should load up on?"

"Nu-uh," he says, refusing to play along. "I wanna know what's going on here first." Pointing back and forth at Lauren and me, there's no pretending I don't know what he's referring to. But it still feels fragile and new. I have no desire for him to get in my head while I'm still getting my feet wet, so to speak.

"None of your fucking business." Standing up, I cross the room and grab a water bottle out of the fridge and toss it to him.

He catches it with one hand, not even flinching. "It

looks like you just moved into my girlfriend's dorm room. Consider me curious."

"I consider you a fucking busybody."

He flips me the bird and cracks open the water. "And you're fucking deflecting. The last thing I heard is you were in a fake relationship with Lauren. Then she gets hurt, you freak the fuck out, and now I walk in and you're holding hands while sleeping next to her."

"So?"

"I'm wondering what changed."

Downing half of my own drink, I wipe my mouth on my sleeve before answering. How do I explain how wrong I was about Lauren? About how I missed all her awesome personality traits simply because I was afraid of being screwed over? About how when I finally peeled back some of her layers, I found a kindred spirit in an amazing woman who is just as afraid as I am? I don't know how to put any of that into words, and frankly, I don't want to. Those are things I want to say to her, not to my obnoxious best friend. So, I shrug and play it off the best I can.

"I like her. That's all."

Jax looks at me for a beat longer than is comfortable. "I don't buy it."

"I don't care."

"I'm not judging you, Germaine. I like Lauren. She's a little out there, but she's good people. I'm glad you finally figured that out. Took you long enough."

I nod because he's right. It took me way too damn long to see Lauren for who she is.

Pointing at me, his face hardens. "Just don't hurt her."

"Fuck you, man," I say through clenched teeth. It pisses me off he'd even think that about me.

"As long as we understand each other."

Pushing aside my hurt feelings because, let's face it, he's got a right to be weirded out by my rapid one-eighty, I move on. "Anyway," I say deflecting again, "about your health."

Jaxon groans and runs a hand down his face. "You're not going to drop this are you?"

"Turnabout is fair play. You rag on me, I rag on you. That's how it works. So, spill. What do I need to know about your diet?"

He sighs and finally placates me. "Lots of leafy greens. Lots of meat and poultry. Lots of beans. It's basically like our current diet except on steroids. And no cheese."

I snicker. "That really pisses you off, doesn't it?"

"I love cheese, man. Maybe more than I love Annika. How am I supposed to survive?"

Out of nowhere an idea hits me. One that might be fun for all of us.

"What if we take a cooking class?"

He reels back, looking like I've lost my mind. "What the hell are you talking about? Since when do we fucking cook?"

"Since we won't have a dining hall cooking us three square meals a day forever," I say, waving my hand around and ignoring his attitude. "We can go to one of those places that have the cooking work stations, and we stay for a few hours while a chef teaches us how to make a meal." He still looks lost. I roll my eyes. "They have them at those fancy grocery stores like Whole Foods and whatever. It's like four hours and they teach you how to make something fancy."

He still looks lost.

"Do you ever watch television? Or read a book? Is your world really this small?"

"I didn't think so, but now I'm starting to wonder."

"We can take the girls."

Jaxon's eyebrows creep up and his expression changes like he's finally starting to catch on. "Like a double date?"

"Sure. Why not? We'll learn how to cook something healthy to help appease your girlfriend and probably your daddy." I duck when he grabs a pencil off the desk and throws it at my head. "The girls will be happy, and we get to eat a fancy meal. Everybody wins."

He bobbles his head while he considers it. "Sounds kind of fun actually. Annika's been dying to go out, but you know she's not a partier."

I look over at Lauren who is still knocked out. "Not like Tiny over there can party for a while anyway. We can set it up for a couple of weeks from now. At that point, I'm sure she'll be itching to get out. It'll do her some good to still be active." When I look back over at Jaxon, he's smirking at me again. I roll my eyes in annoyance. "Do not say a fucking word."

He holds his hands up in defense. "I'm saying nothing. You'll talk when you're ready. I'm just gonna sit back and enjoy the show."

Picking up the pencil that happens to have rolled next to me, I launch it back at him. "This is not a show. Especially now. Let us figure this out and how it's going to work before invading our privacy, okay? Just like I did with you."

"Yeah, okay fine. I get it. But you can't blame me for not seeing this coming."

Looking back over at my new legitimate girlfriend who is still knocked out, my lips quirk up at the corners. "Neither did I, man. Neither did I."

NINETEEN
Lauren

"**A**re you sure you're okay pushing? Why don't you let me push for a while?"

"I got it."

"Are you sure? You haven't let me help at all."

"I said I got it."

I roll my eyes and bite back a quip, but the bickering is about to drive me up the wall.

I love Kiersten. And I... well... really, really like Heath. But the two of them together are getting on my last fucking nerve. It's been non-stop squabbling since Kiersten showed up for a visit yesterday like she promised.

I was so excited when she walked into my dorm room and ran over to give me a hug. She's always been my best friend and my rock, so having her here to distract me from my new sedentary lifestyle seemed like a great idea. My spirits lifted immediately.

Then she saw Heath and her eyes widened. With all the reorganizing of my life, I'd completely forgotten to tell her about him.

Fortunately, he had to get to practice which gave me ample time to catch her up. I told her all about how good he's been to me and how many nights he's stayed over just to give me pain meds in my sleep. I told her about his head rubs that relax me right into slumber. I even told her about the workout schedule he put together. She smiled and said she was happy for me, but I don't think she truly understood the level of effort he has put into my care. And I don't think she was expecting him to not relinquish control just because she showed up.

"Okay, well, be careful around that corner," Kiersten advises. "It's a small space in here."

"It's fine, Kiersten," he responds through gritted teeth, and I can practically hear him biting his own tongue to keep from lashing out. I'm starting to wonder if Heath always has issues getting used to new personalities and that's why he resists meeting new people. The only other possibility is that everyone in the *world* is annoying, and I don't think that's accurate.

"Ohmygod, would you two quit bickering?" Finally, someone other than me loses their shit over these two. I just didn't expect it to be Annika. She's usually the most even-keel of all of us. "Kiersten, I know you came to help, but Heath's got it. He's been maneuvering around our little dorm room for weeks now. Plus, he's big and strong and can lift her way better than the rest of us. Let the man do the physical labor. You have fun distracting Lauren with conversation."

I can't see her face, but by the way Kiersten immediately shuts up, I suspect she's stunned by Annika's outburst. Unexpected or not, I flash Annika a grateful smile. As much as I'm glad my best friend is here, she's disrupted our carefully crafted routine, and due to my lack of mobility, I can't get away from the tension.

Two weeks ago, when my second set of x-rays came back with no damage except the initial spiral fracture and small hairline fracture above it, I was rendered completely immobilized in a toe-to-thigh cast. Being that I'm not allowed to put any pressure on my leg yet, my doctor prescribed a wheelchair for me to get around. Sounds nice in theory, but not in a dorm room. And knowing my mother would turn into a helicopter mom, I declined her offer of help. Heath's offer sounded way better.

Every morning, he comes over to lift me out of bed and carry me to the bathroom. Fortunately, having strong quads means I can do my business by myself, but that's where my luck runs out. Annika has to help me get dressed, which sounds more humiliating than it actually is, thankfully. Then Heath carries me to my wheelchair, which he has waiting in the hall and wheels me to class. We do a similar reverse version at night, including Annika standing in the bathroom while I shower in case I fall and can't get up.

It's not convenient for anyone and takes more time than we've got, but it works, and I'm so grateful for their help.

And then Kiersten came in like a Tasmanian devil, determined to take charge. I love her. I do. But she has gotten in the way of our routine more than once in her haste to be the supportive friend she's always been.

Honestly, I get it. Until Annika came along, Kiersten was the only true friend I had. If there was a crisis, she was the one who helped me fix it. But now I have both Annika and Heath. And if it's something really important, Jaxon, too. It's going to take a while for Kiersten to recognize I've got a much larger support system now. I just hope she doesn't feel shoved aside because of it.

"Kiersten, can you find out which station we're going to be at?" I suggest, knowing that's a task she can accomplish without driving Heath to alcoholism as a coping mechanism.

"Sure!" She bounds away to find the instructor while Heath carefully maneuvers us against a wall and out of the way of anyone who may accidentally run into my leg. As he situates the chair, I hear him blow out a frustrated breath.

"Let it go, Heath," Annika warns before I can say anything. "She's not trying to get in the way. She's just a little lost as to how she can best help."

"Shower duty," he grumbles. "Give her shower duty. I can't be in there anyway."

Annika laughs lightly. "I already did, you grump."

He sighs and puts his hand on my shoulder, squeezing gently. I've noticed he does that a lot—just touches me for no reason. I didn't expect him to be so physically affectionate when I agreed to the change in our relationship status, and I'm hoping it's not because of my injury. I kind of like it.

"I'm sorry. I'm just tired."

Grabbing his hand with mine, I look up at him. "You don't have to stay over to make sure I get pain meds, anymore. Let Kiersten do it. You take advantage of her being here and get some sleep."

"You mean with Annika sleeping in my room?"

"Hey now," Jaxon interjects. "I take issue with that."

Annika rolls her eyes and lightly smacks him on the chest. "Then, it's a good thing I'm going to stay at my place while Kiersten is here. Then no one can complain."

Both guys begin to protest, because they're apparently big fucking babies who can't sleep alone, when Kiersten rejoins us, a smile on her face.

"I told the instructor about your leg and turns out they have a station with a lower counter we can have."

"Oh, that's great!" Annika exclaims. "So how are we splitting up?"

"Well, we could do girls and guys…" I start and am immediately interrupted when both men begin to protest again.

"Nope." Jaxon shakes his head vehemently. "If I have to give up my bed partner, I'm keeping her for my cooking partner."

Annika purses her lips at him. "What is your deal? When did you become a clingy little brat?"

"When I looked at the calendar and realized I have one week left with you before we have to leave for the holidays. Besides, this is supposed to be a double date."

She rolls her eyes. Hard. I'm not terribly surprised. She's been really moody lately, her outburst a few minutes ago proof of that. I chalked it up to finals and shark week. Not a good combination.

"Okay, well you're irritating the shit out of me so I'm

changing it to a girls' night before I smother you with a pillow in your sleep." Turning to me and ignoring the fact that her boyfriend's jaw just dropped, she asks, "Where are we going?"

"Um…" Kiersten stumbles over her words, as stunned as we are over Annika's behavior. "This way."

Heath allows Kiersten past him so she can take over wheelchair duty. Without saying a word, the three of us make our way through the maze of workstations before ending up off to the side. Our station has regular sized counters, but the end has been modified so a wheelchair can roll right up to it. I won't be able to put anything in the oven or use the cooktop, but at least I can help chop and prep.

The guys are on the other side of the room. Heath is looking through all the supplies while Jaxon has made himself comfortable on a stool, sulking.

"Annika, what was that about?" I finally ask, because we all want to know. It might as well be me who gets it out of her.

She peeks inside the oven for whatever reason as she nonchalantly answers me. "What was what about?"

I look at Kiersten, who has the same confused expression on her face. She shrugs at me.

"Do you not see your boyfriend pouting over there?"

Annika takes a quick glance before continuing her inspection. "Oh that. He's fine."

Now I'm even more confused. Jaxon and Annika are the most lovey-dovey couple I've ever known. For them to be at odds is, well, odd.

"Uh oh," Kiersten says more to me than Annika. "Sounds like there's trouble in paradise."

That seems to snap Annika back to reality as we see it. "What do you mean? There's no trouble."

"You sure about that?" I ask. "You just threatened to kill your boyfriend in his sleep because he's making you crazy. That's a little dramatic, even for you."

Annika sighs and sags down onto a stool. "You're right. I blame the drama on Auntie Flo." Kiersten's expression changes briefly, but it happens so fast I barely notice. "Plus, I'm overly tired."

The guilt hits me like a slap to the face as I see the dark circles under her eyes that I hadn't noticed before. "God Annika, I'm so sorry. I didn't even think about how hard this would be for you when I told my mom not to come. Maybe I can call her, and she can get a long-term hotel room or something…"

Annika holds up her hand to stop me. "I'm not tired because of you, Lauren. I mean, I haven't gotten to sleep in or anything lately. But no. That's Jaxon's fault, too. I spent a lot of weeks sleeping like shit because I was worried about his health and he wouldn't do a damn thing about it. And I'm more stressed about finals because of my degree, and you know how hard it is to get into the kind of physical therapy I want to work in." She sinks down even further on her chair. "I'll be fine, I'm just cranky today."

"You may want to go explain all that to your boy toy." She huffs at my term of endearment. "He's probably as exhausted as you with how low his iron is."

"And whose fault is that?" she grumbles. Then she looks at my eyebrow which is clearly indicating my lack of agreement at her unnecessarily cold attitude toward him. She lets her head fall back while she groans. "Fine. I'll go make up with the big baby."

Sauntering over as Annika stomps off, Kiersten crosses her arms and leans against the counter. "Wow. Look at you playing therapist."

I puff a small laugh through my lips. "Hardly. I just feel bad for Heath. He doesn't need whiny Jaxon in his dorm room tonight. He's got enough on his plate."

My evil plan is already working. Annika has her arms around Jaxon's neck, his around her waist as they talk quietly, Heath ignoring them.

"Yeah about that." My attention reverts back to Kiersten, a grin on her face. "What's the story with Heath?"

"What do you mean? I already told you about him."

"Sure. You told me what you thought I wanted to hear. But the last few times I've been here, you guys were at each other's throats. Now, suddenly, you're dating. How did that happen and no bullshit this time?"

For a split second, I consider telling her the truth—he was my fake boyfriend until suddenly, he wasn't. But I realize how shady it sounds, and I don't want her to think Heath is anything like the other dickheads I've gotten involved with. I think in a subconscious way, that's part of why I never told her in the first place. That, and the fact that it wasn't a big deal. We were helping each other out. It didn't turn into anything more than a relationship of convenience until recently.

So, I take the coward's way out and stick with a partial truth. "The more we got to know each other, the more we liked each other. Simple as that."

Not really and by the look on her face, I'm positive she doesn't buy my crappy answer. But she doesn't have time to question it with the instructor calling the class to order.

"Good evening, everyone. My name is Lisa." She's wearing a white chef's coat and matching chef hat, a polite smile on her face like she's indifferent about being here. "Tonight, we're going to make a high-protein dish that's as tasty as it is healthy. To get started on our corned beef and cabbage, I want one of you from each station to go get a Tupperware out of the fridge."

"This isn't over," Kiersten whispers harshly and heads toward the wall of appliances while Annika finally returns from her lovefest.

"Is he all better now?"

Annika shrugs one shoulder sheepishly. "Yeah. I apologized for being a huge bitch. He's fine."

"And you're fine, too?"

"Yeah. I'm kind of looking forward to spending the night in my bed alone."

"Annika!"

"What? I can't starfish in a twin with him next to me."

I shake my head in amusement. Just a few months ago, she was complaining about how much she missed sleeping next to him. Now she's excited about sleeping on her own. Can't say I blame her. I thoroughly enjoyed sleeping next to Heath when he was on the other side of our makeshift bed.

"Does this smell rancid to you?" Kiersten drops the container on the counter. From this vantage point, all I can see is meat, but I assume there are vegetables or something in there, too.

Annika leans over to take a quick sniff. "No. Smells like raw beef."

"Are you sure?" Kiersten barely leans in to take a whiff before popping up, ramrod straight. "Ohmygod, that's going to make me sick."

Confused, Annika picks up the bowl and sniffs again. "I don't smell it. Maybe it's me?" She hands it over to me and I warily take it, not wanting to smell but also not wanting to get food poisoning from cooking bad meat either. Best to sort this out now.

Quickly, I inhale but smell nothing. I do it again, but for longer. Still nothing. Feeling confident, I lean in and take a giant whiff before giving my verdict.

"I wouldn't want to eat it raw, but it smells pretty fresh to me," I say with a shrug and hand it back to my roommate. Kiersten gets that weird look on her face again. "What? What are you thinking?"

As soon as I ask, she schools her features and smiles, waving me off. "No, nothing. Maybe it's because it's already been brined."

"It has?" I ask, trying to look back in the bowl, but Annika's too busy doing her own inspection.

"You may have noticed our corned beef has already been seasoned," Lisa announces to the class confirming Kiersten's assessment. "That's because it takes five to seven days to brine. 'Corned' literally means preserved. That's where the flavor comes from." Who knew we'd be getting a vocabulary lesson along with our cooking?

"We're still going to learn how to make the brine, though," Lisa continues. "You'll be able to take it home to use the next time you make this dish. So, to begin, let's pull out the smallest frying pan from the drawer at your station."

I can't help with anything on the stove, so I take a moment to look over at the guys. Jaxon is smiling as he claps Heath on the back, chattering away about something while Heath pulls out the supplies as Lisa calls them out. It's not necessarily an unusual scene. I've been hanging out with them for long enough that I've seen them interact before. But for whatever reason, I'm struck by how perfect it seems, watching these two best friends as they work together.

Or maybe it's because I'm only watching Heath.

He's just beautiful. His dark skin in contrast with the red t-shirt he's wearing, the sleeves tight around his biceps as he involuntarily flexes when he moves. The way he bites his plump bottom lip as he tries to mimic the instructor's actions. The quirk of his smile when Jaxon makes a mistake and curses.

And then he glances over and catches me staring and his expression changes to one that is definitely more sexually charged. What I wouldn't give to be able to jump out of this wheelchair and into his arms so he could sweep his counter of cooking supplies and ravage me.

There may be a good chance that all the making out we've done lately is making me horny.

I startle when a small stone bowl is plunked down right in front of me. "Jesus, Annika you scared the shit out of me."

"I wouldn't have if you weren't having sex fantasies about your new boyfriend during class." I gape at her. How did she know that? She rolls her eyes. "It was written all over your face, friend. Just a few more weeks until you get that cast off and you can make good on it." She pats me on the shoulder and turns back to the meat, which is now being put in water or oil or something. I have no idea. She's right. I was way too distracted.

Paying attention again, I begin pouring the now cooked spices into the stone bowl to mash into a finer powder. Annika is working with the meat on the stove and Kiersten.... Actually, Kiersten doesn't look very good.

"Kiersten?" She looks at me, eyes wide and breathing

heavily.

She begins looking around frantically, and I know instinctively what's about to happen.

Finding what she needs next to me, I thank my lucky stars for my flexibility so I can grab the trash can off the floor and hold it out to her.

"Here!"

Kiersten grabs it and pulls it to her face just as she begins to throw up. Her heaves can be heard by everyone, and the room goes silent except for some sizzling pans and her sickness.

"Sorry, Annika," I say absentmindedly. "You may want to bunk with Jaxon after all."

My roommate just nods as she carefully removes the pan from the stove and turns the burner off. Girls' night is officially over.

TWENTY

Heath

Squeezing us all in my truck seemed like a good idea at the beginning of the night. The three women are all small enough they can sit in the back. Lauren just has to sit sideways to get her cast in the right position, but with three of them, it also makes it harder to jostle her around, so it works to her benefit.

What I didn't count on was Kiersten, who is driving me up the wall anyway, to start hurling during our double date plus one. Now I feel like I'm trapped in this small cab while she breathes flu germs or whatever all over.

Like I said. It seemed like a good idea a couple of hours ago.

"I'm so, so sorry," Kiersten says for the millionth time since we were kicked out of our cooking class. "I swear that meat smelled rancid, and there was so much of it."

"Just fifty bucks down the drain. No big deal," I say under my breath. Jaxon punches me on the shoulder to get me to shut up. He's as pissed as I am, probably because that food smelled good. But he's got the good sense to not piss off his girlfriend any more tonight.

"It's okay, Kiersten. You didn't know you were going to be sick." Leave it to Lauren to be the voice of reason.

I like her no-nonsense attitude normally, but tonight my frustration level is topped out. "Let's just stop at a pharmacy on our way home. I'm almost out of ibuprofen anyway."

This is news to me, but I'm more than happy to take the hint. If I'm being relegated back to my own room for a couple more days, I want to make sure Lauren's stocked up on everything she needs.

Pulling into the parking lot of the first place I see, I quickly park and turn around. "Okay ladies, Lauren needs ibuprofen. Kiersten, what do I need to get you? Something for your stomach?"

Kiersten sniffs like she's about to cry. Recognizing her best friend is about to start blubbering again, Lauren reaches over and grabs her hand. "It's okay, Kiersten. No one's mad. I promise. We'll get you some Pepto and maybe some cold and flu medicine in case it gets worse overnight, okay?"

Kiersten sniffs again and I feel like this whole night has been one dramatic emotion after another. It actually kind of reminds me of living with my sisters at home.

And isn't that just a great way to think about my new girlfriend. Rubbing my hand down my face, I shake my head to get back on track.

"So Pepto and cold medicine?"

Lauren nods while Kiersten shakes her head. As if I'm having a psychic premonition, my stomach drops. It's like I know something big is coming. Something that will change everything.

"Um…" Kiersten says with another sniffle. "I uh, can you get me a pregnancy test?"

Yup. Get me a 1-800 number and call me Psychic Heath. I knew something was up.

"What?" Lauren whispers at the same time Jaxon breathes, "Jesus Christ." He's promptly rewarded with a smack on the back of the head by his own girlfriend.

"I… um… it wasn't until Annika mentioned her being on her cycle that I realized I've missed a couple of periods."

"Oh honey," one of the girls says, but I have no idea who. I'm too busy fist-bumping Jaxon for it not to be one of our girlfriends who is knocked up. Insensitive? Absolutely. But considering I've been avoiding hearing these words anywhere near me for years, it feels oddly victorious. Part of me wants to jump out of the cab and do a victory dance while singing, "My swimmers didn't do it! My swimmers didn't do it!"

I control myself, however, instead turning to face the back seat. Pulling myself together, I school my features and bring out supportive Heath. "Any particular kind? I can get whatever you need."

Kiersten shrugs and begins to cry lightly. "I don't... I don't know."

The girls immediately start hugging and discussing the merits of a plus sign versus pink lines versus blue lines. I zone them out, instead watching Jaxon as his emotions play all over his face. He is freaking. The fuck. Out.

I can practically hear the calendar of all their sexual escapades flipping in his brain as he tries to nail down dates.

Catching his gaze, I mouth *Shark Week*. He nods vigorously, understanding exactly what I'm saying, but it's not changing how he feels. This one is too close for comfort. Way too close. Less than two feet away from us close.

Finally, someone is patting my arm to make sure I'm listening. "Okay, see if you can get one that actually says the words *pregnant* or *not pregnant* on the stick," Lauren instructs. "It'll probably cost a little more, but it's better to be able to read it one way or the other so we know for sure right away."

I nod in understanding. "Annika, you need me to get you any girly supplies while I'm in there?"

She smirks, probably knowing I'm offering more for Jaxon's mental wellbeing than hers. "No, I'm good. But thank you."

"Cool. Come on dude." I whack Jaxon on the shoulder. "Let's go. You need some air."

Climbing out of the truck, we leave it running, Annika leaning over to lock them in while we go spend money we don't have on supplies we never thought we'd need.

"You okay, man?" I ask once we make it through the sliding doors into the building. It's too hot in here, but I'm not sure if it's the temperature or if my body is having a physical reaction to Kiersten's news.

"Too close man. I know she's not my girlfriend, but there better not be something in the water."

"I thought you couldn't have kids because of the chemo. Did I make that up in my head?"

Jaxon shakes his head, still shaken but starting to calm down now that we're away from the source of his stress. "I don't know if I can have kids or not but hearing someone say the words 'pregnancy test' that close to my girlfriend reminds me that I don't know. I might be able to."

"And you would be that upset if you got Annika knocked up?"

He shoots a glare at me. "I didn't think so. Until suddenly it's right in front of me. Oh hey. It's this aisle."

Jaxon makes a quick backpedal so we can find what we're looking for as fast as possible. Unfortunately, nothing about this is fast. We peruse all kinds of items I've never had to worry about before to even find the pregnancy tests. I'm suddenly grateful we seem to be the only ones in the store.

"Okay we've got a blue box, a pink box, a white box—holy shit, there are so many boxes." Jaxon wipes a hand down his face, as overwhelmed as I am. "How are there so many brands? And why the hell does anyone need a—what is this called? A multipack?"

"Hell, if I know," I grumble, grabbing it off the shelf to inspect the picture. "It's got little lines on it anyway so it's not what we need."

I put the box back and we continue staring at all the choices before us, completely bewildered as to what the girls want. It doesn't help that Jaxon practically had a meltdown a few minutes ago. His brain isn't firing on all cylinders yet, so I'm basically going it alone.

Thankfully, the lone employee must have figured out how useless we are when it comes to this kind of thing.

Walking down the aisle, he heads straight for us, a giant smile on his face.

"Hey, you're Jaxon Hart, right?" I glance at Jax who grumbles, "Oh shit," before pulling himself back together. This situation just went from bad to worse.

"Uh yeah. Nice to meet you, er…" he looks down at the guy's name tag. "Donald."

Donald looks over at me and his eyes widen. "Holy shit. And you're Heath Germaine."

I close my eyes briefly. Normally, I can go about my business with just a few whispers every now and then. It's a college town, so it's a given there will be football lovers milling about. But, of course, the one time Jaxon and I are trying to buy a pregnancy test, a random guy who is clearly a huge fan of the team catches us. I have a bad feeling this is going to end up all over social media before we get out that door.

"Yeah. You been to a game this year?" I don't care if he has or not, but if we're going to get out of this aisle without picture evidence, I need to deflect.

"Nah," Donald says with a wave of his hand. "I can't afford tickets at my pay scale. Besides, they let me watch the games while I'm here. I'm okay with getting paid to sit in front of the TV. No one ever comes in on game day anyway."

"Cool." I stand there awkwardly, hoping Jaxon will take the hint and maybe chat with the guy since I'm not sure what else to say. No such luck. Donald didn't just come over to talk shop, apparently.

"Anything I can help you guys with? Are you looking for anything in particular?" He looks down at the shelf next to us and his eyes widen as he finally puts it all together. "Oh. Well that's um… unfortunate. Any kind in particular you need, or maybe a multipack so you can make absolutely sure?" He winks at us, which goes way past being creepy.

"That's what they're for," Jaxon blurts out, completely missing the psycho wink, and like we're not about to start getting calls from some very pissed off parents and coaches when this guy spreads the word.

No turning back now, though. We were sent on a mission and frankly, with how moody she was tonight, Annika scares me more than my coach right now anyway.

"All I know is they said something about it saying the actual words *pregnant* or *not pregnant*. Something about it being easier to read."

"Ah." Donald looks over and scans the shelves until he finds what he's looking for and grabs the box. "This one. It's a popular brand this close to campus."

Surprised, I open my mouth to respond but stop myself. The more I think about it, the more I realize we probably aren't the first two football players to come in here to buy pregnancy tests. Hell, I bet he sells them weekly to some of my classmates. So I just close my mouth and take the box from him with a nod of thanks.

Task complete, we follow Donald to the register, snagging some ibuprofen on our way, so we can get the hell out of here and put this night behind us. Donald doesn't seem to notice or care that neither of us is in a chatty mood, and he seems to have some boundary issues.

Pressing a few buttons and scanning the items, he asks, "So which one of you is this for, anyway?"

"What?" Jaxon starts to look a pale shade of green again. It'll be a wonder if he doesn't start throwing up, too.

None of that overshadows the irritation I feel at Donald's question, though. "I don't think that's any of your business."

"I didn't mean anything by it," he responds nonchalantly, like his question wasn't totally inappropriate and once, again, creepy. "I'm just curious which one of you is gonna be a daddy. I'm hoping it's you, Jaxon, because that would suck if your career got derailed by this, Germaine."

It's like he's trying to go for solidarity and is failing miserably. At this point, I'm not sure if I'm angry or want to laugh.

"Listen, Donald," I say as calmly as I can, as I hand over my credit card. "I appreciate your—concern, or whatever." He smiles at me, completely missing my tone. "But there are three women in my car. Since this isn't my story to tell, your guess is just gonna have to be good enough."

Donald's eyes brighten and he whistles through his teeth like I just gave him some coveted insider information. "Three women? Everyone thinks you'd sworn off the ladies. Wonder what they'd think of this."

He hands me back my credit card and the bag, which I snatch out of his hands. It appears Jaxon isn't the only one who has a few screws loose tonight.

"Okay. Well, thanks. Let's go, Jax."

We walk out the door, finally free of Donald's questions. Although I'm not convinced he didn't sneak some pics of us. It's only a matter of time before Jaxon's phone rings.

Jaxon is still tense, but probably more from the shock of this scare than realization of the backlash we're about to face.

"Relax dude," I say as I clap his shoulder. "Not your girl. Not your problem. Let's drop them off and go unwind with a beer."

"Or three."

I laugh, feeling grateful for the camaraderie. "Works for me."

It takes a few seconds for Annika to realize we're waiting by the doors, but she finally unlocks it so we can get in. I toss the bag to the back and pray this one is up to par for them. "Please tell me this is the kind of you were asking for."

Lauren catches my desperation first. "Shopping didn't go well?"

"The one time I do an errand like this, a fan catches us." The girls burst out laughing, even Kiersten giggles through her tears, as I grumble, "Coach is gonna fucking kill me when he starts getting calls from the dean." That only makes them laugh louder.

I shake my head and look at Jaxon. Just as his phone rings. We both glance down and see the word "Dad" displayed on the screen.

"I told you," I say with more force than necessary as

the girls roar in the back.

"Shiiiiiiiit," he groans before taking a deep breath and swiping right. "Hey, Dad."

That's it. I'm done. I don't care if this is the right test or not, I need to hit that bar and now.

Backing us out of the parking space, I head us toward campus as Jaxon says things like, "It's not for Annika, Dad," and "You're really asking if I use condoms?"

Jaxon was right. Three beers sound much more beneficial. Fingers crossed Uber is out tonight because I need to kill a whole lot of brain cells at this point.

TWENTY-ONE

Lauren

Pregnant. My best friend is pregnant.

That's the only thing I've been able to think about for the last couple of weeks since all her tests came back positive because it could have been any of us and then what? Life as we know it would completely change.

Talking her through it has been eye-opening and thought-provoking. Selfishly, it's also been a needed distraction during the holiday break.

Actually, that's a lie. I was only home for a week, but it felt like a year, phone calls or no phone calls. The most rest I got was in the car while my mother drove, because I can only fit in the back seat so I could pretend sleep. Otherwise, I was a victim of my surroundings.

My mother hovered. My sister bitched. And I spent the entire time stuck on the couch, unable to get away from either of them. I have never wished for painkillers more simply so I could drug myself to sleep. Not the most appropriate course of action, but no one would blame me for acting in that kind of desperation. Not if they spent more than ten minutes with my family over the holidays.

Fortunately, scholarship athletes are required to practice weekly, even while everyone else is on vacation, so my time at home was cut short. No, I'm not a scholarship athlete per se, but I was still able to sweet talk my way back into the dorm knowing Coach wouldn't kick me out when I showed up at practice today, even though I can't do anything except back extension rolls at this point. For the record, a knee-to-toe cast makes them much harder to do. Thank goodness the doctor replastered my leg a couple of days ago. I can only imagine how much worse it would be if I was still casted up to mid-thigh.

While I enjoy being back at the gym, the real bonus of coming back yesterday is getting to see my boyfriend again.

Boyfriend. That word is still hard to wrap my brain around, but the more we're together, the more I'm confident that Heath is the real deal. That he means everything he says. He's always asking my opinion on things and wanting to study together. He touches me randomly just because. And don't even get me started on how he immediately moved into my dorm room yesterday to make sure someone was with me overnight in the event of an emergency. I have no idea what kind of emergency he's anticipating with almost no one here, but I don't care. I like having him around.

And yes, Annika's bed immediately moved right next to mine as well.

I admit, it was nice having him with me last night. It's also why I'm sitting on this bench, the lone woman in a gym usually occupied by only the football team, stifling a yawn.

Hands on his hips, breathing heavily after finishing a round of pull-ups, Heath smirks at me. "Losing steam already, Tiny?"

As soon as practice was over, Heath came to get me and brought me here to implement the workout regime he had planned a few weeks ago. Now that I've been given the all-clear for upper body workouts, as long as I put absolutely no pressure or strain on my leg despite my new and shorter cast, the plan is for us to work out together. Basically, that means we set up weights side-by-side so he can stare at me, ready to jump in should something go wrong, like I get a sudden desire to run across the room or something. I'm not positive, so I'm humoring him.

I'm also giving him my best half-hearted glare even though we both know he's teasing me. "First, you shouldn't call a short woman 'tiny.' It gives us a complex." He snorts a laugh. "Second, I'm only tired because you kept me up all night, you asshole."

His eyes flare with desire and I know what he's thinking—we're getting close to crossing that all-important physical line. If it weren't for this damn cast, there would have been no stopping it last night. I'm honestly not sure the cast is going to be a deterrent much longer.

Stalking toward me, he leans forward, resting his hands on the bench right in between my legs. It's a very small area, and I'm very, very aware of how close his hands are to the part of me that wants him most these days.

Making sure he's eye level, Heath whispers, "I didn't hear you complaining. Especially when I rubbed my hand up the side of your knee."

"Only because that knee hasn't been touched by anything except gauze for the last few weeks."

He takes a slow, deep breath. "Okay. I can keep my hands to myself tonight if that's what you want."

I narrow my eyes because he's not playing fair. We only got as far as petting over clothes and some serious ass grabbing, but he's right. I was as into it as he was. But I won't admit it. At least not now.

Instead, I shrug playfully and say, "I don't mind if you move that bed back to its spot across the room."

He responds with a growl and his giant palm quickly ends up on the back of my neck, gently pulling me closer. "That is not going to happen." His gaze drops to my lips and the clink of the weights and buzz of chatter fades away.

His lips drop to mine and there is no hesitation when I respond. Kissing Heath is one of the most amazing things I've ever experienced. Not just because he's a fantastic kisser, but because I know it means something to him. He doesn't run around making out with just anyone, so I have no doubt this is as special to him as it is to me.

It's short-lived, however, when the whistles and cat-calls cut through our haze filled bubble.

Pulling back, he rests his forehead on mine and smiles. "We've only got one more set, Tiny." I respond with a tiny growl of my own which elicits a chuckle from him. "One more then we're done."

I nod and take a breath, stretching my arms over my head as he moves behind me. I half expect his teammates to continue harassing us, but no one does. We've all got a job to do here, and they have better things to do than mess with us much more than that.

Within seconds, Heath picks me up and holds me in the air until I have a solid grip on the bar above me. Then he slowly lowers me until he's confident he can let go and I won't fall.

It's oddly sexy the way he can just toss me around like I'm a waif. I'm used to being spotted by coaches, but it doesn't feel the same when Heath does it.

"Just fifteen more, Tiny, and you're done for the day."

I ignore the nickname and concentrate on contracting my muscles, pulling my entire body up until my chin is over the bar. Slowly, I lower back down. I know these football players speed through chin-ups, but I'm not trying to build bulk. I need the strength. The control.

My lack of speed during this exercise doesn't seem to bother Heath. Quite the opposite. He's murmuring words of encouragement and praise as I slowly pull up… and release just as slowly.

"Come on, Tiny. Just one more."

Breathing heavily, I strain as I pull, gritting my teeth as I go. Just as I reach the top, I feel his big hands encircle my waist, but I don't stop. I finish the move all the way to the bottom.

"Ready?" I ask with a pant.

"Gotcha," he responds so I let go, knowing there's more than one way to interpret his response.

Gently setting me back down on the bench, he hands me my water bottle.

"One last set, Heath. You got fifteen more in you?" I ask with a smile, as I bring the bottle to my lips.

"I think I should get out of this last one."

"What? Why? You can't tell me you're tired."

"Because I forgot the extra work-out I was going to have picking you up every time it was your turn."

I shrug. "You're the one who decided on chin-ups. I'd have been happy with some dumbbell presses while sitting right here on this little bench."

He shakes his head playfully and turns back to the bar. I pretend to be resting while he finishes his last set, but really, I'm watching. Watching his shoulder muscles pop with the movement. Watching his core tighten and his abs flex in the mirror.

I bite my bottom lip, internally screaming at myself to calm the hell down. This relationship is based on friendship. It's supposed to go slow and steady to build a solid foundation.

Oh, who am I kidding? My boyfriend is hot as hell, and I'd love nothing more than to race back to my dorm and strip us both naked so he can show me exactly how much power he has behind those thigh muscles.

"Why've you got that look on your face, Tiny?"

I look up at him through my eyelashes realizing I've been caught. I was so into my ogling, I didn't realize he was done.

Licking my lips, I allow my stubborn streak to come out and refuse to give him the satisfaction of knowing I'm embarrassed about being caught in the act. "Just a long day. I think I'm ready to go home and rest for a while."

Heath smirks and rubs his nose with his thumb. "Okay. Let's finish up and get you out of here."

Stretching doesn't take that long for me. Since I can only work out my upper body anyway, there's not a lot of muscles I need to stretch out. Mostly I just watch Heath cool down. And maybe I eyeball him a little more. I can't help it. His body is practically a work of art. Long, lean muscles, almost no fat on his body, strong thighs, strong back, strong shoulders. His dark skin practically glistens from the slight sheen of sweat covering his body.

I've dated athletes before, but something about Heath's build is more rugged. Like the way he's cut in all the right places are less because of lifting weights and more the way his body naturally sits. It makes me wonder what his dad looks like—if he's just as lean and strong.

Soon enough, we're crossing the campus again. Me in the wheelchair, Heath pushing me. I sigh dramatically.

"What's wrong? In pain? Did I push you too hard?"

"No," I grumble. "It was actually a good workout. I'm just tired of being in this chair. I wish the doctor would give me a boot already so I could walk."

Heath chuckles behind me like it's no big deal that I'm still sitting around. He's not the one getting restless. "It'll be soon. The x-ray showed its healing up nicely, right?"

"Yeah," I admit half-heartedly. "Not as fast as I'd like, though."

"A spiral fracture is nothing to mess with. It needs to heal up well if you're going to keep throwing those flips and spins and whatever the hell it's called."

"It's called tumbling. Just say that," I advise, trying not to laugh. If I'm stuck being sedentary, at least Heath keeps me entertained.

"Whatever. I know you're frustrated, but if I've learned anything in all my years of football," I scoff at his over-exaggeration, "it's that you can't rush an injury."

He's right, so I don't say anything. With the way I've been feeling, it'll all sound bitchy and ungrateful anyway. I'm sure the feeling will pass, but it's like my anxiety has ratcheted up a notch and is coming out as anger. It's not about Heath, though. It's about losing my competition spot for the season, feeling helpless, and probably some worry for Kiersten.

I don't even want to think about that. She swears the dad, Chad or whatever, is being supportive and wants to raise the baby with her, but I have my doubts. Call me pessimistic, but I know very few guys our age who would step up to the plate after a couple of quick fucks. I'm hopeful, of course. Just... not convinced.

I push thoughts of my best friend out of my mind. Right now, I need to focus on the immediate future—getting out of these sweaty clothes and into the shower.

Heath and I maneuver the wheelchair into my dorm past what's-his-name reading *GQ* this time and into my room. I push myself to standing and Heath helps me to my dresser where I pop one of my anxiety pills and gather my clothes for my shower. While I'm glad we got an en-suite this year, it still sucks having to hide my shower supplies from our thieving suitemate. Speaking of things that suck, I just realized we may have a problem.

"Um… Heath?" I say quietly, not sure how this is all going to play out. "We forgot something."

"What's that?" He's already taking my stuff out of my hand, prepared to set me up in the bathroom. As he turns for the door, he stops in his tracks. Turning slowly, he looks at me and takes a deep breath. "Annika's not here to help you in the bathroom."

I nod, nerves taking over. "I mean, it's not a big deal. I can probably do it on my own." I don't know why I feel this way. He's my *boyfriend.* Hell, he felt me up last night. But for some reason, I feel shy. Like sharing my body with him is important. I want it to mean something.

Oh god, no. I can't be falling in love with him, can I?

I roll the thought around in my brain for a second. Is that a bad thing? To love Heath? I don't think so. He's a good man. Kind and loyal, hardworking and with a lot of drive, full of integrity. He's horrible about showing everything he's feeling on his face, but as far as flaws go, I wouldn't consider that more than an annoyance sometimes. If I'm going to fall in love with anyone, he deserves it the most. It just makes things more complicated. And complicated makes me nervous.

"It's okay," I say with resolve. "I need to start doing things on my own again, so it'll be good for me to try."

Heath bites his bottom lip and looks around the room like he's trying to figure out the best course of action. "Are you sure?" he finally says. "I don't want you to lose your balance and put pressure on it or fall over."

"I'm sure." Not that I have much of a choice. "I'll take it slow, and if I run into problems, I'll call you."

He pauses, hands on his hips, before finally conceding. "Okay. Let's get you set up."

He quickly deposits my clothes on the bathroom counter and shampoo on the edge of the bath while I hobble behind him on the crutches I rarely use. They're fine for my room, but anywhere outside the dorm is too far for me to get to.

I grab the plastic leg sleeve that will cover my cast so I can shower without it getting wet. It's a pain to get on and off, but a necessary evil.

Looking around the room, Heath finally seems satisfied that everything is ready for me. "Okay. I think you're good. I'm gonna be right out the door, so if you need anything, just yell."

I flash him a smile because he is the sweetest. "I will. Promise."

He nods once and out the door he goes, closing it softly behind him.

Getting my sports bra off is easy. My shorts, however, are a little more difficult. It takes some maneuvering, and thankfully, I'm flexible, but I'm finally free of them and sitting on the edge of the bathtub. Yes, it's gross, but again, necessary evil.

Grabbing the plastic sleeve, I scrunch it up and lean over to get it situated over my foot. Unfortunately, that's the easy part. Getting it much past that isn't working.

I grunt, trying to contort my body into a different angle to get the damn thing over my heel and around my ankle, but I can't find the right position.

"Shit," I grumble and take a few breaths. I never expected to feel winded from trying to get on the equivalent of one pant leg.

"Are you okay?" Heath calls from the other side of the door. "It's been a while, and I haven't heard the water running yet."

"I'm just having some issues with the plastic sleeve."

He pauses and I already know why. This might be a

two-person job. And he's the only other person here.

"Um…" I hear his throat clear, a strong tell that he's nervous. "… Do you need my help?"

I drop my head back and close my eyes. Do I need his help? Most definitely. But do I want it? Most definitely to that question as well. Is it a good idea, though? That's what I'm unsure about. Because I want Heath. And I want to cross that line with him. I do. I just don't know what happens after that, and that scares me.

Regardless, I can't just sit here naked and dirty. I'm going to have to suck it up, cross my fingers, and hope he's truly the man he claims to be.

"Yeah. I think I do."

Another pause as he processes my words. "You're already naked, aren't you?"

A giggle bursts out of me because I can almost see his shocked face as he said that. "Typically, that's what we do when we're getting ready to shower, yes."

"Okay, well, um… maybe put a towel over you so I don't see anything. That I shouldn't. Or that you don't want me to see. Or whatever."

The way he stumbles over his words has me feeling more confident. Knowing he's as nervous as I am makes me feel safe, in a weird way.

I grab the towel and drape it over me as best as I can. My hip is still exposed but it's the best I can do with the size towel I have. I knew I should have asked for oversized fluffy towels for Christmas.

"You can come in," I finally call out and brace myself for his perusal. Will he like what he sees? Will my body turn him on? Will my lack of boobs make him laugh? They're all irrational thoughts, but that's me—irrational when I'm scared.

He shuffles in the room taking one glance and quickly looking away. I know it's his way of trying to protect my privacy in a very non-private moment. Instead, he looks down at my leg. "You almost got it over your heel," he says with a small smile that relaxes me.

"I know they have to make the rubber at the top tight to

make sure water doesn't get in, but could they not have figured out an easier way to get it on?" I joke as Heath squats down in front of me. I suck in a breath because I'm very aware of how close he is to my very naked private parts. Based on the leap of the muscles inside me, my private parts are also very aware of how close he is.

The air in the room practically crackles with tension as he gently reaches for my foot and rests it on his leg. The move causes my legs to spread apart and I'm once again hit with how intimate this moment feels. I watch his face, his jaw tightening and nostrils flaring. Try as I might, I can't stop my eyes from dropping to look at his crotch, where his shorts have suddenly gotten tighter.

This situation isn't supposed to feel sexual, but our bodies don't seem to care.

"Try not to move your leg," he commands when he gets a good grip on the rubber. We work together, my eyes locked on his face as he watches what he's doing. It takes effort, but he finally slides the sleeve into place, his fingers grazing the back of my knee as he makes sure the seal is correct. The feeling makes me gasp and almost as quickly, his eyes snap up to mine.

I can see every emotion on his face, every battle he's having in this moment as his fingers continue moving gently over my skin. The lust. The desire. The respect. And I think, unless I'm totally off base, I think I see love.

I can't move my eyes from his. Can't tear away from his gaze as I come to my conclusion.

I want him. I want him now. I want him here. I want him forever.

"Heath," I say quietly, barely above a whisper.

His hand drops and he pushes to a stand, trying and failing to discreetly adjust himself in his shorts. He looks away and clears his throat. "I'll uh... I'll be outside the door."

Before he can move, I grab his hand. Standing up, I pay no attention to the towel that just dropped to the floor. Heath, on the other hand, looks directly at the towel then up at me very obviously avoiding looking at my body. His attempt at respect is appreciated but not needed. This is Heath. I trust him.

Balancing on one leg, I grab the hem of his shirt and lift it up. With the height difference, he has to help me pull it over his head. I can still see the question in his eyes. The concern that he's misinterpreting my actions.

Hooking my fingers in his shorts, I slowly push them down, never taking my eyes off his. "Stay," I breathe. "I need help, but more importantly, I need you."

His big hand comes up to cup my jaw. "I don't want to hurt you." We both know there's a double meaning to his declaration and his concern is what cements my decision.

"Then don't."

My words seem to spur him on because suddenly, his shoes and socks are off, the water in the shower is on and he lifts me up, chest to chest, as he steps over the lip of the tub and into the spray. The water is warm enough but it's the heat of his skin that has my body practically burning up. Still, Heath is determined to take things slow.

With eyes locked on mine, he takes his time soaping me up, his strong hands grazing over my skin as he works. When his fingers make their way to my breasts, he rubs in gentle circles, once, twice, and allows his thumbs to rub over my nipples before pinching them between his thumb and forefinger. The sensation makes me gasp and his breath hitches as he watches my face.

He adds more body wash to his hands, rubs them together to create more suds and down my body they go, over my flat stomach, the swell of my hips, moving over so they can circle my thigh and continue sliding down until he's on his knees in front of me. Seemingly unable to resist, he kisses my pubic area, just above where the small landing strip of hair leads down to where I want him the most. It's pure, unadulterated torture when he stands and makes quick work of washing the rest of me.

He reaches to grab the body wash again, but I touch his arm to stop him. "My turn."

Biting my lip, I make sure to have a good amount of lather. It's my turn to explore the dips and curves of his physique, and I don't want to waste time having to lather up again.

Placing my hands on his neck, I begin the trek downward with the back of his shoulders, around to his biceps, over to his pecs. His abs flex at my touch, and the shadows behind the heavy curtain combined with his dark skin make even the few scars marring his body seem to glow. His hips cut down to the "V" that guides me like a map.

And then my fingers are wrapped around him and he gasps as I stroke slowly. He's proportional for his body size, and he's built like a football player, so I have to remind myself that means he's probably bigger than I've had before. The thought could scare me but somehow, I know this means more to him than a quick fuck. He'll be gentle until I tell him not to hold back. Because this is the beginning of making love.

He allows me to peruse for a few more minutes before he grasps my wrist tightly. "Enough," he demands. Quickly, he shuts the water off behind me and grabs a towel, wiping us both down and tossing it aside. When he's satisfied that I'm dry enough to not get any residual wetness in my cast, he positions himself to remove the plastic sleeve off my leg.

The care he takes to make sure he does it right, combined with the cool air, make my nipples even harder. I don't understand how he's made clunky, awkward moves with my cast sexy, but he does. I have no doubt it goes back to the fact that he loves me. He hasn't said it. He may not even know it. But he certainly treats me like it.

When I'm finally free, he hoists me up, his hands underneath my butt and kisses me. We are a mash of tongues and lips, soft moans and pulls of hair. He walks us back into my room and gently lays me down on the bed.

"Are you sure?"

I nod vigorously because I'm more sure about him than anything in my life.

That's all he needs before the foreplay begins again. We spend what seems like hours tasting and teasing, exploring the most intimate parts of each other, always aware of my injury and making sure the only thing we feel is pleasure.

When he finally pushes inside me, I gasp. No sexual experience has ever been like this. I've never felt this kind of intimate love before, and I only want it like this from now on.

As we push and pull and thrust into our joined ecstasy, a single tear slides down my face from the pure, unfiltered joy I feel as my orgasm rocks through me. Nothing has ever felt so right, and I'm so grateful to be here in this moment.

When we're able to catch our breath, he kisses me gently, hovering over my body. Then he rolls next to me and pulls me to him.

"You okay?" he whispers in my ear, brushing my hair off my neck so he can kiss me gently.

"Yeah," I say, snuggling into him. "I'm more than okay."

As I lose consciousness to sleep, I force my negative self-talk out of my head. There's no way this was just a one-night stand. And if I have my way, I won't have any of those ever again.

TWENTY-TWO
Heath

"Ooof!" I grunt as I slide along the turf, football secure in my arms. I wasn't expecting to be hit from that angle.

"You're not paying attention to your left side," Jaxon bitches as he puts his hand out to help me up. Not sure how he got to his feet before me, but it's nice to see some of his speed back.

Reaching up, I pop to my feet. "Well, it's been a while since I've had a reason to look for you."

I toss Jax the ball and he throws it back toward the line of scrimmage, not that they need it. Coach is on the field, talking with the QB about some plays he wants to try. It's been happening all day. Now that the regular season is over and we didn't get a spot in a bowl game, practice is a little lax. We're still pushing ourselves, but we're trying some new stuff. There's always another season to prep for.

I'm not complaining about getting a bit of a break. I just can't afford to get lazy. I've still got decisions to make.

"Seems like those iron pills are finally working for you."

Jax pulls his helmet off and runs his fingers through his sweaty mop. "Really? We're gonna talk about my health instead of your skills?"

And my best friend is finally back. Thank god. "No. We're gonna talk about how nice it is that you're not being a pussy anymore. And before we change topics, I'm gonna say this one time." We stop walking and I get right in his personal space and point at him. "You ever pull that shit again and not take care of yourself, and we're gonna have problems. I let it go once. I won't do that again. I care about you too much."

He puts his hands on his hips and nods once. "I hear ya. It won't happen again."

"Good." I punch him on the shoulder and go back to the task at hand. "Now tell me what I did wrong on that play."

We spend the next few minutes discussing some small tweaks Jaxon thinks I should make based on my archrival's most recent game. In true Jaxon form, he's finally back to watching stats and crunching numbers. Add onto that, his anatomy class has him observing the human body in a different way. It's oddly helpful. It's also good to see him feeling better. Even Annika seems more relaxed on the side of the field as she watches.

We head back to the line, expecting to go again but instead, Coach calls it for the day. I'm a little peeved that I don't have a chance to redo the play, but it happens. Besides, I'm not gonna complain about getting to the gym to pick up my girlfriend a little sooner than normal. If I'm lucky, she'll be showing off her flexibility when I get there.

Visual images of exactly how flexible she is come racing back into my mind. Oh yeah. Dating a gymnast is a very, very good idea.

"Have you decided what to do yet?" Jaxon asks, as we slowly make our way back to the locker room. I'm grateful for the distraction so I don't embarrass myself with a public erection. I'm not, however, excited about this change in topic.

I haven't told anyone other than Jaxon about being invited to the combine yet. Coach obviously knows since he's the one who handed me the invitation the other day.

but I'm still on the fence about it so I haven't made it public information. I didn't want input and pressure from people whose opinions don't matter while I make the biggest decision of my life so far.

"I don't know, man. I have a couple of weeks to decide before the registration deadline," I say as I strip my jersey off and fling it onto my shoulder. "I thought for sure I'd jump at the chance, but I'm having second thoughts."

"How is that even possible? It's all you've talked about for the last three and a half years."

"I know. But if I get drafted now, I won't be done with my degree."

"That's because you double majored in business and finance, you dumb ass," he jokes. "If you'd done one degree, you'd be done."

I shoot him a glare. "Says the guy who changed his major to pre-med this year." He shrugs but doesn't respond because he knows I'm right. "I don't know, man. I don't know the right thing to do. I could take another year to improve my performance, maybe add a few pounds, get my degree."

"Hang out with a certain gymnast a little longer…"

I shove him which makes him laugh. "She doesn't have anything to do with this decision."

"Oh, she doesn't? Because the way I remember it, a few months ago there was no question that you'd go if you were invited. Now suddenly, you're spending every night in her bed, taking care of her while she's injured, and considering spending another year in college where she'll be."

He's right. As much as I don't like it, Lauren is part of my thought process. I just found her. I just fell for her. And now I'm considering moving away from her? It's unlikely I'll be drafted to the team that's moving to San Antonio since they haven't even completed construction of the new stadium yet, which means no matter where I go, it'll be far away.

I pull open the outside door that leads into the locker room as I continue to think. Throwing my sweaty pads down, I start stripping. The cooler temps outside feel good to work out in, but don't make much of a difference in the sweat department. What I need is a hot, hard shower spray to pound against my shoulders and give me some time to think.

There doesn't seem to be any privacy for me, though. Jaxon plops down on the bench next to me and begins unlacing his shoes. "Listen, man, I'm not judging you for having feelings for her. I like Lauren. Always have. It's just a complete one-eighty for you. You've spent a lot of time avoiding women to keep your focus on playing ball and now, you're having conflicting feelings about the combine."

"That has nothing to with her. I've always been conflicted about whether or not I'd go at year four or five."

"I know that. But take her out of the mix for one second. If she was still that annoying roommate of my girlfriend that you couldn't stand, what would you do?"

I look at the floor and try to imagine if I were in that situation. Would I stay for a degree and make sure I had a back-up plan for retirement? Or would I go so I have the ability to support my family now?

"It's not that simple," I finally admit. "I've been so focused on getting into the pros, I forgot about life."

"Nope. Don't know. Explain."

I blow out a breath as I come up with the words. "I think maybe when Lauren broke her leg, I realized that could've been me." As the words come out of my mouth, I suddenly understand exactly where my hang-up is. "In my mind, there is nothing beyond playing ball. Nothing. But what if I'm injured before then? Hell, what if I'm in a car accident? Or get bitten by a dog."

"What? Who do you know that has a dog?"

I roll my eyes. He's not following anymore. "My point is, there's no guarantee I'll even be strong enough or healthy enough to play. If I leave now and something happens, I won't even have a degree to fall back on. I'll have to re-enroll in school to get the degree so I can get a decent job. I don't want that."

"So, you think concentrating on your back up plan is

the way to go?"

"Yeah. Maybe? Hell, I don't know." I rub my hands down my face in frustration. "The only thing I know for sure is I need a shower, stat. And then I need to get my woman from the gym and take her back to the room."

Jaxon narrows his eyes and stares at me. He's assessing me. It kind of weirds me out. And then he blurts out exactly what's on his mind. "You finally hit that, didn't you?"

I shove him off the bench and onto the floor. "Shut up, man. I'm not answering that question."

Stripping off the rest of my clothes, I wrap a towel around my waist and head to the showers. He just laughs behind me.

I'm glad someone is amused. Me? I'm still just… confused. I've been dreaming of the combine for as long as I can remember, but for some reason, it doesn't feel right. I've gone over it in my head a million times, and I can't figure out why. The only thing that's different in my life, the only thing that's changed, is Lauren.

As the water rains down on me, I think about what an unexpected blessing she is. She's understanding of my schedule and supportive of my career. She's an athlete herself so our priorities align. And she's just… fantastic.

Smart and funny and feisty. Lauren keeps me on my toes and makes me laugh. But I also have the need to protect her. And I'd be lying to myself if I said I didn't hate the idea of leaving her so soon into this relationship.

Still, is that a reason to put my dreams on hold? Is that even why I'm considering waiting another year? Or is she a convenient excuse for what I should be doing anyway?

Sighing, I shut the water off and grab my towel. The one thing I know for sure is I can't make this decision without getting some input from an expert. I don't know anyone who has trained more players for the NFL than Coach.

Having made one decision, although it almost seems like a delay tactic in some ways, I head back into the locker room where only stragglers remain. My guess is most everyone went straight to the gym to lift. I think I'm better off waiting for that, especially since I want to have this conversation sooner rather than later, and I don't want Lauren to have to wait for me.

I get dressed quickly and grab my phone to shove it in my pocket, but the flashing blue light stops me. It's not unusual for me to have a text or two, but this time feels different. I can't put my finger on why, but it's like a sinking feeling in my gut. Psychic Heath is back.

Unlocking the screen, I have five missed calls—three from my mother, two from my oldest sister—and a string of texts telling me to call home asap. I don't bother listening to the messages, I just dial my mom.

"Shit," I grumble as it goes straight to voicemail. Hanging up, I call Jackie instead.

It barely rings once before she answers. "Heath?"

"What's wrong?" I bark out, terror racing through my body.

"You gotta... come... home...." She says through her tears. "It's... it's Dad."

That's all she says before I race out the door, singularly focused on getting to my truck and getting on the road.

"What happened?"

"He had a heart attack."

My breath whooshes out of me and it's all I can do to keep myself from collapsing as she speaks.

"It was bad, Heath. We called an ambulance, but he stopped breathing and he turned this weird color."

This isn't happening. My dad isn't dying. There's no way this can be happening...

"By the time the ambulance came, Mom was doing CPR and the girls were screaming. I'm in the hospital waiting room, but they won't let me go back to see him."

I begin running across the campus. My truck is only half a mile away, but it feels like my legs can't get there fast enough. I don't know how I'm going to survive driving for hours, but I don't have a choice. I need to get home. I have to get home.

"Where's Mom now? Is she okay?"

"Yeah." My sister sniffs and her voice calms down a bit. "They're a little worried about her blood pressure, so they

took her back to make sure it's coming down. Heath…"
A sob breaks out of her and it only fuels my desire to get
there faster. "I'm so scared."

"I know. I'm on my way now, Jackie. Just hold on."

I have to get there as fast as possible. I won't let my
family down. Not now.

TWENTY-THREE

Lauren

"Careful, Lauren. Stay tight," Coach's voice is more like background noise in my ear as my body swings around the bar, his instructions just reminders of what my muscles already know to do. "Good. Hold the handstand. Hold. Hold. Come down slowly."

Instead of completing another giant and swinging all the way around again, I slowly lower my hips so I'm resting on the bar.

"Ohmygod, that felt good," I say, a huge grin on my face making my coach laugh.

Allowing my body to fall backward until I'm hanging, I'm careful to scoot my way over to the side where Coach helps me get down safely. I'm still not back to normal practice, but when the doctor cleared me for some bar work, I almost hugged him. Bars isn't my favorite, but I'll take anything at this point.

The only stipulation is I can only use the single bar over the foam pit, just in case I fall. I won't be allowed to dismount on purpose for a while, but in the meantime, if something goes wrong, at least there's less of a chance of reinjury if I land in a pit of foam squares. Not that I'm physically able to fall. Coach insists I use the straps to keep me securely in place. I almost rolled my eyes at him, but the idea of having something to do besides back extension rolls and conditioning overshadowed his helicopter coaching.

Plus, I get it. I was *this close* to earning a top spot. He doesn't want me reinjured any more than I do. I may have missed my goal, but he could be missing fractions of a point for his team. As much as we like to pretend this sport is all about the individual, reality is, funding for his program relies on a good team outcome as well. Not having the best competing makes an impact on him, too.

Unwinding my hands from the straps, I drop when I feel his hands on my waist helping guide me to the floor.

"How did it feel?" he asks. "Too much with the weight of the cast?"

"Not at all." I balance on one leg as he hands me a crutch to lean on. "It definitely feels different. I won't be doing any release moves with this baby on, that's for sure. But it feels so good to be doing some actual gymnastics again instead of just weights."

He smiles in understanding. As a former gymnast himself, I don't know how he isn't just itching to get on the apparatus sometimes, even at his age. "I can tell you've been keeping up with your work-outs. Your shoulders look strong."

"That would be all my boyfriend's doing," I say with a laugh. "He's been researching various upper body and core exercises. I'm just following the program, so I don't get lax while I wait for this leg to heal."

Coach pats me on my shoulder and gestures with his finger for the next person to climb up. "Just don't overdo it. The last thing you need is a shoulder injury as well."

"Noted." I pick up my second crutch and slowly make my way to the opposite side of the room. It's slow going without an even surface to navigate. Mats and pads are everywhere. Usually, I wouldn't even notice. But for whatever reason, crutches make you feel everything.

I finally reach my goal, as in the wall, and drop the

crutches to balance on one leg. Flipping myself over, I push into a handstand against the wall and begin doing pushups while upside down. Sounds crazy, but it's like a reverse pull up. Great for the shoulders, back and arms—no impact on the legs. And one of the few exercises I'm allowed to do.

I may hate them, but at this rate, bars may become my best event simply from all the new muscles I've been building.

I crank out twenty push-ups and carefully step down, very aware that the blood is now rushing out of my brain. Hands on my hips, I take a slow, deep breath and relax.

"How does it feel to be back on bars?" Ellery skips up to me a smile on her face. "You looked great up there."

I smile at the only friend I have on this team. It doesn't bother me that no one talks to me again. It's way better than being harassed on the regular. Besides, none of them matter in the long run anyway, and clearly my injury took away whatever threat I was. Whatever sneers I used to get are non-existent now. Essentially, they just ignore my existence. So, there you have it. I have one friend, possibly some enemies, and a whole lot of who-gives-a-shit. Works for me.

"It was fun. There's only so many giants you can do, but hopefully Coach will let me out of those straps now that he sees I haven't been slacking on my weight training."

We both take a breath and simultaneously step into handstands to begin more pushups. I do more than she does, probably due to my new muscles, care of the football team, but when I step down, she still has a smile on her face.

"What has you so happy today?" I ask as I lean my hand against the wall for support.

She bites her lip and then blurts out, "Can I ask your opinion on something?"

That's odd, but I guess you can't tell who is on your side on this team anyway. Maybe it's not as weird as I think. "Sure. Do you want me to be honest or validate how you already feel regardless?"

I have to give Ellery credit—she pauses to think on my question. I appreciate that about her. Not a lot of people want the truth no matter what, but she seems to.

"Yes. Yes, I want honesty. Even if it's painful."

I'm not sure if she's trying to convince me or herself. That has me concerned. "I don't want to tell you something that will hurt your feelings."

"Oh no." She grabs my arm like she's trying to comfort me from some big disappointment. "It's not even about me. It's about someone else."

I wish I was a better person, but now she has me intrigued. She wants my opinion on a person? A person in this gym? I have zero problems with honesty about that.

Holding in a laugh, knowing I'm the only one feeling amused by this, I plaster on my best supportive friend look. "Sure. Who do you want the skinny on?"

"Kevin," she gushes, a starry-eyed look on her face as she turns to watch him work out.

I'm a little confused as to why my opinion matters, but for some reason, it does. Judging by the swoony expression she's sporting as she watches Kevin on the rings, I'm guessing she wants me to say he's a good guy.

Truthfully, he's not a *bad* guy, especially compared to just about everyone else in this room. He did hand me my clothes when Con had no problem letting me lay in his bed, vulnerable and humiliated.

But Kevin didn't stand up for me either. Never told them they were being douchebags. Never stopped them from treating me like trash.

Still, that doesn't make him the ringleader or even part of the treatment. It just means he's kind of a pussy and not strong enough to stand up for something that isn't right.

I guess they all can't be Heath Germaine. And doesn't that make me a lucky girl?

"Yeah," I finally say carefully. While Kevin isn't

my choice personally, Ellery's not me. They may end up being perfect together. Who knows—maybe she'll be the one he feels strong enough to fight for. "He's a decent guy. I don't know much about him truthfully."

"He's so great," she gushes, eyes still on the man of her dreams as he holds a front support, body inverted, his arms out straight. He looks a little wobbly if I'm honest. Could probably benefit from Heath's exercise regime. *Wobbly or not, at least he gets to dismount*, I think to myself irritated but plaster a smile on my face when Ellery finally tears her gaze away to engage in our conversation. "He called me the other day after I fell on beam and made sure I was icing the bruise. And then he brought me some Icy Hot after I was complaining about a knot in my shoulder."

That may possibly be the worst attempt at wooing I've ever heard in my life, but it seems to be working on her. I pick my words carefully to make sure I'm being truthful without ruining her current fantasy.

"Of all the guys in this gym, if I had to choose one of them for you to date, it would be Kevin."

She beams at me, although I know her smile is more about the idea that she and Kevin are a match made in heaven than my approval. I just gave her the confirmation she so desperately needed. And I'm sure there is an element of relief that I don't have some random tidbit of juicy gossip that unravels her impression of him. She knows if I thought Kevin was horrible or abusive, I would tell her. I learned my lesson about not paying close enough attention to my girls and the men they are involved with, and Ellery, in her own odd way, has become one of them.

Nudging her on the shoulder, I say, "Come on. Let's do one more set so we can stretch and go home."

She bites her lip and sighs one last time before joining me in more pushups.

Cool down doesn't take very long. There's not much for me to do except stretch. Even then, the cast gets in the way of most of my usual exercises, so before I know it, I'm back in my chair, fighting with the door so I can leave.

"Got it," a deep male voice says.

I look up to find Kevin pushing the handle, so the door doesn't fall on me. Ellery is right behind him, nodding with excitement at how helpful he is. I can almost hear her thinking, *"Isn't he so great? He noticed you were struggling and helped you."*

If only she knew that he doesn't get much more helpful than this.

No matter. He's her problem, not mine, and as long as he doesn't hurt her, I don't have an issue with him.

I thank him as they wave and walk away together. They've only gone a few steps when my phone starts vibrating against me. Speaking of fabulous boyfriends...

"Hey babe," I say with a smile on my face, excited to hear from him. How girly am I that just getting a phone call makes my day?

"Lauren."

My good mood immediately changes. His voice sounds off and the hair on the back of my neck stands up. Something is wrong. "Are you okay? Did something happen?"

"My dad had a heart attack."

I suck in a breath. I don't know much about his family, but I know they're close. This is a huge blow. "Ohmygod. Tell me he's okay."

"I don't know. He's alive. That's all I know. I have to go. I have to go to Lubbock today. Now."

"Yes. Yes of course you do."

"I can't come get you."

"Heath, don't worry about me. Just be careful, okay? Is Jaxon going with you? Can you even drive?"

"I'll be fine. They know I'm coming, and my mother already threatened to whoop my ass if I get in a wreck on the way there."

I laugh lightly. "Well, of course. She doesn't need any more to worry about, so don't give her a reason to take her mind off your dad."

"That's exactly what she said."

He takes a deep breath and I just let him be silent. I'm sure his thoughts are racing, and he feels helpless. The only thing I can do is be here and allow him to feel what he feels. Finally, he clears his throat, probably of the tears he's allowing me to be part of, even if it's only over the phone.

"I should probably pay attention to the road, so I'm gonna go."

"Okay," I reply quietly, my heart breaking for him. "Keep me updated, and let me know when you get there, okay?"

"Yeah. Okay. I will."

"And Heath…"

"Yeah?"

"He's going to be fine, okay? If he's anything like you, he's strong and stubborn. He won't go anywhere until he says it's time."

An emotional chuckle is his response. "Yeah."

"Drive safe. I'll talk to you soon."

"Okay. Bye."

The phone disconnects and I sit there staring at it, so many emotions running through me. I'm sad for him. I'm afraid for his dad. I'm worried about his drive. And I'm pissed off about my injury.

I was never excited to get hurt, but now more than ever, I'm cursing my own inability to do things. I wish more than anything I could go with Heath, help him share driving duties, make sure he gets there okay and comfort him along the way. Instead, I'm stuck like this—needing to stay out of the way as he deals with this blow.

Sighing to myself in frustration, I drop my phone in the fancy fabric cup holder attached to the side of my chair. I need both hands free if I'm going to wheel myself across campus.

Too bad I did all those inverted pushups. My shoulders are going to get a double work out today.

TWENTY-FOUR

Heath

The normally seven-and-a-half-hour drive, not including stops, took me six and a half with two pit stops. Once for gas and once because I didn't want to run into the hospital covered in my own piss if my bladder were to explode. It still took too damn long to get here.

I race to the information desk, trying very hard not to look wild and crazy. It may be how I feel, but hospitals don't care for the dramatics.

"My dad," I say carefully. "He's having heart surgery right now. Where is the waiting room?"

She gives me a sympathetic smile and stands from her rolling chair. "Oh, I'm so sorry to hear that. Go down this hall to the elevators," she points in the general direction, "And head up to the fourth floor. Follow the signs to the surgical wing."

I nod my understanding. "Thank you."

"Of course. I'll be praying for him," she calls out, as I pick up the pace quickly reaching the elevator doors and pressing the call button several times.

Lubbock may be conservative to a fault, but for the most part, the people here are genuinely kind and will pray for anyone at the drop of a hat. Most times I don't notice it. Today, I'm appreciative. My dad can use all the prayers he can get.

Getting impatient, I press the call button again. It took me almost seven hours to get to the hospital. It figures it'll take seven more to get to the fourth floor.

As if it can feel my impatience, the elevator doors finally open, and I step inside the empty carriage, anxious to reach my destination.

Fortunately, it takes very little time to get to the right floor and the signs to the surgical wing are pretty easy to follow. Finally, I see my sister sitting in a chair alone scrolling through her phone.

"Jackie!" Her head whips over and she stands when she sees me, pulling me into a tight hug as I reach her. "How is he? Any news?"

"Nothing yet. He went back about twenty minutes ago, so you just missed him." She pulls back and puts her hand on my chest. "The doctors say he's going to be fine. Prognosis looks good."

"But the surgery. What are they doing? Replacing a valve or… or…"

"It's a routine thing," she says gently, which does nothing to calm my nerves. "It's called a thrombolysis or something. It's like an injection of an anti-clotting agent to get his artery clear. But the doctor said dad's going to be fine."

I take a minute to let her words absorb in my brain. "He's not going to die?"

"You know Dad," she says with a watery smile. "He will not go until he's good and ready."

I sink down into the waiting chair, my body relaxing for the first time since I got the call. "Oh, thank God." Rubbing my hand down my face, I finally allow myself to say what I refused to even think the entire time I was driving. "I was so afraid I was going to be too late."

Jackie sits in the chair next to me and grabs my hand. "You know Dad is too stubborn for that. Doesn't matter if he got hit by a bus. He would refuse to die until he got the last word in about being respectful to Mom and not to ever, under any circumstance, root for the Cowboys."

I chuckle because it's true. The man doesn't hate much, but he harbors a scathing resentment for Jerry Jones that we've never been able to figure out. We finally gave up trying.

"Speaking of Mom, where is she?"

"I finally convinced her to go down to the cafeteria to get some coffee."

I widen my eyes, looking appalled. "You didn't go get it for her? What kind of daughter are you?"

"The kind who knows Mom sits too much as it is and is gonna get a blood clot in her leg if she stayed next to his bed for much longer. She'll be back soon. She just needed to let her muscles stretch out. Maybe people-watch for a while. It's been an emotional day for her."

"And the girls?"

My sister laughs and shakes her head. "Supposedly doing homework after a long day at school. At least that's what Maggie was instructed to do when I left this morning. But if I had to guess, I'd say the two of them are on the couch right now, piled up next to each other catching up on *Teen Mom*."

"Hold up. Mom lets them watch that trash now?"

"Nope. Bunch of opportunists." She shakes her head in disappointment.

I nudge her shoulder with mine. "You're salty because they're watching without you, huh?"

Her lips quirk to the side just a bit. "Maybe."

I laugh and put my arm around her, kissing her on the top of her head. For barely eighteen, Jackie is mature for her years. I blame that on the fact that she's in charge of our two younger sisters while our parents work. It kills me that she's had to grow up so fast and reminds me of why I can't get off track.

A few minutes go by in silence as I quietly get lost in my thoughts. The last conversation I had with my dad was discussing my invitation to the combine. He was as excited as I was when the invite came, and I expected him to encourage me to go without a second thought. Instead, he played devil's advocate and kept asking questions about when I'd go back to get my degree, weighing the risk of injury versus the probability of a better deal, tossed out retirement plans. The conversation was unexpected. And it made me think.

"I hear you've got a girlfriend."

Pulled back to the present, I feel like I've been kicked in the gut again as I remember why I'm here. And then guilt hits me. I haven't called Lauren since I hit the road. I haven't responded to any of her texts yet either. I should at least tell her I made it safely. But for some reason I can't explain, I don't. It's not that I don't want to, it's that right now I feel like I need to be here for my family, not flirting with Lauren.

"Sort of." The words pop out of my mouth before I even think about why I'm not telling the whole truth.

Jackie knows me better than that, though. "Sort of? Does she know that she's *sort of* your girlfriend?"

"No, you're right," I backpedal. "She's definitely my girlfriend. Made a public declaration in front of our friends and everything."

"So why didn't you just say that in the first place?"

I rub my hand down my face, partially from exhaustion, partially from irritation. I forgot what a ball-buster my sister can be. "I don't know. I'm just not thinking straight right now. My head's kind of spinning."

"Mine, too," she admits. "So, I need you to talk to me about stuff that doesn't involve me getting worried about Dad."

I nod in understanding. "You're right. Sorry, uh… what do you want to know about Lauren?"

"Oooh…. Lauren," she singsongs. "Is it serious?"

Damn. She just goes straight for the jugular, doesn't she? "I mean, I don't how serious it is. We're dating and we like hanging out."

"And sleeping with her. You like sleeping with her."

There's that guilt again. This time it's from knowing I'm sleeping with Lauren but my automatic answer to the question of if we're dating is 'sort of'. Shit. I'm a dick. "Let's not even go there."

"Whatever." Jackie rolls her eyes but thankfully drops that particular subject. "How did you meet anyway?"

Stretching my legs out, I get comfortable. I know how this grill session is going to go. "She's Jaxon's girlfriend's roommate."

Jackie has to pause and think that one through. "Jaxon's... girlfriend's... Okay got it. Is she cute?"

I smile thinking about Lauren's feisty little attitude. "Yeah."

"Show me a picture."

"Just look her up on the school website."

"The school has all the students on the website?"

I laugh softly. "No, dork. She's a gymnast. Everything you want to know about her academic and athletic careers will be listed in her bio."

My sister's eyes widen as she pulls out her phone and starts typing. "Oh, she's a gymnast? How cool! I wonder if she knows Simone Biles."

I snort a laugh. "Yeah. Just like I know JJ Watt. Because all athletes know each other."

"You don't know." Jackie tosses her sass my way. "A lot of elite gymnasts opt for college instead of the Olympics. They could have trained together at some point."

"I'm impressed you know that."

"Whatever. I know things." She goes back to scrolling through her phone until she finds what she's looking for. "Oooh, she's cute." Jackie shoves her phone in my face to show me the headshot.

I push her away since I can't see anything that's two inches away from my face anyway. "Don't ever let her hear you call her 'cute'. She'll kick your ass."

Pulling her phone back, Jackie examines the picture more closely. "Yeah, I can see that. She looks like she could unleash some anger if she needed to."

The thought of my five-foot-two girlfriend whopping my five-foot-eight sister brings a smile to my face. "She'd definitely try."

Clicking her phone off and dropping it back in her purse, Jackie continues, interrogation apparently not over.

"No seriously. How did you go from being the roommate's best friend's I don't even remember what you said, to dating? Was it romantic? Did you woo her?"

I shift uncomfortably in my seat, not sure how much I should say. It was an unconventional beginning, to say the least.

"It started out as a fake relationship."

From the change in expression, I can tell that got her attention. "What do you mean?"

I stop to choose my words carefully. Yes, Jackie is eighteen, but she's still in high school and she's still my baby sister. "She was just a friend and she was being harassed by these guys on the team. But when they thought we were dating, they backed off. We just kept up the charade."

"What the hell? Why would you do that? I mean, it's noble and all, but it seems kind of out of character for you."

A serious expression on my face, as the memories of Jackie's turmoil assault me. Regardless of what I feel for Lauren now, there's no denying it started because her situation triggered a part of me that needed to be unleashed. Jackie can understand that, so I turn and look her dead in the eye. "I couldn't protect you. I wasn't here to protect you from those jackasses. But I can protect her."

Jackie sits back in her chair, fire in her eyes. "I didn't need you to protect me."

"Of course, you did. You were devastated and there was nothing I could do. I was off at college playing football and living my best life and you were stuck here…" I wave my hand in no general direction. "… putting up with it day in and day out without support from me."

She drops her head and sighs heavily. Not the reaction I was expecting. I thought she'd be more understanding of where I'm coming from. Maybe even appreciative of my desire to protect her. Not this irritation. "Okay, first of all, I'm not the first woman who is going to get played, and I won't be the last. It happens all the time. To almost everyone."

I look at her like she's nuts. "No, it doesn't."

"Big brother, I love you. And I know you're super

smart. But if you seriously think mine was an isolated incident, you aren't paying attention to what goes on around you."

Her words hit me like a slap to my face. Is this what women go through regularly? Are they constantly having to question whether a man is being honest with them, or if he just wants to get in her pants? Suddenly Lauren's trust issues make more sense.

"Second, of course I was devastated. Here was this guy that I thought liked me, and instead of treating my virginity like it was something special, he spread it around the whole school."

I feel myself getting angry again. I'm sure she can see the tick in my jaw.

"But I got my revenge," she adds. "And no one bothers me anymore."

My head whips over to look at her. "Revenge?"

She nods, a malicious look on her face. "At first, I was just shocked. I wanted to hide and never show my face to anyone around here again."

"And I wasn't here to help you."

"No. But I started thinking about what Grandma would do."

"Grandma?" I furrow my brow because that's not at all where I thought this was going. "The same grandma who preached about waiting until marriage until her dying breath?"

Jackie cocks her head and drops a huge bomb on me. "Heath, a woman isn't that opinionated about sex unless she's been jaded and has a reason to be. Not even Grandma."

"What?!?"

"Relax. If there's a story there, I don't know it. But I started thinking about how she would handle things, and I realized something important. We Germaine's stick together. We take care of each other. But when push comes to shove, we also know how to take care of ourselves. And that's what I did."

"I'm not sure if I want to know."

"Oh, you do," she says with a laugh. "You see, people kept coming up and asking me about it. Asking about certain intimate details that should never be shared because that's just disrespectful."

My hands start to clench as I fight the urge to punch something.

"Relax, brother. I'm not to the good part yet."

"There better be a good part," I grumble.

"There is. So anyway, at first, I was sad and humiliated. But then this one girl, Tasha, came up and said she heard I made squeaky noises during sex and asked if it was true."

"Ugh!" I throw my hands over my ears. "I don't need to know this!"

"It's important," she argues, pulling my hands away. "Listen! When she said that, it was like Grandma turned on this switch from heaven because suddenly, I was mad. I was so mad. People were walking around clapping him on the back for a job well done, and I was being made fun of. What kind of bull shit was that? So, I turned the tables." Her malicious look turns downright evil. "I turned to Tasha and I said, 'Do you know why I squeaked? I was in such shock to see that his penis was the size of a Vienna sausage.'"

Stunned, my mouth gapes open until I can find the right words. "Ohmygod, you did not."

"I most certainly did. And then I held up my hand and said, 'Seriously. My thumb is bigger. But maybe I could have worked with that except he kept trying to figure out how to get it in my clit. He couldn't even find the right spot.'"

I can't help it. I ignore the part about her lady bits and bark a laugh. "What did they say?"

"A couple of the girls started laughing, so I kept going and told them that he shot his load in about four seconds flat, all over himself. I just kept going on and on about how his face contorted until he looked like Ace Ventura and he sounded like a wounded dog when he came. I don't even know where all my inspiration came from, but by the time I was done, people were laughing hysterically at what a horrible lover he is."

"I can't believe I'm saying this because I don't want to know this much about your sex life, but that was pretty damn clever."

Jackie sits back, looking pleased with herself. Hell, I'm pleased with her, too. "It sure as hell was. He talked to me one more time, demanding I take everything back because he's the laughingstock of the school, but I refused. Told him my mama taught me better than to lie, and then in front of everyone in the hall, swore on Grandma's grave it was all the honest to God's truth."

"You lied on Grandma's grave?"

Jackie flicks her hand at me dismissively. "I figured she wouldn't mind this time. In fact, I'm pretty sure she would have encouraged it." Turning serious, she adds, "See? You can stop trying to protect us girls, Heath. We're strong. We're smart. And we know how to hold our own. I bet Lauren does, too. So, make sure you're dating Lauren because you like her. Not because you're trying to save me by saving her."

Jackie's words cut through me, mostly because I don't know why I like Lauren so much. Is it because we've truly discovered a love connection? Or is this some weird unresolved God-complex I have? I need to think about this some more, but my thoughts fly out of my head when my mother walks through the door.

"Heath," she says gently, arms out for me to give her a hug. Her eyes look swollen like she's been crying, but she's smiling.

I don't hesitate to cross the room and practically fall into my mother's embrace. I didn't realize how much I needed her comfort until she starts repeating, "He's going to be fine. Your daddy's going to be just fine."

It's the first time in the last seven hours that I believe it.

TWENTY-FIVE

Lauren

No tumbling. No leaps. No turns. No vaulting.

Not even allowed to climb on the beam and no bars without being strapped on, which means nothing except giants.

I'm. So. Bored.

Laying on my back, I stare at the gym ceiling. It's amazing how much of our equipment is attached to the steel beams. I think I knew that but for whatever reason, my brain just glossed over it. Makes sense, though. What are they going to attach the rings to? Ceiling tiles? Plywood? With how much force the guys put on the straps when they perform, they'd break a hole in the ceiling within hours. The thought brings a smile to my face.

Ohmygod. This is what my life has come to. Laying here, sprawled out, pretending to stretch, and fantasizing about the male half of our team faceplanting in the middle of a routine. And Heath's not even here to keep my mind distracted with weird and interesting conversation when he comes to get me.

He's only been gone for a few days. After one hell of a scary day, the doctors believe his dad is going to make a full recovery. It's such good news. Heath is still gone and wants to make sure his dad is truly on the road to recovery before heading back. I completely understand and agree under the circumstance. Unfortunately, I got none of this information from the source. Instead, Jaxon has been updating me because Heath has gone radio silent.

I get it. Heath is busy and probably freaking out, but selfishly, this is hard on me. Heath's absence, not to mention his silence, combined with my own restlessness, make my days feel like torture. That's not a good sign that I'm so attached to him when I'm supposed to be protecting my heart. It's also not good for my mental wellbeing to be so idle. Its times like these where I can easily spiral, so I need to pay close attention to my self-talk.

Well, what do you know? At least one thing stuck from all those years of laying on my therapist's couch. She'd be so proud.

Deciding it's time to actually do something beyond just lay here, I bend my arms putting my hands next to my ears, and push up into a bridge. Using the only leg I'm allowed to put pressure on, I push myself as far as my shoulders will allow. Once I feel sufficiently stretched, I lay down and tuck my body. Rolling back and forth feels good enough but does nothing to alleviate my boredom. I might as well leave. Even studying business ethics sounds more fun than sitting around here.

Of course, I didn't put my plan to leave into motion five minutes ago. And for whatever reason, Con has decided now is a good time to come over and converse.

"How's the leg?" he asks, plopping down next to me and straddling his legs, stretching his own splits.

I make a show of looking around before pointing to my chest. "Me?"

He huffs whatever displeasure he's feeling and reaches forward. "Don't act like that, Lauren."

"Like what? Completely and totally uninterested in anything you have to say? Because it's not an act. I truly don't care."

"I liked you better before you got some hotshot football player boyfriend."

"You mean starry-eyed and naïve to the kind of person you really are? Yeah, she's long gone." I push off the floor and grab my crutches to hobble away. It would be a much more dramatic exit if I could stomp off, but this is what I've got to work with, so I try to make the best of it.

Sadly for me, Con still has two working legs and is right behind me as I move. "Come on, Lauren. Don't you remember how good we were together?"

I look over my shoulder and furrow my brow. "Did you seriously forget how horrible of a person you were to me? What's your angle here?"

"There's no angle. I just... I don't know." He steps in front of me and stops, effectively blocking me from getting away. "I just think you should give me another chance."

I don't know what exactly is happening, but I take a deep breath before trying to make myself very clear. "Con, even if Heath and I weren't together, there is no way in hell I would ever go out with you again. So, whatever it is you think you're doing, just stop. You're wasting your breath."

He opens his mouth to respond but is interrupted by our team's unofficial Regina George. Her real name is Ally Chancellor, and she's a huge bitch. I stay out of her way most of the time, not at all interested in engaging in the drama she leaves in her wake.

"Conrad, I need to borrow your car."

Weird. I had no idea they were friends. Then again, I don't pay attention to any of them anymore, content to stick to my own training.

"Why would I do that?"

She doesn't look up from her phone, texting while she talks. It's actually kind of impressive. "Because your mom gave me a gift card for Christmas, and in true Aunt Linda fashion, it has an expiration date on it." Ally presses send on her phone and finally looks up. "It expires tomorrow, so I need to go spend it today."

The rest of their conversation fades into the back-ground as I put some pieces of the gymnastics team drama puzzle together.

Ally has always hated me. She wants an all-around

spot badly but isn't the best, so she could be knocked out if she can't get her floor exercise pulled together.

My specialty is floor exercise, and I've bumped up my points values this year.

Con is her cousin.

Con has spent the last few months trying to throw me off my game.

All of it stopped the second I got injured, which effectively caused me to lose my spot and helped secure hers.

Wait. There is no way the whole flirtation and sleeping with me only to humiliate me thing, was over Ally competing in the all-around. Was it?

Holy shit.

"What kind of *Love Island* bullshit did I accidentally wade into?" I grumble to myself, completely floored by this realization.

"What?" Con asks after telling Ally where his car keys are.

"Nothing. Nothing at all." I crutch my way around him, ignoring him as he tries to engage me in conversation. I've got too many other things to do than sit here and listen to Con feed me more shit. To be perfectly honest, I'm not even interested to know if I'm right in my assumption about why I was his target in the first place.

As I situate myself in my wheelchair, pulling on my favorite oversized Aerosmith sweatshirt and tie on my lone shoe, I think I about how little I care what anyone in this gym thinks of me. It's almost startling how much my attitude has changed in the last few months. Maybe it's because nothing shows you people's true character like a major conflict or in my case, a conflict followed immediately by a major injury. Or maybe it's because Heath's dad having a heart attack put things in a different and more important perspective. Regardless, it's odd knowing how little I care what these people think. Odd and a little freeing.

Shooting off a quick text to Annika, I wheel my way out the door and down the sidewalk, not even bothering to say goodbye. The only person who cares that I'm leaving is Ellery anyway, and right now, she's too busy focusing her googly eyes on Kevin.

I laugh softly to myself as I think about how strange that relationship is. They're cute together and all, but never in a million years would I have put them together. But more and more, I see them catching each other's eye across the room or chatting quietly in a corner during break times. I only hope he doesn't turn out to be a dick. I don't think he is, but at this point, my trust doesn't come easily anymore.

The wheel across campus is flat but long, and I'm out of breath by the time I make it to the dorm steps where my roommate and her boyfriend are hanging out.

"Hey guys. Thanks for waiting for me."

"You don't have to thank us," Annika says as she takes the crutches off my lap and balances them in front of me so I can stand up. "It's kind of nice that you need me again."

"Aw. Were you feeling lonely without someone to care for?" I joke as I push out of my chair and hop around until I find my balance between the crutches. When I'm settled and out of the way, Jaxon folds up the chair behind me.

"Hardly," Annika says with a laugh. "That one right there might be feeling better, but now all he does is whine about all the labs he's doing this semester."

Jaxon pulls the door into the dorm open for us as I carefully navigate my way up the short steps. "It's not whining. It's the realization that I may have bitten off more than I can chew. Advanced Chem is a given, but I had no idea the psychology class I'm required to take would mean extra research projects. What the hell does this have to do with being a doctor?"

"It's called bedside manner," I answer quickly and gesture down to my leg. "Trust me. Not everyone has it, and the ones who didn't were horrible. I don't remember half of what they told me."

"See?" Annika points at me. "That's exactly what I told you. And if you're going to be a pediatric oncologist, you better learn the psychology of kids."

"I should have taken the child psychology class," he grumbles as we clunk our way down the hall. I'm sure we're an interesting sight to see—Annika leading the way, me huffing and puffing on my crutches, Jaxon pushing a perfectly good wheelchair behind me. At this point, I'd hope everyone on this floor is used to us.

"Why didn't you?" I lean against the wall, waiting for Annika to open the door and let us in.

"I will. I have to take both of them, actually. This one fit into my schedule better. Or so I thought."

One by one, we follow Annika inside and I drop myself into the rolling chair that used to come in handy for sitting at a desk. Now, it's used to give me mobility inside this small room.

Jaxon leans the wheelchair against the wall by the door and flops down on my bed. Well, technically, it's Annika's bed, it's just shoved up against mine. "Somehow I missed the part about having double the number of labs when I set it up this way."

Annika pouts her lip in an exaggerated fashion, but I feel sympathetic. I crinkle my nose in disgust. "Sounds like torture."

"Yeah, it's no picnic so far."

"You'll be fine." Annika pats his leg and turns to me. "I don't have anywhere I have to be right now. Do you need help showering?"

I drop my head back and make a face. "Ugh. Yes, I do. But it takes so much effort."

Annika smiles. "I know it's not ideal, but it's not terrible, is it?"

"No," I grumble. "I'm just tired of not doing things on my own."

"Oh really." My best friend crosses her arms and smirks at me. "I don't hear you complain when Heath is the one helping you shower."

"It's way less boring when he showers with me."

"Hey!" Jaxon covers his ears. "I don't need to hear this shit."

Annika grabs his arm and pulls it away from his head. "Oh please. Like you two don't do all that locker room talk when we're not around. I'm not stupid."

Jaxon gets a serious look on his face. "No. We don't."

"You don't?" I don't believe him because what guys don't talk about boobs and butts and getting off? That's just weird.

"No," he responds with a shrug. "It's kind of this un-spoken rule. We just respect you guys more than that."

Annika makes an "awwwww!" sound while I mumble "Buncha pansies." Jaxon rolls his eyes at both of us. Or maybe just me.

"Speaking of," Annika begins now that she's done swooning over her boyfriend for the umpteenth time, "when is Heath coming back?"

"I don't know," I admit, rolling myself to the dresser to gather my clothes. "I got one text last night that said he was hoping to hit the road tomorrow morning."

"Um… he's actually on the road already."

"What?" I whip around to look at Jaxon. "When did he leave?"

Jaxon suddenly looks sheepish, maybe because of the stunned expression I'm probably sporting. "About ten this morning."

"I thought he was waiting for his dad to be released from the hospital."

"He was discharged last night. He didn't call you?"

I shake my head and bite my bottom lip. I shouldn't be surprised that Heath called Jaxon and not me to give him an update. They've been roommates and best friends for years. I've only been dating Heath for a couple of months. And yet, I can't help but feel like I've been sucker-punched.

Maybe he doesn't like me as much as I thought he did. I mean, I assumed after we shared that night together and he made it clear it was about more than just sex, it meant our feelings for each other were deep. But maybe it wasn't as mutual as I thought.

Recognizing my thoughts are beginning to spiral, I reach back into my drawer and grab my meds. I usually take them after practice anyway, but it's hard to forget when I'm doing my best to put a mask on as I fight down the tears of insecurity.

"I'm sure he wasn't thinking, Lauren," Annika says

quietly behind me.

Turning my gaze to her I flash her a wide smile. It's fake, but hopefully I'm the only one who can tell. "Oh, I know. He's got a lot on his mind right now. As long as one of us knows what's going on, it's fine." Grabbing my things off the top of the dresser, I know I can't keep up this charade much longer. "Let's go get this plastic sleeve on my leg, so I can clean up. I'm sure you guys have plans."

Carefully, yet quickly, I push myself to the bathroom, fighting the emotion bubbling up inside me until I can be alone behind that shower curtain.

Suddenly, the words I spoke to Con come racing back to me. Even if Heath and I weren't together, there is no way in hell I would ever go out with you again.

I was speaking hypothetically, but now, I just hope I didn't speak too soon.

TWENTY-SIX
Heath

I trudge up the stairs, backpack flung over my shoulder as I head to my dorm room. I'm fucking exhausted, physically and mentally. I was only gone for four days, but it feels like weeks since I slept. Sitting in a hospital during a crisis, coupled with fourteen hours of driving will do that to a body.

The good news is my dad looks to be out of the woods. The doctor has no reason to believe he won't make a full recovery. In fact, Dad was doing so well, he was discharged earlier than normal. That's my dad for you—stubborn as a mule in all things, including how long his body will need to stay in a hospital bed.

Breathing a sigh of relief to finally be back at my home away from home, I open the door to my room and stop where I'm at. This is not what I was hoping to walk into.

"I knew you guys missed me, but I wasn't expecting a welcome home party." The joke falls flat to my own ears, but I don't have much energy left to care. Certainly not to this many people.

Annika is sprawled out on my roommate's bed with several textbooks open in front of her. Lauren is lounging on mine, only one textbook in her lap but with her phone in hand. Her face lights up when she sees me, and it hits me like a punch to the gut. How did she get so attached to me so fast?

Jaxon is sitting at the desk. At the sound of my voice, he spins around in his desk chair and smiles. "Hey man, you're back." His face falls quickly. "And you look like shit."

I can't disagree. "I feel like shit." I toss my wallet onto the dresser and bag of dirty clothes into the closet and drop onto my bed, as far away from Lauren as I can get without making it look obvious that I'm keeping my distance. I ignore the look of confusion on her face at my lack of greeting. I've got too much on my mind to worry about how she's feeling.

Dick move? Yes. But under the circumstances, I think it's justified.

"So, what's everyone doing in here anyway? Decide to have a party while I was gone?"

"We went to eat and decided a change of scenery would be nice for a while," Lauren says quietly. I don't look at her, just nod at the information. "Was the drive okay?"

"Same drive as always." I know my answers are clipped and by the uncomfortable vibe in the room, everyone else is noticing it too. "I was looking forward to crashing for a while, but I guess that'll have to wait."

Annika sits up quickly and begins gathering her things. "I'm sorry, Heath. We didn't know you'd want to sleep here. We can go."

I run my hand down my face, frustrated by my own lack of manners. "Naw, stay. I'm sorry. I'm not trying to be rude. I have a meeting with Coach anyway."

Pushing myself up, I grab my wallet and shove it in my back pocket.

"You have a meeting with Coach now?" Jaxon sounds confused, which comes as no surprise.

"Yeah, I called him on my way back. He's in the office working on some paperwork so he told me to pop in."

"Let me guess." Jaxon leans back in his chair, crossing his arms over his chest. "You want to talk to him about registering for the combine."

"Yeah. So?"

He stares at me, unwavering. I can tell he's not thrilled by my decision. "Things changed that quickly, huh?"

I stare right back, not even a little moved by his obvious displeasure. "I have a family that needs me, Jaxon."

He nods once and turns back to his books, effectively dismissing me. Whatever. I don't need his approval to plan my future. I never did.

Looking up, my eyes catch Lauren's. She looks hurt by my dismissive attitude. I can't say I blame her. I've been almost non-existent by phone or text the last few days and now, I'm walking out without so much as a hello. I understand, but I can't let it stop me and what I have to do.

"I'll, uh… I'll call you later," I say quietly, trying to push the guilt down, and pull the door open. She nods and does her best to smile, but I see the pain in her eyes. There's just nothing I can do right now to stop it. "Later."

I book it out of the room as fast as I can, ready to get out of such an awkward situation. Plus, I'm feeling an urgency to talk to Coach as soon as possible. I don't need his approval to register for the combine, but I do feel like it's common courtesy to let him know my plans.

Despite my exhaustion, I have a restless energy that needs an outlet, so I jog across campus to the field house. Within minutes, I'm knocking on Coach's open door.

"Germaine." He drops his feet off his desk and waves me in, tossing some files onto the mess of paperwork on his desk. "Come in. How's your dad?"

"He's good, sir. Already home and being pampered by my mother." The thought of how seamlessly they moved into that partnership when he came home brings a smile to my face. "He'll be off work for a couple of weeks until he gets the all-clear from his cardiologist, but there's no indication this will hinder him long term."

"Good, good," Coach responds. I know better than to think he's answering me absentmindedly. And he knows better than to think I'm here to talk about my dad's health. "What's so urgent that you need to talk to me tonight?"

This is it. What I've been working towards and toying with for the last several years. Once these words are out of my mouth, there's no going back. "I wanted you to know I'm registering for this year's combine."

Coach pulls his glasses off and drops them on top of the growing mess, then leans back in his chair. "Is that so?"

"Yes sir."

"You know you don't need me to give my permission."

"I know. But I felt it was only right to give you a head's up. You're already planning for next year, so you need to know I probably won't be here."

"I appreciate that."

"And I want your opinion about it."

I didn't expect those words to come out of my mouth. Up until this moment, I never considered what Coach thought of my prospects. I'm leading the NCAA with most tackles per game and was barely edged out of all-season tackles by Abel Anders. I'm quick, I've got a good work ethic, and my grade point average shows I'm committed. All reasons why I'm a good candidate. Or so I think.

Looking at Coach's expression, though, I'm suddenly wondering if I'm wrong. He's not moving, just looking at me, his fingers steepled and resting against the tip of his nose. I've seen this look before. He only makes it when he's preparing himself to give bad news.

Finally, after what seems like an eternity, he sniffs and drops his hands to the armrests. "I think you need to wait a year."

Not the words I was expecting, but now he has me curious, so I wait.

"Your stats are solid, but you've got room to improve which will give you a stronger showing and will secure a better contract."

"That also gives me another year to risk an injury that could knock me out completely."

"True," he says with a nod. "But right now, you run a greater risk of being injured your first year in the pros. You need to add a few pounds yourself if you're going to keep up with the big dogs. You play with some big guys now, but you know full well how much bigger they are at that level."

My jaw ticks. I don't have a year to wait. I've got responsibilities now. I've got people to help provide for *now*. If I can secure a contract in the next couple of months, my parents can stop worrying about how to make ends meet and they can stop working so hard. If I wait—hell, I don't even want to think about the potential implications on my dad's health if I stay in college for another year.

With that in mind, I ignore his concerns. "But do you think I'll get picked if I go for it this year?"

"Yeah, I do," he says with a nod of his head. "But I've been doing this for a lot of years, Heath. And while you'll get picked up, you won't be in the top ten. I also have reservations thinking you'll do much more than play for a year or two before it's over." He leans forward and rests his elbows on his desk. "Give yourself another year to gain some muscle weight and show your stats are solid, not just a fluke. It'll be better for your career, long term. And I don't just mean that because you'll have a degree to fall back on. That part's an added bonus. I'm talking about your longevity in the pros."

Looking off to the side, I consider his words, but we both know I'm not going to take his advice. Pushing out of my chair, we both stand. "I appreciate your honesty, Coach."

"But your mind is made up."

"Yes, sir."

He sighs and puts his hands on his hips. "I won't say I think it's the right choice, but it's your call, and I'll support you any way I can."

"Thank you."

Coming around from behind his desk he claps me on the shoulder. "Go get some rest, son. You look wiped, and I don't want you to miss another practice. We need to keep you in shape if you're going to put in a good showing in Indianapolis."

I smile at him and nod, the exhaustion I've been holding in beginning to take over. It makes the trip back across campus seem slower.

By the time I'm back at my dorm, my feet feel like they're dragging through cement and my body feels like it's been hit by a bus. I'm behind on schoolwork, I have to register for the combine, and I need to check in with my dad. All I want to do is slow down for a few minutes, but suddenly, all my priorities seem to be moving at the speed of light. The only part of me moving fast is my brain.

Trudging up the stairs for the second time, I can't help but think of how much of a dick I am for hoping my dorm room is empty. I don't want to see anybody. I don't want to talk to anybody. I don't want to do any more talking for the night. Not even with Lauren. I know my bad mood isn't her fault and eventually, it will pass, so at minimum, I need to text her and let her know I'm okay.

That thought is fleeting, though, when I find my room empty of noise and people. Taking advantage of the quiet, I call home to check-in.

"Heath. Did you make it okay?" My mom's calm voice relaxes me. When she sounds like this, her tone gentle and her drawl slow, I know everything is fine.

"It was a long drive, but I made it."

"Good, good. Did you eat on the way?"

I chuckle at her concern. My mother shows love in a lot of ways, but food is probably her favorite. There's a reason I had to be an athlete growing up in that house. I needed to burn off all the calories. "I did, Ma. I stopped and grabbed a burger."

She tsks. "A burger. That's terrible. I should have sent you home with some leftover homemade lasagna."

"Ma, I'm fine. Besides, I polished off the lasagna yesterday. That's not why I called though. I wanted to check on Dad. How's he holding up?"

"Your father is just fine. Still angry he can't go to work tomorrow."

My father's voice belts out through the speaker. "Doctor shouldn't be worried about my heart. He should be worried about me dying of boredom. You left me with all these women, Heath. I'm gonna go out of my mind listening to all their boy talk."

"You hush up," my mother scolds him gently while I smile at their antics. My dad always complains that he's outnumbered now that I left him as the lone man of the house. I never remind him that we were outnumbered four-to-two in the first place. It's all in jest anyway. It was always clear growing up that he was happy to have a boy. But his girls make his face light up.

"Don't listen to your father," my mom says, refocusing her attention back on me. "He's just being grumpy because the doctor won't let him eat fried food anymore."

I let out an exaggerated gasp. "What are you going to feed him now if you can't fry his food?"

"Just because I like to cook in grease doesn't mean I have to." Her voice carries a little more sass now that I've insulted her cooking. "I'm already trying some new marinades for my famous baked chicken. And this just gives me an excuse to learn how to make zucchini noodles like I've been wanting to do."

"Don't you try to trick me into eating green vegetables!" my father hollers in the back.

"Stop interrupting. I'm talking to my son," she argues. "And Amy, don't you dare give him that bell back! I'm tired of him ringing it in my ear when I'm sitting next to him on the couch." I hear rustling around as she probably moves to a different room for some quiet. When things finally settle in the background, she speaks again. "There. I left him in the living room to fend for himself for a while."

I love my parents' relationship. Married for twenty-five years, they've always had eyes for only each other. Apart, they're wonderful people. But together, they're dynamic.

"Now that I can hear you without interruption," she continues, "tell me what's really on your mind."

"What do you mean?" I play dumb, not wanting to add any more pressure to her already stressful life.

She scoffs. "Don't even try that with me. I carried you inside me for eight-and-a-half months, Heath Germaine. I know when you're thinking too much."

I could keep up the pretense, but if my mother is throwing out birthing stories, I'm just wasting my own breath. Leaning back on my bed, I fess up. "I'm registering for the combine."

"Ah." Oddly, she doesn't sound surprised. She doesn't sound happy either, though. "What made you finally come to the conclusion that it's the best course of action?"

Her lack of excitement is disappointing. I thought she'd be happy I was one step closer to the pros. Instead, she makes it sound like it's the wrong thing to do.

"It's time. I'm ready."

"Hmm."

My head falls back, knowing this conversation isn't going to end well. "What, Ma? I know you have an opinion."

"Oh no. No opinion. I'm just curious if you talked to your coach about it."

I don't want to tell her what he said, mainly because I don't want her to be disappointed in me. But I also don't put it past her to call him herself if she thinks I'm being shady. That fear is what kept me on the straight and narrow most of my life. Nothing like being humiliated in the middle school locker room because my mother called to verify my whereabouts, which were not exactly honest, to scare you straight.

"He thinks I need another year."

"Mmm. And you don't agree."

"It's not about if I agree or not, Mom. It's about taking care of my family. It's about making sure the girls can go to college without student loans and making sure you and dad don't have to work two jobs anymore."

I don't mean to spew all my issues at her, but something inside me snaps. Probably because I'm tired of people dismissing my plans. They should be excited about me being an NFL prospect, but instead, I keep getting shit from everyone about it. It's disappointing and angering and actually a little hurtful that the consensus seems to be I'm not ready.

Probably stunned by my outburst, my mother says nothing. Until suddenly, she's laughing. And not just a little. She's laughing so hard she might even have tears in her eyes.

I don't understand. "Why is this so funny?"

"Oh lord, you are so much like your father."

"And that's funny?"

"It sure is. Do you know how many times your father's pride has gotten in the way of him making good decisions, and how many times I've had to intervene so he gets out of his own head long enough to stop thinking like he is the end all-be all of this family?"

Her words stop my irate train of thought. I've never once thought of my dad as being prideful. Proud, yes. But letting pride cloud his judgment? Never.

I want to say as much, but she's not done. "I appreciate how much you want to help, and I know your daddy's heart attack is making you panic—"

"I'm not panicking—" I try to interrupt, but she runs right over me.

"—but if you suddenly paid off our mortgage and paid for your sisters' college, your father would knock your ass out."

Never, in my twenty-two years of life, have I heard my mother cuss. The shock of it deflates any argument I have.

"We don't have much, but we only have a few years left on our mortgage until it's paid off. By ourselves. With no outside help. Do you know what an accomplishment that is and how good we feel about that? And the timing is such that it'll be paid off before Amy goes to go to college, so she won't have to take out any loans."

"But what about Jackie and Maggie? They'll be going to college sooner than that."

"Have you even talked to your sisters about their future plans?"

I shift uncomfortably realizing I've spent so much time on my own goals, I never actually asked my sisters about theirs. "No."

"That's what I thought," my mother says with a sigh. "Jackie wants to be a cosmetologist. She's been taking the classes for the last couple of semesters and will just have a few more things to do to get her license after graduation." That comes as a shock to me, but my mother keeps going. "And Maggie wants to work with animals, but she doesn't like school. She's been saving up money already to become a vet tech."

My thoughts begin to swirl as she feeds me this information. "But... dad works two jobs."

"For the insurance, Heath."

"What?"

"Your dad is a teacher by trade. He loves it and would never quit, but health insurance for a teacher is terrible. The coffee shop provides insurance for part-time employees. So, we crunched some numbers and realized it would cost us less and help us build our nest egg if he worked a few nights a week."

"Wait..." I squeeze the bridge of my nose because this is all new information for me. I'm having a hard time processing it. "So, you guys aren't struggling for money?"

"Well... we have four kids. We're always struggling for money," she says with a chuckle. I'm glad she finds this humorous because I don't find any of this amusing at all. "But we're not destitute. Not even close. How did you even come to that conclusion?"

I have to think about that. I suppose it's from years of my dad bitching about proms and weddings and all the expenses that come from having so many girls. "Just some of the things dad says."

"Heath, I'll let you in on a little secret. Your dad is a whiner." I huff a laugh because I know that. "He's hilarious, which is why I put up with it, because it's just his dark sense of humor."

"So, you don't need my help?"

"Oh baby, no. And I'm sorry you thought we did. I know that put unnecessary pressure on you to get to the next level." That's an understatement. Since high school, I've been working to make things easier on my parents more than to make it easier on myself. "Don't misunderstand. I love your heart and how hard you've worked for us. But if you swooped in at the last minute and took away your dad's chance to write that final mortgage check so he can say he bought this house on his own, he would never forgive you. I suspect you understand that because you are just the same."

She's right. I am. I love the satisfaction of working hard and accomplishing my goal. When it comes down to it, having the best stats in the NCAA isn't that different from paying off a thirty-year mortgage.

"I'm coming!" my mom's voice yells, and I know my time with her is almost up. "Dark humor or not, I'm gonna smack that man upside the head if he gets ahold of that bell again."

That elicits a genuine chuckle from me. If I know my sister's well enough, they'll give it back to him just to see if they can get my mom to lose her shit. She rarely does, so it's a sight to see sometimes.

"Anyway, I'm going to see what he needs and let you get some rest, okay, baby?"

"Alright, Mom. Thanks."

"You're welcome. Oh, and Heath, before you register, just think about what I said. Don't do the combine for us. Do it because you feel it's the best course of action for *you*."

"Okay, Mom. Goodnight."

We hang up and I collapse on the bed, more confused now than I was a few days ago. There's so much to think about, but I'm not sure my body and brain can take much more.

It isn't until the next morning that I realize I fell asleep without taking a shower. Or texting my girlfriend.

TWENTY-SEVEN
Lauren

I click off my phone, disappointment and hurt running through me again. I'm still getting radio silence from my boyfriend, if I can even still call him that. I can see the writing on the wall. I know how this works. He's going to ghost me now that he's gotten what he wants. I should have known better than to sleep with him.

I hate the feeling of defeat it gives me to know I was snowed yet again. It makes me feel weak and insecure. Like when it comes to the opposite sex, I only have one thing to offer. It's a shitty feeling to have.

And yes, I know logically it's not truth, but when that's the only way men ever treat you, it's tough to get logic and emotions to work together.

Squeezing my eyes closed, I vow not to think about it anymore. Not to think about him. I'd rather cut my losses and move on. It shouldn't be that hard to avoid him. Just because his best friend is dating my best friend doesn't mean we all have to hang out anymore. It was easy and convenient for a short amount of time, but we all have our own lives. Right now, I need to focus on mine.

"Thanks for bringing me," I say to Annika, determined to keep my thoughts in safer territory. It's a sad day when the demise of my gymnastics career is a topic I'd prefer to discuss.

Annika is sitting on a rickety blue chair that looks like it could collapse at any moment. It looks uncomfortable, but she doesn't seem to notice, probably because she's reading some sports injury article. Ever since she got into the training program, her obsession with sprains, strains, and ice baths has hit a whole new level.

Looking up from her phone, she smiles at me. "It was no problem. I have some reading to do, so I don't mind the wait."

"And you get to pick the doctor's brain about my injury and the best course of action to help it heal, right?" I prod.

She shoves her hands in between her thighs, probably to warm up her fingers. Even I have to admit it's cold in here and I've got five pounds of plaster keeping one of my legs warm. "You got me. I know it seems like I'm doing you a favor, and I know this is painful for you, but from an educational level, your injury is fascinating to me." She cocks her head in question. "Is it too soon for me to admit that?"

"No," I say with a smirk and a shake of my head. "I get it. We athletes need weirdos like you to help us get better, so observe away."

"I'm glad to be of service."

She's cut off from saying anything else when the door opens and Dr. Copperman walks in.

"Hey Lauren. How are you feeling?" He asks with a huge, blindingly white smile, bypassing me to wash his hands.

Dr. Copperman is a wiry, middle-aged man who seems to have a ton of energy. He's that doctor who pushes himself around the room on his rolling chair instead of standing up and walking two feet. It's a little odd, but I've gotten used to it. It helps that he's also quick with his visits, so I've never had to wait long and he comes highly recommended as one of the best orthopedic surgeons in the area.

"How am I?" I make a show of tapping my finger to

my lips in thought. "I'm bored out of my mind and praying you're going to tell me I can work out again."

Somehow, his smile gets even broader. "Well, then I won't leave you in suspense anymore and tell you no, you cannot work out."

I groan in response as he rinses and dries his hands.

"Based on your x-rays, the fracture is healing nicely, but it's not quite there yet. We want to make sure the bone is nice and solid before putting that kind of pressure on it again."

I give him a wry look, not that it will change anything. I just want to make it clear how unhappy this news makes me.

I jump when his cold hands touch my leg. "Sorry about that. We need to figure out a way to get the water to warm up faster around here." He begins manipulating my leg this way and that, testing my mobility and pain level. "The good news, however, is that you're recovering faster than most people with this kind of injury."

"Is that because she's so active and healthy?" Annika interjects.

Not having seen her before, Dr. Copperman furrows his brow. I wave my hand dismissively. "It's okay. That's my roommate, Annika. She's in the sports training program as of this year so this break has been of great interest to her. You can tell her whatever. I don't care."

"Well, congratulations. That's a hard program to get into," Dr. Copperman says kindly while continuing with his ministrations. "And yes, likely the fact that she's an athlete and treats her body as such is why she's healing so quickly. A normal, non-athletic college student with the same injury likely wouldn't heal as fast."

"Is she still looking at a four- to six-month recovery time?"

"That's the tricky part." Dr. Copperman releases my leg and leans against the table next to me, crossing his arms. "Typically, I'd say yes, but as a gymnast, that means something different than it would to you or me."

"Because of tumbling and vault and dismounts…" I

toss out, as he nods his head with every skill I mention.

"Exactly. Bones have a remarkable way of healing and becoming strong again, but that doesn't mean certain areas won't be weaker than the rest. I don't want you to jump into something and end up breaking it more severely."

That's not encouraging news. "So, there's no way I'll be back, even for the tail end of the season."

"I'm afraid not."

I close my eyes, heart sinking. I knew it was a long shot, but I was hoping I'd get lucky, just this one time.

"The good news is, I think we can officially move to you a walking cast."

My eyes fly open and I look at him in shock. "Really? No more wheelchair?"

"Well, I wouldn't go that far. The trick here is balancing the bone heal with not losing muscle mass that you need to support that bone. You're going to tire easily, and when your leg starts to hurt, use that as a sign that you need to stop walking on it."

"But I don't have to sit all the time. I can shower on my own and walk across campus and stuff?"

Dr. Copperman chuckles at how delighted I am, which I admit to. This is the best news I've had in weeks, and I can't wait to stand upright again.

"If you think that's good news, you're going to be really happy with the next thing I have to say."

My eyes widen. What could he possibly say that would make me even happier than I already am?

"You are still restricted from any sort of tumbling. No vaulting, no dismounts, nothing that could put pressure on that bone."

"So, no leaps," I offer up, just to show I'm a team player.

"Correct. However, I understand you guys have a foam pit, right?" I nod, keeping my fingers crossed about where this is going. "I'm clearing you for bar work, as long as you're over the pit."

Normally, I hate bars, but right now, this is the most exciting news he could have given me. Clasping my hands together I clarify, "Release moves and everything?"

"Only if you're over the pit."

I squeal and clap my hands. I can't help it. Even if it's not my preferred event, it's a huge step in the right direction. "I promise I won't do anything more than that. Do I just go without the walking boot or wrap my leg or anything?"

He sits down on his chair and rolls himself to the computer on the desk, using his badge to log in before making some notes while he talks. "I'm ordering you a specialized brace to wear during workouts. It won't do anything about the pressure of walking, but it'll keep your tibia from rotating in ways we don't want. So, it'll feel a little restrictive."

I scoff. "Not nearly as restrictive as this cast." I knock on the plaster for effect.

"True. I also want you to start working on building up the muscles in your shins so we're sending you to physical therapy."

He takes the next few minutes to explain what exercises he wants me to do until I can get in with the PT, while Annika takes notes. Not that it's hard to remember the various versions of calf raises, but who knows. She may need that information for a test, and I'm sure she'll be passing the info along to the training department so they can work with me as well.

Since it's pretty simple to explain, he's not there long before his assistant comes in with an electric saw to cut this baby off me. I'm ready. Not just so I can have my leg back, but because I want to shave. Casts are itchy to begin with. Adding stubbly leg hair only makes it worse.

By the time it's cut off and my leg cleaned of the nasty funk that no one enjoys smelling, Dr. Copperman is back with a walking boot in one hand and brace in another. "It's your lucky day! We had both of them in the office, so you don't have to wait."

Carefully, he shows me how to use each of the devices. The hardest parts are figuring out which strap goes where, but I pretend to listen intently anyway. If I have questions later, I'm sure Annika is still taking notes.

Finally, after what feels like hours, I'm ready to walk out of here on my own two feet.

"I want to see you back in two weeks so we can re-x-ray and see how it's going, okay?"

"Absolutely," I agree. Pushing myself to standing and testing out my new footwear, I let out a sigh of relief. "You have no idea how good it feels to stand up without crutches."

I ignore the sounds of amusement and march out the door as best I can. Walking in a boot is going to take some getting used to, and I can already tell I'll have to work through some soreness, but I'm ready. For the first time in days, a genuine smile crosses my face.

"What do you want me to do with your crutches?" Annika asks as we head out the door and to the car.

"You can toss them in a dumpster or set them on fire for all I care." Not the most responsible answer but at least it's honest.

Using the key fob to unlock the car, she opens the backdoor. "Interesting ideas, but I think I'll just put them back here instead."

"Works for me." It takes a little bit of finagling to get myself in the front seat, only because I'm not used to the kind of bulk this new device has, but I have no complaints. It's so much more comfortable than the cast was already. "I've never been so excited to shave my legs!" I shout when Annika gets situated next to me.

She giggles right along with me. "I've never been so excited to not have to see your hoo-ha anymore."

I throw my head back and laugh, releasing all my pent-up stress. And then my phone vibrates against me and the good times come to a screeching halt. It's a text from Heath.

Hey. Call me when you can.

I shake my head and shove my phone in my pocket, ignoring him. I'm having too good of a day today to think about him. I'm done being treated like I'm disposable. I won't allow it to happen anymore.

Not even by someone like Heath Germaine.

TWENTY-EIGHT

Heath

During practice, I was okay.

During weight training, I was okay.

During class, I was okay.

I was even okay when I sat down to catch up on some of the outstanding assignments I have.

Now, I'm not okay.

I have texted Lauren five times and called three. No, I didn't leave a voicemail that last time, but after saying the same thing seven times, it started to feel redundant.

Now I'm getting antsy. My first assumption is something happened to her, but since I never got a frantic call from Jaxon and now, he's sitting across the room head bopping around while he studies, that's unlikely. It also leads to the only other conclusion:

She's ignoring me.

I don't like it.

Tapping my pen on my desk, I run the last few interactions through my brain. Yes, I was short with her yesterday, but I was exhausted and on the verge of making a major, life-altering decision. I explained as much in my second voicemail. Under the circumstances, that's a forgivable offense, right?

"You gonna keep fidgeting over there, or are you going to say what's on your mind?" Jaxon doesn't bother lifting his head or taking off his headphones, his words confrontational enough.

"I'm not fidgeting," I grumble and toss my pen down. For the millionth time, I pick up my phone to check for a response. Still nothing. Huffing my frustration, I toss it down, too.

Jaxon finally looks up. "Dude. The vibe you're giving off is making it impossible for me to concentrate on the structure of microorganisms."

"I don't even know what that means."

"What it means is you're driving me up the fucking wall. What gives?"

Knowing exactly how petty I sound, I grumble, "Lauren won't text me back."

Jax pulls his headphones off finally. "I'm sorry, what?"

I sigh and lean back in my chair. "My girlfriend. Lauren. You know her. She won't answer me. I've texted and called all day, and she's ignoring me."

"Ah." Jaxon puts his headphones back on and turns back to his work.

"That's it?" I grab a piece of crumpled up notebook paper off my desk and toss it at his head. It misses, but he flinches. "That's all you have to say about it?"

"Do you blame her?" Jaxon asks without a hint of sympathy.

Anger runs through me at his response. "My father had a heart attack, Jaxon. He could have died. Do I not get a little bit of understanding for being in my own little world because of it?"

"She understands, Germaine. We all do. But I understand where she's coming from, too."

Crossing my arms, I lean back again, glaring at him. "This ought to be good." I wave my hand for him to continue because I'm kind of itching for a fight. Maybe it'll take the edge off. "Please, go on."

He scowls at me and drops his headphones on the textbook in front of him. "Okay. Here it is. You went through a terrible ordeal. You didn't know if your dad was going to survive, so you took off. I understand that. But when you got there and found out he was going to be fine, you didn't bother to update anyone. Not even to say you got there safely. We were sitting down here worrying about you and you just went radio silent."

"I was at the hospital," I say through gritted teeth.

"So was your mother, but she answered when I called." I clench my jaw. He has a point and I don't like it. "And then he was discharged, but instead of calling your girl-friend or even texting her, you called me."

"So what? I didn't have time to call everyone in my contact's list, Jaxon."

"No. So you should have called the most important people on that list. And if my name is before Lauren's, you damn sure shouldn't be sleeping with her under false pretenses."

His words stop me, my mouth agape. "You think I tricked her into having sex with me?"

"You tell me."

The challenge in his eyes makes me want to haul off and punch him. My nostrils flare and I have to concentrate on slowing my breathing down. "Never once, *never once* have I tried to get in someone's pants just to say I scored."

"So, you're telling me you have real feelings for her."

"I'm telling you I'm in love with her."

His eyebrows move up just slightly in surprise. I don't miss the reaction probably because it's the same one I'm having internally, except I'm battling myself right now. I love her, I know that. But I'm also pissed as hell.

Jaxon doesn't miss a beat when he finally drives his point home. "And yet, you ghost her for days after she finally sleeps with you."

I want to deny it. I want to tell him he's wrong. But I can't.

"Sounds a hell of a lot like what that dick on her gym-nastics team did to her, huh?"

I lose my breath, like he punched me in the gut. All my bravado just dissipates. "It's not the same."

"No?"

"No," I practically yell, not sure if I'm trying to convince him or myself.

"Because I was there after you picked her up that morning, pretending to be asleep because I didn't want to deal with you. And I've been with her since you took off for home the other day. And from my observations, she's taking your dismissal even harder than last time."

My eyes close and chin drops to my chest as the memories of the morning I picked her up on the side of the road assault me. I remember how shattered she was all those months ago. Her normal self-confidence was nowhere to be found, stolen by a guy who didn't deserve to get that intimate with her. And now I've done the same thing. It doesn't matter that the intentions were different. The damage is still identical.

"I have to fix this," I say softly to myself, my anger dissipating and feeling a sudden urgency to get to Lauren and beg her forgiveness.

"Glad you finally figured that out." Jaxon turns back to his textbook, finally having said his piece.

Standing up a little too quickly, my chair rolls backward and hits the wall. "I need to go see her." Frantically, I grab my keys and phone, shoving them in my pocket. "I need to get to her dorm."

"They aren't there."

"What? Where are they?"

Still not looking up, Jaxon says the last thing I expected. "They went to some club."

It takes a few seconds for the information to register. "They did what?"

Jaxon finally looks up as he explains. "Apparently, Lauren likes to dance whenever she has a bunch of anxious energy built up, so Annika took her to a new place. Sante? Sanve? I don't remember the name of it."

"Wait. They went by themselves? They didn't want us to go with them?"

He stares at me blankly.

"No, I get that they don't want me around. But... Annika's okay with this?"

The side of Jaxon's lip quirks up. It almost looks like pride that his girl is venturing out without him again.

"It's been eighteen months since she was attacked. She figured tonight was the night to go for it. So, fair warning, if you plan on staying here, she may have some nightmares. Or she may be fine. We'll see."

I feel my own burst of pride at this new development. Annika is one of the best people I know, so for her to feel comfortable just hanging out with her friends at a club again is pretty awesome.

"That's great, Jaxon. I'm happy for her."

"Me, too." He picks up his phone and waves it at me. "Of course, she's texted me about a dozen times since they got there, but baby steps, right?"

"Yeah."

"Plus, Paul works there now so he's keeping an eye on them. From what I understand, he's only serving her bottled water."

"Good ole' Paul," I say with a chuckle, but then I remember my other concern with the girls going out tonight. "Did Lauren take her chair or just use crutches?"

Jaxon shakes his head, his disappointment returning. "Had you not been such a jackass, your girlfriend probably would have reminded you that her follow up doctor's appointment was today. They took her cast off."

"What?" This is great news. News she didn't think I'd be interested to know about. The thought puts a sour taste in my mouth. "She's not wearing heels, though, right? She's not ready for that."

"Calm down. She's in a boot for the time being. I think she just wants to see how long she can wear it before she has to stop. And that whole anxious energy thing."

Again, I feel like the wind is knocked out of me. This is huge news and she didn't tell me. Either she didn't feel the need or didn't think I'd care. Either way, I know I've screwed up badly.

My phone chimes and hoping it's my girlfriend, my heart jumps. It sinks just as fast when I realize it's just

Jaxon.

"That's the address to the club," he says as he clicks off his phone. "Go fix this with her."

"I will." Quickly, I set the GPS to figure out where I'm going. Shoving it back in my pocket, I head toward the door again. "And thanks, man."

"Germaine." I stop in my tracks at the tone of my best friend's voice.

"Yeah?"

"You got in my face when I was treating Annika in a way she didn't deserve. Consider this payback." I nod in understanding. "But know the same rules apply. You pull this shit again, and I'll personally kick your ass."

"Noted and appreciated, brother."

He nods once and turns back to his book, probably smiling like he just single-handedly fixed my relationship. I'll let him have his moment. I've got to do my part to make it right, too.

TWENTY-NINE

Lauren

The beat of the music feels so good as it pulses through my body. It's like a part of me that has been missing is finally back. Maybe not the music. My trusty sidekick, Steven Tyler, has been with me all this time. But being able to *move* to the music has been long overdue.

I'm a little clunky with this boot, definitely not graceful, and people are giving me a wide berth, but I don't care. Being able to put on a pair of silk shorts without worrying about them snagging on plaster and an off-the-shoulder crop top without thinking about crutches, then getting gussied up for a night out feels like a dream come true. I don't even mind that I have to wear flat shoes with my boot. Well, one flat anyway. It's a small price to pay to get off campus and dance the night away.

This new place is okay. It's like a cross between a club and a bar, with a decent-sized dance floor in front of a stage. A giant wooden bar is off to the side and there are tables anywhere the dance floor isn't. It's almost like the venue is having some sort of identity crisis. It wouldn't necessarily be my first choice of places to frequent, but Paul, Jaxon's old boss from Ambrosia, is here, making it the perfect place for Annika and me to go by ourselves.

And the fact that it's not nearly as crowded as an actual club keeps me from worrying too much about me or my boot getting stepped on.

I move my hips, arms above my head, which is just about all I can do. Spinning around or getting too crazy throws me off balance, but I can turn just enough to see Ellery.

When I asked her to come along with Annika and I to celebrate my newfound freedom, I knew she would get along with my best friend. The more I get to know Ellery, the more I like her. I thought a night out would help us get to know each other better outside of our sport. It worked.

And then Kevin showed up. I don't know if she invited him or if he crashed our girls' night, but they've been inseparable ever since. I'm not mad about him being here. It's cute watching them. They're terrible dancers, but Kevin looks at Ellery like she hung the moon. That's all I want for my friend, so I have no resentment about dancing by myself.

Now that I see she's fine, I glance over where Annika is sitting. As always, she'd rather be at the bar watching some football game than shaking her groove thing. When she catches my eye and tips her bottled water at me, I smile. It's our new signal that everyone we came with is okay. We use it often. No girl will ever be left behind again.

Turning my attention back to the music, I let it take over me, flowing through me as my body sways to the beat. My mind begins to clear, my emotions calm, as every problem fades away. Every hurt and concern melts until I feel centered, a small smile tugging at my lips.

That's when I feel strong hands on my hips and a large body behind me. I don't startle because I know without a doubt who it is. My assumption is only confirmed when I'm suddenly encased by his arms. I only fit this way with one person—Heath.

I should push him away. I should demand an explanation. Tell him I won't ever be treated that way again. But there's time for a strongly worded conversation later. Right now, all I know is I've missed him, that I feel safe when

I'm around him, and that he's here. He sought me out.

Intertwining our fingers, I allow myself to melt into him, getting as close as I can on a public dance floor with a boot in the way. He gently picks me up, placing my feet on top of his much larger ones, allowing him to lead us more gracefully now that my boot is out of the way.

It also gets him a couple of inches closer allowing him to lean down and say, "I'm sorry," in my ear.

I respond by running my hands up to his biceps. I don't question his apology because Heath's never been anything except honest with me. Honest when he's struggling. Honest when I'm driving him crazy. Honest when he's screwed up. But I also don't let it go just yet. We have some talking to do and some decisions to make.

Later. Right now, I just want to dance.

I lose track of time as we move, bodies fully aligned. My body and thoughts battle each other, wanting to fall back into old patterns and be with this man in every sense, but knowing I deserve to be more than just a vessel for stress relief. I want to trust that Heath would never use me like that, but the last few days have been brutal. For my own sense of well-being, I have to be careful. Yes, I love him. There is no doubt about it. But love isn't enough for me. Six months ago, genuine affection was good enough. Not anymore.

I could dance for hours, but just as Dr. Copperman predicted, my leg begins to ache. I tap Heath's arm gesturing for him to lean down.

"I have to stop. It's starting to hurt," I say in his ear.

Heath immediately turns me around and picks me up so I'm off the floor. We're face to face, arms around each other. It's unexpected and makes my stomach flip.

He presses his lips to mine, and I melt into his kiss, opening for him so his tongue can sweep into my mouth. The kiss is quick so he can get me off the dance floor. But he never puts me down, just whisks me across the room to the stool next to Annika's.

"Time to go?" she asks as soon as I sit. I just nod, my eyes still trained on him. "I'll go get Ellery," she says and leaves us to this moment.

I can see his apology in his eyes. See how sorry he is. That look makes me realize how imperfect he is. He doesn't do relationships so he's going to make mistakes. But his intention was never to hurt or dismiss me. That realization makes a huge difference to my already healing broken heart.

He kisses me again, this time a peck before pulling back and once again whispering, "I'm sorry." I put a finger on his lips to stop him.

"Not here. Let's talk at home, okay?"

He nods and kisses my finger, then turns to look around the room like he always does when we've been out together. It's another reminder that old habits die hard with this man.

I try hard to make sure my nerves don't take over as we wait for Annika. I have no reason to be worried. Heath isn't like the others. He's honest and kind and good. Still, the question of how he disappeared so easily starts to fester the longer we sit, and it gets harder to control. Like a tiny ripple in the ocean that picks up speed as it gathers other ripples, trying to turn into a giant wave that will roll over and over until it crashes into me, drowning me.

Somehow, Heath must recognize my internal battle because he grabs my hand, pulling it to his mouth to kiss my knuckles. "You okay?" I nod and smile, but it's a little too reactionary. We both know it. "I know I screwed up, babe. I'm here to make it right."

With those words my anxiety relaxes, the wave slowing down until it's nothing more than a ripple again.

"Ellery's staying here," Annika announces as she saunters toward us, looking at her phone. "Kevin's going to take her home."

"I figured that would happen. They've been stuck to each other like glue all week."

"They're kind of cute together." Annika and I both look back over at them doing some weird cha-cha move on the dance floor. "In an odd kind of way."

I stifle my giggle because the last thing I want to sound

is condescending. "Let's go. I need to get my leg up."

We wave at Paul who nods his goodbye and Heath scoops me up in his arms, carrying me to Annika's car first, making sure she gets inside safely. Not that he can do much about a potential attacker while he's holding another human being, but it's still a welcome gesture.

Once she's gone and he finally has both of us settled in his truck, he shoots out a quick text and tosses his phone in the cupholder.

"Sorry," he says as he fumbles around in the center console. "Just wanted to give Jax a heads up that Annika's on the way. I'm going to follow her home if that's okay with you."

"Of course, it is. Although you may have to catch up to her."

"I'm not worried. Worst case, we catch up to her when she's walking through the parking lot. Good enough for me. Besides, it gives us more time to talk. But first, take these." He pulls out a bottle of ibuprofen and shakes out a couple, handing them to me along with a water bottle.

I smile at his thoughtfulness and do as instructed. When he's satisfied I'm settled, he cranks the engine and heads out of the parking lot. Placing his giant paw on my thigh, he squeezes lightly.

I turn to look at him, taking in his features. He's got bags under his eyes and his skin is a bit on the sallow side. He looks drained. I can only imagine how exhausted he must feel. And yet he still came for me. Despite his need for sleep and probably to catch up on work, he made it a priority to make this right.

I'm still not sure what that means, exactly, but it makes it easy to forgive him. Now, I just need him to forgive himself.

"How is your dad, anyway?"

To my surprise, Heath smiles broadly. "Feisty. Driving my mother crazy with all his bitching about his diet changes."

"That's good, right?"

"Really good. His doctor doesn't see any reason he'll

have any more trouble if he just gets his cholesterol and eating under control. Yes, it was a heart attack, but comparatively speaking, it was the best outcome we could have asked for."

"That is such good news," I say and squeeze his hand. I can't imagine how much of a relief it is for him. For the entire family. "And how are *you*?"

The smile fades as he answers me with brutal honesty. "Shook."

He pulls my hand to his lips again and kisses gently several times. "I'm so sorry, babe. I was so scared he was going to die that I lost track of everything else until I got there. And then I was so relieved he was going to be fine, that I shifted into this weird, I don't know, like... planning mode or something. I kept thinking, 'But what if it happens again? How can I make sure this doesn't happen again?'. All I could think about was the combine, and how I needed to focus everything on football again."

My heart sinks. These are the same reasons he had originally for not dating. I thought his thought process had changed. That he felt differently—like maybe I helped him keep his focus and reach his goals. It turns out, I was wrong.

Pulling my hand from his, I push my hair behind my ear and fidget with my shorts. "I understand."

Heath looks over at me once, and then a second time, as he tries to keep the truck in between the lines. "I don't think you do, Tiny."

Pulling into the dorm parking lot, he drives to the front in time for us to see Annika being let in by Jax. He waves when he sees us, and I know I probably won't see my roommate again for the night.

In true Heath Germaine fashion, he watches until the door closes behind them before throwing the truck into park. Then he turns to face me full-on, his stare intense. Maybe more intense than I've ever seen him before.

"Lauren, I've spent years singularly focused on my goals so I can provide for my family. My parents work so hard, and I don't want them to have to do that anymore.

But I've been so fixated on reaching the pros, I've pushed anything and anyone away that I can't use to my benefit."

"Ouch."

"What?"

"It sounds an awful lot like you just said the only reason any of us are your friend is because you can use us."

He huffs and turns his head, eyebrows furrowed. "I am fucking this all up. You have to know that's not what I meant."

"No, actually. I don't."

Licking his lips, he nods. Whether it's in understanding, agreement, or to pacify me, I'm not sure. "Let me try this again. With the exception of a very few people, I've pushed everyone away. But I started to relax a little. Let my guard down. Fall for you."

My head whips over so fast, I almost give myself whiplash. "What?"

A small smile tugs at his lips. "This isn't the most romantic way to tell you I love you, but I think you need to hear it right now."

"I need to hear it now because you're breaking up with me so you can shift your priorities around?"

He reaches for a lock of my hair and gently plays with it. It feels so good but doesn't distract me from my confusion. "I'm not breaking up with you. I'm trying to tell you that I got scared."

"Why?" My voice is nothing but a whisper as he shares his fears with me.

"Because I've never felt so deeply about anyone. When Jaxon told me where you guys were tonight, I almost lost my shit, thinking about you being at a club without us there."

I roll my eyes and laugh. "I know that's been our routine for the last few months, but we're not totally incapable of going out without an escort."

His bright white smile practically lights up his face with my poking fun. "I know that. But it still didn't feel right. It doesn't feel right when we're not together. Whether it's walking home from practice or being in the same room while we're studying, I just want to be with you." He takes a deep breath and I let him take a moment to finish whatever he's going to say. "I'm sorry it took me distancing myself to figure that out. I guess I just needed a kick in the ass to get my head on straight."

"I'm curious who did the ass-kicking."

"Jaxon and my mother."

"Ooh, that's rough," I say with a laugh, the mood in his truck lighter than it was before.

"Hell yeah, it was!" His tone turns serious. "But I needed it. And Lauren, I can't promise I won't screw up again, but I'll never push you aside like this again."

"It's not that I expected you to call me constantly. I just want to be there for you when things happen. Good and bad. To help you through them. To help you stay focused. I understand your dreams. I want to help you reach them. Because I love you, too."

Immediately, it looks like a boulder has been lifted from his shoulders. His whole body relaxes in one breath. Satisfied that our first real problem is sorted out, he leans over and kisses me again.

"Would it be okay if I stayed with you tonight?" he asks against my lips. "As much as I love Jaxon and Annika, it's just weird sleeping in the bed across the room when they have a sleepover."

Smiling against his lips, I nod. "I think I want a sleepover of our own tonight."

He gives me one more quick peck before pushing away and yelling, "Let's go!"

I laugh as he pretends to peel out of the parking lot, anxious to get me home.

THIRTY
Heath

"You know the doctor said I can walk right?" Lauren teases, as I carry her down the hall to her dorm room. "He gave me a walking cast for a reason."

"And did he also say when it starts to hurt you need to get off of it?" She says nothing. "That's what I thought. Besides," I give her a quick peck, "I like carrying you around. It's like an extra bicep workout."

She smacks me lightly on the shoulder, grinning as she does. I gently lower her to the floor when we get to her door, allowing her to let us in.

Lauren limps through the door and I know she needs a break. Scooting around her, I situate the pillows on her bed so she can prop her leg up.

"You certainly didn't waste any time taking our love nest apart. Is this going to happen every time we fight?" I ask it playfully, but knowing the makeshift double bed was pulled apart in my absence stings a bit.

Lauren peeks up at me through her lashes, giving me a knowing look. "Annika doesn't always stay with Jaxon. As much as I love her, it would be weird to wake up as her little spoon."

"It would be weirder if you woke up as her big spoon, but hey," I hold my hands up in mock defense, "no judgment from me." Sitting down on her bed, I plump up the pillows a little more. "How are you feeling? Does it hurt a lot?"

She rubs just above her knee, probably trying to relieve some of the tension. "It just aches. Dr. Copperman said it would be like that for a while until my body gets used to being fully upright again."

"When can you start back at the gym?" I move her hand out of the way so I can take over rubbing her leg and loosen the straps on her cast a bit. She moans and drops her head back, clearly enjoying my touch. It makes my libido stir but I have to keep it under control. She's in pain and I just apologized. Tonight, isn't about sex. It's about taking care of her needs, physical and emotional.

"Tomorrow."

I can feel my eyes light up. This is what she's been hoping for. "Really?"

A huge smile crosses her face. "Yep. I mean, with restrictions. No tumbling, no dismounts, no vault, basically nothing that will put unnecessary force on the bone. But I can go back to bar work and some basic beam stuff."

"Hey, that's better than nothing."

"Tell me about it." Suddenly, she sits up straight. "Oh! I forgot to show you. I got a new brace for the gym. It's even smaller than the boot."

I can't help but laugh. "You are really excited about this."

"I am. And only another athlete can understand why. Wanna see?"

"Sure," I say with amusement and move out of her way so she can carefully stand up. "Let me see this sexy new cast." I smack her on the ass, making her squeal.

"Ow, you asshole." She rubs her ass as she hobbles into the bathroom. "I have to pee, too. I'll be right back," she announces and shuts the door.

Leaning back on her bed, I close my eyes and lay my clasped hands on my chest. It feels so good to be back with the one person who loves me for me, not what I can provide them in the future.

Okay, I guess that's not fair. I never gave anyone else a chance to get to know me, but it's too late now. I can't believe a fake dating relationship turned into something more. Into something real. But it did. Lauren matters to me, more than I ever thought possible. And I'm oddly grateful to my roommate for threatening to kick my ass for her.

I hear a door click and I slowly open my eyes only to see a vision standing in front of me. Lauren is sporting her new brace, but that's not the part I'm concentrating on. All I can see is the black lace thong and matching sports bra. I didn't know they made lace sports bras but I'm not complaining. The outfit, or lack of outfit, accentuates the muscles she's worked for so many years to build, and somehow makes her body look softer. Curvier.

And suddenly, I'm harder.

I lick my lips because damn. My girlfriend is fucking hot and I am currently visualizing about four million different ways I can strip her of that lace.

"What, um…" I clear my throat because suddenly my mouth has gone dry. "What are you doing, there, Tiny?"

"What does it look like I'm doing?"

"It looks like you're about to reinjure yourself."

Her immediate frown makes me want to laugh. My feisty girl is back. "I want to try out my new brace before practice tomorrow. See what it can do."

I can't help it. I throw my head back, a belly laugh bursting out of me. My reaction makes her smile even more. "Are you sure, baby? This is not what I came here for. Lord knows I don't deserve it today."

With no hesitation, she limps over to me and climbs on my lap, carefully straddling me so she can take my face in her hands. "Heath, stop. I understand."

"Doesn't excuse what I did."

"No, it doesn't. But you explained it. You apologized. Now you have to let it go."

I think back to what my sister said at the hospital. About

letting the past go when it doesn't affect anyone anymore. She's right. Both of them are right. I have to stop carrying the weight of everyone else on my shoulders. Especially if they're fine getting around on their own.

"You're pretty smart, you know that?"

"It's why I'm a business major."

"Oh, is that so," I say with a chuckle.

"Yeah. Now shut up and kiss me."

Leaning forward, I capture her lips with mine, not holding back. The kiss is hard and deep and passionate. Not just making love but making up for hurt feelings and disrespect.

Lauren begins clawing at my shirt, trying desperately to remove it. I lean forward and in one swift movement, rip it over my head and toss it to the floor. Her moan of relief when skin touches skin takes any hesitation I was feeling before and smashes it to pieces. I love this woman and now more than ever, I need to show her how much.

I run my hands across her rib cage, down her hips, around the globes of her ass. When I get to her legs, I remember we still have to be careful.

"Does it hurt?" I ask quietly as my hand caresses the brace over her calf.

"A little," she admits. "I think maybe I should be on bottom this time."

A laugh rumbles out of me. "Are you sure it's because of the pain and not because I can hike that leg over my shoulder?"

She shrugs coyly. "Maybe a little of that, too."

Carefully, I flip us over until I'm lying on top of her, between her legs, exactly where I want to be.

As we continue to make out, mouths fused together, her hands reach down and push my shorts over my hips. They don't go very far before I have to help out. Once I'm free, her small hand wraps around my girth and begins stroking slowly, her thumb gently rubbing over the tip every time she strokes upward. It's enough to make me almost lose my mind, and my load all over her.

Pulling away, I rest on my knees and look down at my

beautiful girlfriend—her hair splayed out on the pillow, chest heaving, cheeks flushed. "God, I love you."

She smiles and raises an eyebrow. "You just want to get in my pants."

Perusing her body with my eyes, I purse my lips. "I'm a little beyond that, at this point."

"Shut up and make love to me," she demands. Can't argue with that.

Hooking the waistband of her panties with my thumbs, I slide them down over her legs, taking special care to get over the brace. Her range of motion is definitely better in this thing, but I still don't want to push it. "This comes off, too." I reach my arms around her and with her help, unclasp the fancy lace bra.

We're both fully naked with nothing between us. I pause for a moment to kiss her well and truly before grabbing a condom from the bedside table and sliding it on.

When I finally push into her, we groan simultaneously. I don't know how I ever thought this woman was anything more than perfect for me. But she is. She's sassy and feisty and her body fits perfectly with mine. As I thrust in and out, her leg hooked above my shoulder as promised, all I can think about is how much I love her. And how much nothing means as much to me as she does. My new goal isn't to reach mine. It's to help her reach hers.

Right after I help us both reach our orgasm.

Within a matter of minutes, we fall into a heap of limp bodies and loose limbs, physically and emotionally relieved of the stress that has been plaguing us.

Pulling Lauren to me, I wrap her up in my arms kissing her gently on the neck before relaxing and closing my eyes. She wasn't kidding that her new brace gives her a much better range of motion. The Velcro burn I'm going to have on my ribs is well worth the pain.

I lie still while her fingers gently trace up and down my arm. I'm almost surprised she's not asleep from so much physical exertion today, but I have a feeling her brain won't shut down, so I let her stay lost in her thoughts until she's ready to talk.

I am on the verge of passing out myself when she finally says my name.

"Heath?"

"Hmmm..." I don't open my eyes, way too comfortable. Briefly, I wonder if I'm still wearing a full condom but then remember I pulled it off just before collapsing on the bed. Thank goodness that trash can is still close by.

"When is the combine?"

"The end of the next month."

"Oh." Her hands continue to rub my arm and I begin to fall asleep again. "How long will you be gone?"

My eyes fly open. Shit. Once again, I forgot to let my girlfriend in on the plan. I'm not just bad at this boyfriend thing, I'm downright shitty at it. "I'm not going."

Her hand stills for a beat before she rolls over to face me. "What do you mean you're not going? You've been working your ass off for this. Is it because of your dad? Are you needing to make sure he's better before having to move, or something?"

I run my hand down her back, enjoying the feel of her silky-smooth skin. "It is because of my dad. But not the reason you're thinking."

She furrows her brow, the concern on her face evidence of how much she loves me. How much she cares about my future.

"I had an interesting talk with my mother during all this, and it turns out that I may have been pushing myself to reach my goal for the wrong reasons."

"How so?"

I sigh and run my fingers through her hair, prepared to share how much has changed in such a short amount of time.

"My dad has worked two jobs for as long as I can remember. My mom works long hours, too. And I just wanted to help alleviate some of their stress."

"I think it's honorable that you want to help them."

I give her a quick peck on the lips for being so supportive. "Apparently, they don't want my help."

Lauren pulls back and sits up, leaning on her elbow.

"Wait, they don't want you to go to the combine this year?"

"They don't care if I go this year or next. It's my goal either way."

"Right."

"But I may have misunderstood why they work such long hours and possibly inflated their need for help."

Her eyes widen slightly in surprise. "Well, that's good, right? That takes some of the pressure off."

"It should. I think I'm still trying to wrap my brain around something my mom said."

"Which is?"

"That they don't want my help, and if I try to pay off their mortgage, they'll never speak to me again."

Lauren bursts out laughing and then turns serious. "Oh, man. What are you going to do with all those millions if your parents won't take them? Must suck to know you'll be set for life."

I pinch her rib making her squeal and giggle. "Okay, smart ass. I'm fine with it. It's just... I don't know, I guess it's a different way of thinking. For so long, I've been trying to go pro to take care of my family and now I can go pro just for me. Is it weird that I feel kind of selfish?"

She lays her head down, hands underneath her face. "No. I think maybe it's going to take some time to wrap your head around it. Like with my leg. I've been so singularly focused on competing on floor, I never thought about trying for bars. Now look at me. The only thing I can do is bars. It's kind of... I don't even know how to describe it. It's just different than what I thought it would be." She shifts closer so our legs are intertwined. "What does your coach say? Does he think you should do it?"

"He thinks I need another year."

"Yeah?"

I nod. "I told him I didn't care what he thought, and I was doing it anyway."

"And now you have to go tell him you changed your mind again."

"Yeah. I'm not looking forward to that."

She gives a small shrug. "Just tell him you got caught

up in the Germaine pride. I'm sure he'll understand."

I make an amused sound and grab her ass, shifting her leg over my hip. "But do you? Understand?"

Her eyes soften and her lips tilt up. "I do. And I totally and completely forgive you. As long as you don't pull away from me like that again."

I clasp her hand and pull it to my lips, grateful that this amazing woman loves me in spite of my flaws.

"Never."

"Good. Now, let it go so we can move on."

I kiss the inside of her wrist, trying to keep things light before we fall asleep, but the feel of her skin on my lips and the relief I feel from her acceptance have the opposite effect on my body. So, I kiss up her arm, to the inside of her elbow, over her bicep, her shoulder, her collarbone, the side of her jaw, and finally take her lips with mine.

"I love you so much."

I can feel her smile against my lips. "I love you, too. I'm kind of excited I get to love you up close and personal for a whole extra year."

"Let's not waste any more of it."

"Agreed."

So, we don't.

EPILOGUE
10 months later

Blowing out a breath, I shake my hands and legs trying to get the nerves out of my system. I know this new routine like the back of my hand, but that doesn't change the anxiety I'm feeling. One year ago, practically to the day, I broke my leg in this very arena. My routine is completely different now, but it doesn't keep me from battling the memories.

Anxiety is a bitch like that.

Fortunately, all I need is to look up in the stands to see my boyfriend sitting there cheering me on, and suddenly, I feel more centered. The quick thumbs-up he flashes me helps as well.

We've been going strong since last year, taking everything from our studies to our training day-by-day. It became clear very quickly that staying in school for an extra year was the right choice for Heath. He's added about twenty pounds of muscle, which I didn't know was even possible, and his stats are through the roof this year. No one else in the NCAA even comes close to his numbers. The chatter on all the sports stations is he could easily be a top ten draft pick. Maybe even top five. But until the official combine invitation comes in, he's just keeping his head down and working hard.

And of course, supporting me by still picking me up at practice and coming to my meets. There's only been two so far, but somehow, I think he'll be showing up at the rest of them. It's one of the perks of having two completely different seasons.

Seeing my signal, I salute the judges and strut onto the floor, getting into position for my routine. I only catch a glimpse of Kiersten, who drove in with her beautiful three-month-old baby boy just for today.

I suspect she's here because she needs the support. Raising a baby on your own with almost no job experience and no baby daddy is tough. The sadness in her eyes and deep circles underneath are testament of exactly how rough it's been.

Refocusing my attention on the job at hand, I freeze in position and wait.

As the first beats of my new floor music begin, I let my body take over. A few dance moves strategically designed to get me to the corner of the floor where I take a deep breath…and LAUNCH!

Three steps…

Hurdle…

Round off…

Back handspring…

Whip back, whip back…

Back handspring…

Double back…

Land that baby and immediately launch again back to the other side…

Round off…

Back handspring…

Shushunova…

I barely hear the cheers from landing my first and most difficult combination tumbling pass. Because of the way my leg broke last year, I was nervous to land any twisting elements, so we changed the skills and beefed it up. There's more room for error, but the point value stayed about the same, so it works.

Plus, I love my new music. Christmas Eve Sarajevo is something I've always envisioned doing a kick-ass floor routine to. Turns out, I was right.

Once I get to the complicated series of turns and the final tumbling pass, I already know it was the right choice. I nailed this routine.

Finally, we reach my favorite part and it goes right along with the music.

Wolf jump...

    Split jump...

        Straddle jump...

            Shushunova...

            Roll to my back and arch up, one leg bent and freeze...

The music stops, the crowd cheers, and a smile breaks out on my face.

As I salute the judges, I look up in the stands to see my friends all on their feet cheering loudly. They know the same thing I do... I've done it. I've secured my competition spot on the event I love.

It's exciting and I don't mind reveling in the moment.

Ellery runs to me when my feet hit the concrete floor and hugs me tightly. "You did it!" she squeals in my ear. "You nailed it!"

I just smile, trying to catch my breath while we wait for the score. It doesn't take long...

9.925... easily the highest score on the team.

Ellery jumps up and down squealing again, some new members of the team coming over to give their congratulations as well.

It's welcome, but not needed. Something's shifted in the last year, and I no longer need anyone else's approval.

I'll always struggle with anxiety. It's just a part of me. But I'm confident in myself. I'm confident in my skills. And I'm confident that I've surrounded myself with the best support system I can have.

That's all that matters to me.

The End.

Matters to You

Sneak Preview

Want to know more about Kiersten and how she ended up a single mom? Then grab *Matters to You*, coming January 2021! Here's a sneak peek:

Spence chuckles and I can't help but think about how lucky I am that he's so good to me. To us. Things could have turned out so much worse.

"Alright, alright. Just take it slow and I'll be there as soon as I can, okay?"

"We will. I promise. Text me when you get there and we'll meet you at the front so you can have your turn with the scanner gun."

"Will do. And take care of Baby Archie for me."

"We're not naming him after a prince!" I argue. Again.

"He doesn't have a royal title so he's not a prince! Loveyoubye!" Spence yells back and hangs up on me.

I stare at the phone, mouth agape.

"He got the last word in about the baby's name again, didn't he?" Lauren asks, smiling as she lifts her travel cup of water to her lips.

"Every. Single. Time." I toss my phone on the couch and settle in. We still have some time before we have to leave for the appointment. "How's it feeling?" I gesture to Lauren's leg as she massages just above her knee. The tibia fracture that knocked her out of the entire gymnastics competition season last year is finally healed. But from the looks of it, it still bothers her. "Does it ache?"

"Mostly when it's going to rain."

"Or if you do too many tumbling passes?"

She smiles sheepishly, knowing she's been caught. "Just don't tell my coach, okay?"

"You should be more worried about me telling Heath."

Lauren shrugs. "He's an athlete. What's he gonna say? 'Don't work out so hard'? He knows I'll throw that right back at him the next time he's bruised up from a game."

"This is why you two are perfect for each other. You understand each other."

"You have no idea," she murmurs and reaches over to the table, picking up a notebook.

I don't know that I'll ever understand how Heath and Lauren ended up together. Heath doesn't seem to like anyone except a very few people and they used to verbally spar with the best of them. But I suppose once your perception of someone changes, well, everything changes. And now they're what I like to refer to as a power couple; cheering each other on at every game or meet, pushing each other during work outs, making sure they're both stocked up in IcyHot and ibuprofen. It's fun to see Lauren happy and in love. She deserves it.

"I can't wait for you to see my new floor routine. *Christmas Eve Sarajevo* is amazing music for tumbling. And the turn sequence at the end makes me feel like I can do anything."

Thinking about the music, I can envision how Lauren turned such a powerful song into an equally powerful routine. For just a split second, it makes me yearn to dance again.

But then the moment is gone when Lauren flips open the cover and poises her pen into the ready position. "Okay. Baby shower. I need a list of people to invite."

"Just do me one favor." She nods and gestures for me to continue. "My sister really wants to help. Or at least feel like she's helping. I know she's still in high school but can you call her and ask her opinion on things? Just a couple times."

Lauren doesn't skip a beat. "Of course. I'm glad Nicole is so excited. Is she going to be able to come?"

I shake my head because I don't really know. "That's the million dollar question. I almost positive my mom won't be there. But I'm hoping she'll at least let Nicole come. Even if it's just to report back on how horribly bloated and exhausted I look and how much better off I would be if I'd just lived life their way in the first place."

Lauren laughs through her nose. "Sounds... stifling."

I shrug. "Their loss. Either they'll know their first grand child or they won't. At this point, I don't really care."

I might eventually, but not today. Today is all about celebrating my little boy's birth.

Lauren and I spend a good thirty minutes discussing baby shower guests and games. I try to veto the one where everyone has to cut off the same amount of ribbon as the width of my belly, but apparently this isn't a democracy and she's going to do it anyway. As long as there's cake, I guess I'll survive.

"The only thing we need to really figure out is where to have this party," Lauren remarks as she continues jotting down ideas. "I don't know the area well enough so I might need to defer to you on this part."

"I bet the community group on social media would know."

"You think?"

"Oh yeah. People are always asking for venues and specific businesses. Hang on."

I find the page I'm looking for and begin, searching for a decent venue to hold a party. I know I've seen a whole thread about it before. But then one post in particular catches my eye.

CAUTION! AVOID AVENUE R AT THE CORNER OF CINCINATTI! MAJOR ACCIDENT!

"Well shit," I grumble.

"What?"

"There's a car accident close to here. I think we have to

go that way to get to the store. Let me see how long ago it was. Maybe it's cleared already. Otherwise we need to go soon so we can find a way around it."

"Is it bad?"

"I can't tell yet. Just says its major."

I click on the post and my heart stops. A picture of the wreck has been posted in the comments and it looks like Spence's car. With a black sheet over it.

My breathing speeds up as I zoom in but can't see enough of the back window to tell if the spot in the bottom right corner is his favorite radio station sticker or something else. Surely it's something else. It's someone else's care. I can't be Spence's. I'm just overreacting. Honda has lots of cars out there. Millions. It could be a million different people. Not my Spence.

The comments, though, do little to ease my mind.

It's going to be here a while, guys. An ambulance came out but they never took anyone away and they've stopped working. Pray for these people.

I'm here. Overheard an officer say they're waiting for the medical examiner.

Y'all pray for the families. That black sheet isn't a good sign. Usually that's only to cover the scene when someone has died.

"No, no, no, NO!" My voice sounds shrill as I close the app and try to call Spence.

"Kiersten, what's wrong?"

I know Lauren is trying to talk to me, but I can barely hear her over the sounds of his phone ringing and my own heartbeat.

"Pick up, Spence. Come on, baby. Pick up."

Finally someone answer. "Hey, this is Spence. You know what to do."

Dammit. I hang up, uninterested in leaving a voice message. I need to hear him, alive and breathing.

Dialing again, I continue my ministrations. "Come on, Spence. Answer the phone. Pull over if you have to. Please answer."

Matters to You, coming January 2021.

ACKNOWLEDGMENTS

It would not be an M.E. Carter book without about a zillion people to thank because gratitude is what I feel for each and every one of you.

First up is **Brenda Rothert** for her constant cheerleading, her constant advice and her constant discussion of storylines and how to "fix" my stories when they get bland. I couldn't do this without you. Especially not sports romance!

This book would not be what it is without the help of my former teammate, **Martha Jenkins**. As teenagers, I was in awe of you and your skill, always wishing I could be as good as you, while simultaneously just enjoying watching the beauty you brought to the sport. And I distinctly remember sitting in front of my TV watching Nationals when you got injured during your floor routine. I'm pretty sure you still won the all-around title! I remember squealing on the inside and thinking, "I KNOW HER!!!!" It was so cool. Through the magic of social media and the desire to provide for our families, I'm proud to now call us friends. Even if part of me still wants to fangirl every once in a while. Thank you for all the wonderful team memories and your insight into the world of college competitions. And for introducing me to the magic of Sol-U-Guard. ;)

I knew **Wanda Curry** would know all about the current terminology and skill levels. She is more obsessed with gymnastics than any other person I know. Thank you for pointing out the errors I made so they could be tweaked and updated for the current college generation. Wow, it's weird saying that. I love you so much, friend. And I thank you for always loving my flighty self, even though I may call every day for a month and not again for six more. You've always understood me. Oh also... you still owe me a pickle.

Next is **Amie Moore** for reading through this with a fine-tooth comb and making sure the innerworkings of an interracial relationship were correct. You said, "If anyone can tackle this and get it right, you can." I can never thank you enough for having confidence in me. My fear is always that I'll get it wrong or that I'll screw up my characters. But you totally understand my desire to get it "right" even when I struggle to express myself the correct way. Not everyone sees my heart. So thank you!!

I can't forget **Hazel James** and her red-lining the first draft. Trust me, I'm not mad about it! It was perfection so that I didn't end up with a shitty book. I see a beautiful crit relationship forming!

Marisol Scott would blow up my group if I forgot her. Thanks for your insight, your feedback, and always helping me come up with the organization for take overs and Carter's Cheerleaders. It is much appreciated!

Erin Noelle, as always your editing is both infuriating and exactly what I need. How I fix certain bad habits while creating new ones, I'll never know. Keep calling me out! Eventually we'll get there!

Thank you, **Janice Owens**! For our first time working together, I feel like it was really smooth. You put the finishing polishes on this baby and I'm so grateful.

Alamea and Jasper, holy smokes you guys. I am so appreciative of you both jumping in at the last minute to just triple check my snafu with positions didn't screw everything up. This is what I get for not stopping to verify my own information when I'm writing. You're welcome on giving you a fun "couple's project" to do during quarantine. Lol

As always, **Mom**, you found the final few mistakes. Were you an editor in a former life? I'm starting to think so. Thank you for using your skills on this one.

And of course **Alyssa Garcia**, not just for formatting and helping me with promo ideas, but just for being you. A friend, a cheerleader, a confident, a woman of integrity who shares her knowledge just because she's a good person. You are a true gem in this community and I would be lost without some of your advice and assistance. Especially with, ya know, newsletter imports and crap like that. lol

Carter's Cheerleaders, you are the best bunch of assholes this side of the nuthouse (Clark Griswold, anyone?).

You make me laugh every single day. And I'm so happy not just to call you readers, but friends.

The Walk, you know who you are. Thank you for keeping me on track and focusing on what's truly important –

God. Who I am so grateful to for gifting me with a job that provides for my family without sacrificing their well-being. I will continue to do my best as long as you let me.